The Clouds in Memphis

The Clouds in Memphis

stories and novellas

C. J. Hribal

University of Massachusetts Press   Amherst

This book is the winner of the
Associated Writing Programs 1999 Award in Short Fiction.
AWP is a national, nonprofit organization dedicated
to serving American letters, writers, and programs of writing.
AWP's headquarters are at George Mason University,
Fairfax, Virginia.

Printed in the United States of America
Designed by Mary Mendell
Set in Melior by Keystone Typesetting, Inc.
Printed and bound by Thomson-Shore, Inc.

Library of Congress Cataloging-in-Publication Data
Hribal, C. J.
The clouds in Memphis : stories and novellas / by C. J. Hribal.
p. cm.
"Winner of the Associated Writing Programs 1999 award in short
fiction" — T.p. verso. Contents: The clouds in Memphis —
The last great dream of my father — Consent — And that's
the name of that tune — War babies.
ISBN 1-55849-266-6 (alk. paper) I. Title.
PS3558.R52C58 2000   813'.54—dc21   00-030278

British Library Cataloguing in Publication Data are available.

To Krystyna, as always,
and to Tosh and Roman and Hania

Acknowledgments

"The Clouds in Memphis" originally appeared in slightly different form in *TriQuarterly,* no. 95 (Spring 1995). Portions of this novella were reprinted in *A Broken Heart Still Beats: After Your Child Dies,* ed. Anne McCracken and Mary Semel (Center City, Minn.: Hazelden Publishers, 1998).

"Consent" originally appeared in *Witness* 9, no. 2 (Fall 1995).

"The Last Great Dream of My Father" originally appeared in slightly different form in *The Sycamore Review* 8, no. 1 (Spring 1996).

Chapter 7 of "War Babies" (under the title "The Everfresh Canning Company") originally appeared in *Witness* 10, no. 2 (Fall 1996).

"And That's the Name of That Tune" originally appeared, in a different form, in *Witness* 12, no. 2 (Fall 1998).

"And That's the Name of That Tune," in a different form, also received the Eleanor and Larry Sternig Award for Short Fiction for best short story published by a Wisconsin writer in 1998.

Thanks to Ann Bowe for assistance on matters of legal procedure, and to Krystyna Kornilowicz, for her careful reading of the manuscript. Grateful acknowledgment to the Wisconsin Arts Board for an Individual Artists Fellowship, which allowed this book to get started, and to Marquette University, for funds to allow its completion.

C. J. H.

Contents

The Clouds in Memphis

1

The military payloads always come through at night.

Janie walks toward the hollow clanking of the trains with her arms crossed and the wind whipping her hair wavy and seaweed-like over her face and shoulders. It's cold for October, maybe only the high forties, and the wind on her cheeks makes the world go blurry. Birds, hundreds of them, fly straight up out of the oaks and magnolias, then get beaten back or sideways. It's as though they're launched, then tail away, lacking the power, the velocity to get anywhere near where they want to be. They should just stay in the trees, but then it's her startling them that makes them burst from the trees with that sonorous beating of wings.

At first, watching their strange flights, their sudden cutaways and swoops, Janie thought they were bats. Do bats congregate in Memphis? Later she finds out they're a kind of thrasher or catbird. Or grosbeak. Whatever somebody tells her she forgets. She's like that. *They're beautiful,* she thinks, but just as quickly *They're only birds.* And under the magnolias and oak trees they make such a terrible mess. See? The wrought iron fences are chipping, and the sidewalks are gouached white and black and purple.

Still, at least they weren't bats.

Janie hugs herself as she nears the railroad tracks. You can't go very far in any one direction in Memphis and not run into them. They're everywhere. The switching yards seem to expand in girth every time you turn your head. All that growth, like rings on a fat man's stomach. Somebody tells her no, nobody's added lines in years and years, but she simply won't believe them.

The backs of her hands feel good underneath her armpits. She's pleased at the way her workouts make her feel less rubbery. Janie is a rangy woman. Some might call her petite but she gave up that way of thinking years ago.

She takes a deep breath. The roaring of wind and the rustling of leaves is tremendous. It is the kind of wind that whips birds out of trees and the moisture from your eyes. Her feet on the cement sidewalk don't even sound like her feet. They sound like they're coming to her from some distance away; they are somebody else's feet and they're coming up behind her, or obliquely from across the street. She turns quickly, expecting to see someone or something approaching, but there's just the scattering of yellow ginkgo leaves that have already fallen and the tumble of dirt and grit they always get mixed up with.

Rufus is snapping at a whorl of leaves and grit. He barks twice at the foot-high dust devil, then yips as it blows right past him. Rufus is the reason she can walk at night. He's a black collie mix, five years old, the result of one of Stephen's prized bitches getting out at night with the neighbor's black Lab. Stephen was going to throw the whole lot into the river. His standard practice with accidents: take the entire litter of yelping pups, cinch them inside a burlap sack, and heave the whole thing into the Mississippi. "What you can't help, you correct with dispatch," he says. Janie hugs herself tighter and hardens herself again and again against him. What does he say about Stevie then, or Peter? Dispatch. She bets it's something they say with pride down at the office.

2

Every day Stephen comes to the trial, but leaves early. They neither speak nor sit together. Stephen is not a man who likes inaction, and sitting with his hands folded in his lap or his head inclined in his upright palm, his feet jiggling, he is the picture of something wild and untamed, forcibly restrained, his obedience temporary, reluctant. Janie can't help sneaking sidelong glances at the woman next to him, a blond in a blood red suit whose gold and diamond brooch is nesting where the lapels on her jacket cross. Her skirt and jacket match her lipstick and her hair is done up in that poofy-curly style favored by homecoming queens and cheerleaders. She is the type of woman for whom sitting next to Stephen is a kind of apotheosis, something for which she has trained and studied and denied and maneuvered herself, and Stephen is the result of that denial, the indulgence she gets in exchange for her self-mortification.

Which makes what Janie has done a kind of apostasy.

As often as not Stephen leaves at the first lull. He gets up, the blond gets up, and then Stephen crosses the aisle and presses his card into Janie's hand. "Call me if something develops," he says. He has given her the card twice now. The blond, who's very tall, waits with her overcoat draped over her forearms. Janie wonders if this woman thinks she's stupid or a basket case or just forlornly unlucky or what. It bothers her she even wonders what this woman thinks. She—the blond—is probably a woman to whom Stephen gave his business card only once, and even that was superfluous. The card, or his number if he wrote it on a napkin or envelope, went immediately into the Rolodex by her phone. Janie, however, who married him, is given his number weekly. This is Stephen's way of saying he remembers the startling rapidity with which pieces of paper get buried under or fly out of Janie's life. No doubt the tall, lemon-haired woman has been told this. No doubt Janie must appear to her to be a very dreary woman. It's evident in the way she stands, one wool and silk sheathed thigh canted slightly in front of the other. "Oh, yes, the wife." She's behind Stephen, her unspoken, "Oh, do let's get on with this, Stevie," is communicated by her posture.

Only a tall drink of water—Stephen has always referred to his women as something consumable—in a blood red suit could get away with calling Stephen "Stevie." It's probably a liberty with which she experiments.

"Call me if something develops," Stephen repeats. His blunt-edged fingers drill his card into her palm. He's making sure she acknowledges that he's leaving. She knows Stephen. He has no interest in process. Results, verdicts, decisions—now there's something to concern yourself with. He wants to make sure he's there when the decision is reached. Since he cannot make the decision himself, he at least wants to be there when they reach it. The difference between reach and make is the difference between approximation and creation. All a jury can hope to achieve is approximation, a confirmation of what he has already decided. And his appearance, his being there (he believed this about their marriage, too) will be the cause, the instrument by which judgment is reached and justice rendered. Reasonable doubt and due process are obfuscating intrigues. If he knew this judge he'd have called him already.

Pity there has to be a jury.

This is one time Janie agrees with him. She would like to skip completely this business with juries and advocates for the defense and plaintiff, this whole courtroom procedure where the simplest facts get worried into meaninglessness or badgered into nonexistence, where every possible permutation the sequence of events could take is given weight and credence, where the trivial "*might coulds*" concerning her son's death are examined discussed analyzed reanalyzed and cross-indexed for reference. And yet the facts of this case are simple: a drunken boy in a Plymouth convertible struck her son and killed him. What else is there to know? She wants to stand up and scream at the jury, *That boy killed my son! What else is there to know?*

The card from her husband is made of one of those new materials they use in papermaking now. It's translucent as rice paper and feels flimsy enough you might poke your finger through it. Or it might dissolve in water. But you can't rip it, tear it, or make it go ragged in any way. It is indestructible.

She leaves it on the bench when they break for lunch, folded like a white crow.

3

You cannot get "Nightline" in Memphis. Instead you get reruns of "Perry Mason." Until recently Janie always pitied Della Street. Admired her, too, for her beauty and perseverance until one day she simply shouted at the screen, *Wake up, would you! He's not ever going to love you. He's just your boss!* and she realized with shame that she was pulling for the impossible, for something the writers hadn't even conceived of, so intent they were on making sure Perry had no life outside his cases. Della Street is an employee, and Perry's relationship with her is totally, inexhaustingly professional.

Isn't that a laugh?

4

It's usually after "Perry Mason" that Janie takes her walks. With Rufus nosing the bushes, she's given up being scared of what most women at night are scared of. She even walks on bad streets—anything south of Central is questionable—and delights in the tiny thrill that no one else she knows would be doing this in daylight, much less at night. But it's at night when the most trains come through. The military payloads are the richest. Camouflaged jeeps, half-tracks, tanks, personnel carriers, whole boxcars in dull green with black stencilling: TOP SECRET, and PROPERTY: U.S. GOVERNMENT. They are long, lumbering affairs, these trains; the wheels click and clack with a sleeplike rhythm that's broken only occasionally by the shriek of a crossing whistle. Two long, deep hooooonnngs! Then a short toot. Then a final, long hoooonnng! As a teenager, Janie had been a ham radio operator. The very idea of speaking to someone in Peekskill, N.Y., or Kingston, Ontario, or even someplace in South America excited her. Each time she got her chance at the key she was giddy, though her brother Spencer usually hogged it. From eight to thirteen she studied Morse code religiously. By age eighteen she had abandoned it completely. A whole piece of her life simply gone. It was the same way with her belief in God. Walking toward the hoooonnng! she wonders why trains sing out at crossings with the International Morse Code for "Q." It's as though the train itself were a question.

At the corner of Melrose and Central she pauses. The lawn at St. Paul's Episcopal Church is uncut and littered with leaves and dancing candy wrappers. The stop signs shiver, and the amber and cherry stoplights flashing over the intersection are uncertain discs swaying in the wind. They don't look capable of slowing down or stopping anybody.

And then the train goes past, and its irregularly regular clacking sounds like drunkards in tap shoes struggling to form a kick line.

Janie is filled with a sadness she cannot fathom.

5

Thirteen months ago she was just another divorced mother of three. She was having trouble with the rent and the school payments (St. Catherine's for Nikki, Memphis University School for

Peter, special ed for Stevie); utility bills, bank statements and magazine subscription notices—*Interview, Newsweek, Southern Living, Architectural Home Digest*—all tended to go in a pile by the door. She kept a pigeon-hole writing desk there, a big one with a high back, and at one time she took great delight in keeping everything separate and prepaid. She filled the empty holes with shells from trips to Biloxi and Miami Beach and the Gulf coast of Alabama and the Florida Panhandle. That was back when she was married and even after, before Stephen realized, or decided, that he could wrench control of her life from her simply by delaying or skipping or scrimping on the child support payments. Stevie's medical bills were questioned constantly. *He can't breathe!* Janie shouted at Stephen once when he asked about the latest round of tests. They say he's got weak lungs and the air is too moist for him. *Don't you remember when he was a baby? He can't breathe! He's never been able to breathe!*

"I remember," Stephen said. "I'll have a check for you next week, Wednesday or Thursday at the latest. Some things need to clear this week yet." Stephen was a contractor. He inherited his hardware store from his father and had then gone into real estate development. He made his money building in Whitehaven and Collierville and Germantown—places where people paid good money to stay away from Memphis proper (though that had failed in Whitehaven; it was mostly black there now and the name seemed a cruel joke). At any given time Stephen had six or eight projects all going on at once and all of them, he claimed, required his capital.

"I need it *now*, Stephen. The children can't—"

"*Can* wait. People are used to waiting. Or at least they should be. Patience, after all, is a virtue, and whatever happens quickly—" Stephen went off on one of his important-sounding drones. Janie tuned him out. This was the man who spent ten thousand dollars getting hair to grow on his head, then complained he didn't have any money to send Nikki to a good college preparatory school in New England.

She couldn't believe she had married him, but things were different then. She had been on a spring-break trip with two other women and two men from a fraternity, who had traveled down with them. She was rather taken with George but she ended up marrying Stephen. Stephen, unlike George, was serious. He was tall and thin and wore his hair short about the ears and neck, but long on top and slicked tight to his skull. On the beach, though, his carefully plastered hair whipped about his face and long strands of paleness littered his shoulders as they broke off, bits of scalp still attached to the root ends. He was going to bald early and it touched her seeing it fall off like that. She believed she could fall in love with him in time, especially since he set himself up as Janie's protector, warding off bullies and generally acting chivalrous.

When he first kissed her and she had to pry open his anuslike pucker with the silvery worm of her tongue, she knew she would have to show him everything. But then he wiped his clamlike lips and was on her, her silence a kind of permission. He blundered into her with eagerness and love and came out again with grateful torpor. Eight months later they were married. The delay, Janie was sure, was caused by his mother's hounding him to drop her. But despite the quiet, diffident manner he assumed when in his mother's presence, Stephen stuck by her. I love her, Mama, he told her one night after dinner while they sipped tea on the porch swing. I love her and I will always cherish her.

Sex, Janie gleefully decided at the time, is stronger than blood.

A lot of things Janie used to believe have proved erroneous, but that is one idea she has not had to amend. So many things she treasured have been undermined, but that casual, defiant assertion made when she wasn't quite twenty still nags her. It's like with mosquitoes. You slap them and slap them and yet they're still buzzing, peppering you with bites that swell the longer you scratch them.

Sex is stronger than blood. Janie knows that, the secretary knows that, every trophy who ends up a wife worried about the next trophy knows that. Even Stephen's mother, who was cordially distant to her from the very first, knew it. She would never do anything so impolite as tell Janie what awful thing Janie had done, but it was clear that the horrible thing was not something for which she would ever be forgiven. On the morning of the wedding, though, Stephen's mother took her aside and issued what Janie at the time took to be a warning, but years later decided was a brief upwelling of compassion.

"Remember, dear," Stephen's mother had said, "the diamond is never big enough."

6

Stevie was a blue baby. He kept passing out as an infant and had to be revived with respirators two or three times a day. Stevie would cease breathing and his color would change the way figures in cartoons get hot or angry: the rapid progression through the hues of red to umber, to purply brown, to a midnight blue that looked like it came from a fountain pen. She went with even less sleep than she had anticipated; she was endlessly checking on him, putting her hand on his back to feel the tiny bones rise and fall, or failing that, shoving a compact under his nostrils. Once she brought iced tea out to the yardman and passed the time with him a little, talking of nothing in particular, when she was suddenly seized with dread. Back in the nursery Stevie was a blue ball, curled tight as a shrimp.

"There might be some damage," the emergency room doctor said. Janie looked at him blankly. "The brain. When he passes out like that he's not getting enough oxygen to his brain. We'll have to wait and see."

"Oh," Janie said, and found herself biting her lips until they were lumpy and sore and her mouth was filled with blood.

When she found out later, Janie wondered which was worse—

that her lack of watchfulness when Stevie was a baby meant he'd always be slow, or that Stephen used Stevie's slowness as a reason to sleep with his secretary? She didn't find out until the twins were three. She'd had inklings of it early in the pregnancy, but had said nothing. She was afraid to believe it was true. When she finally confronted him about it he said, "Yes." And Janie in a blind rage told him to move out. To which he said, "Thank you." For years, he said, he'd been piling guilt upon guilt until he was freighted with a moral heaviness so great that he was grateful Janie had given him the green light to shed it. Now, he said, he could live with himself. He could live with his secretary.

And Janie was left biting her lips again, wondering how he'd managed it, a getaway as clean as God's.

7

The switching yards are so close to Central Gardens that some mornings when Janie's working she can hear the click of wheels and the boom and bang of metal coupling with metal. It's as though the trains are lovers slapping each other, provoking desires where none exist.

Janie thinks things like this while she's doing these people's houses. She has overheard enough arguments to know that more slapping goes on in the world than you'd think possible. Knows, too, that every bit of violence that ends in love-making is a kind of rape the wives won't admit but acquiesce to. Sometimes there's a crack, a sharp little cry, and then the warm noises of two bodies struggling to overcome their own separateness. The warm humming noises of people desiring to meld flesh with flesh into a single flesh. As though such a thing were possible. As though the shouts and cries and exasperated gasps that Janie hears from two floors away don't give testimony to the fact that this cannot be so. Janie, listening to them, can look out the windows and see clouds above the treetops, gray cottony clouds stretched until they're shredded. On other mornings she sees high cirrus clouds that look like the pale skeletal bones of long, broad fish. It's on mornings like this that she keeps the windows open and listens to the trains coupling. They make a more distinct noise than people. But to get the windows open she has to argue. Most people for whom she works like to keep their windows closed. They have radiator heat and central air and big square rooms with high ceilings. They believe the noise of their house's machinery will drown out the noise of their love-making. And besides, why let the outside air in anyway? For ventilation, Janie will say. I need to breathe. And sometimes they relent.

Actually, there is precious little love-making in Central Gardens. Mostly she hears it in the newer suburbs where the nouveaux riches believe they're being racy. In Central Gardens she's only heard it twice, and both times it was after she started the air compressor, then shut it off to bleed the hoses.

Central Gardens is an old neighborhood, and except for the modern conveniences they keep to the old way of doing things. The houses are brick or pink granite or white stucco. Built at the turn of the century, they are now occupied by the descendants of the families who built them. There are a few Philadelphia attorneys and chiropractors sprinkled about, but most of the new money lives out east, in Germantown or Collierville. Janie used to live in Bartlett, and worked for all those people out that way, but she wanted to be closer to the river, closer to downtown, in a neighborhood where there were sidewalks and where people walked, at least occasionally, for groceries. She also wanted to get away from a neighborhood that was constantly reminding her of the accident. That's what she calls it, though it hardly seems accidental when you drink on purpose, as that boy had. But "accident" is as good a word as any for encapsulating grief, for letting her speak of what happened without feeling the jagged tear raging inside her.

Even if it doesn't work.

Some mornings at six A.M. it's only Janie and the live-in maids. The day maids are dropped off at six-thirty or seven by men in boatlike Chryslers and Cadillacs seven years out of fashion. The cars sputter away from the curb spitting oil like outboards, and with their ruined shocks and the suspension's swing and sway they really do look like boats riding low in the water.

The maids, if they know Janie's coming, will sometimes have a biscuit and coffee waiting for her. Then they retrieve the morning paper while Janie unloads her eight-year-old Datsun crammed with ladders, paint cans, shellacs, glues, and varnishes. She has wood crates filled with brushes and sponges, drop and oil and tack cloths, varnish removers and paint thinners, scrapers and steel wool, and plastic sheeting and rags. Also a box or two of medical examining gloves. Often the owners want the woodwork redone to go with their newly textured walls. They decide this once Janie's already painting. Then they say they'd like everything finished by Friday, Saturday at the latest. They're having a dinner party that evening and need the day to air everything out. Could you come in early? they'd like to know. We'd be ever so grateful.

Janie, letting her voice go good-old-girlish, says she might could, then quotes a figure that would put a strain on most people's gratefulness if she weren't so sure they'd smile knowingly to themselves if she asked for less.

Janie used to worry whether she was charging the right amount, too high or too low, and then found out that she was charging what a black painting crew grateful to get the work would charge. She discovered that she could get more work, or the right kind of it, if she priced herself nearer to exclusivity. There was a certain pride for her clients in agreeing to swallow too high a fee. But it took her years to figure this out.

She comes home most evenings eager only for a light beer and something nonthreatening on TV. For Janie, comfort is a major issue. It disappeared completely when Stephen left and she has spent years scraping herself and her family back into the middle class. At one point, right after Peter, she thought God was punishing her for trying to be comfortable. For merely wanting it. But then she thought, given what her clients make, her prices are fair and life isn't. So they're not connected. Bad things just seem to happen to her. It's a little the way she is—scatterbrained—and a little the way the world is. She locks herself out of her apartment, out of her car, leaves her car's lights on till the battery's dead, leaves money at the automatic teller machine. The machine she uses is called "Anytime Annie," and sometimes this alone so infuriates her that as she's walking away, she leaves her keys and her money right on the tiny aluminum shelf they provide for just such stupidities. Later she'll find her keys are being held by a security guard inside the bank, but her withdrawal has vanished.

Some people are just singled out, it seems. Major griefs and minor inconveniences: it's only by size that you can distinguish them. In the year after Peter was killed, Stevie had his truck wrecked by a couple of drunk teenagers in a stolen car, Nikki had her car stereo stolen, and Janie herself had backed into a light pole and sideswiped a neighbor's car while parallel parking. There'd also been a break-in at her studio and her cat had been run over right in front of the house. Renting in a block where everyone else owns, she had already felt singled out. Now she's becoming known as "the catastrophe lady." The people in the apartment upstairs, a history professor and his wife, talk about her. Recently, when she was backing her car out of the curved driveway—she had snapped the mudflap off previously, and was now smashing in the wheelwell—a deadfall from the pin oak in the front yard landed smack on the hood of her car. The professor's words to his wife and guests (they were having drinks on the front porch before the Memphis State–Old Miss game) floated out to her. "Some people," the professor said, "just aren't born to luck."

8

It was while she was still married to Stephen that she got interested in painting. Stephen thought this was something wives went through, a phase coincidental with pregnancy and childbirth and postpartum depression (he'd been reading up on this), so he made the arrangements for a nanny, and three mornings a week Janie drove the Volvo to Memphis and took classes at Memphis State. But Janie got good at it—watercolors especially; they were nontoxic, and with kids that mattered—and once Stephen moved in with his secretary, Janie moved to Memphis and finished her degrees. In graduate school she was drawn to oil and clay. Something tactile, thick under her fingers, that she could touch the painting after it was dry and feel the bright dark whorls of color: that was something. A small gallery in Miami took one of her pieces, "Evening, Lake McKellar," for an exhibit of *Art by Southern Women: Reforging the Chains,* and a Chattanooga collector bought another entitled "Lost at Sea." This pleased her but she was still dependent on Stephen's irregular alimony and child support checks, which were likely to arrive five, eight, fifteen days late, if at all. Stephen would make a big show out of making it up to her—buying her dinner in East Memphis, springing Mall of Memphis shopping sprees on the kids—but the ripples from this largesse were also meant to sustain them long after the wake of his passing had died against some far distant and unseen bank. His attentions were lavish but infrequent; the local Toyota dealer did better by him than they did.

She and Peter and Nikki and Stevie were still living in Bartlett then. One of Stephen's townhouses. The children were in a Catholic elementary school. Even Stevie. This was a sign of her rebellion against Stephen, who once commented that a Catholic woman had worked as a receptionist in his office for a time, and she seemed very nice. The lay teacher who had Stevie in her class, however, said Stevie might be best served by placing him in a special class. He's slow, the teacher explained, he needs special attention and care that in a class of forty-five I can't give him. Janie called Stephen.

"Stephen," she said, biting her lips, "Stephen, we need more money for Stevie. He's been tested, Stephen. He needs special schooling."

"Special, huh?" His tone was more impatient than malicious. He believed discipline and hard work could make even the slow adequate.

"Stephen, please. His teacher, the nuns—they all say he needs special attention."

"Hand-holding," Stephen said. Then, more softly, "What's this special attention going to run me?"

She quoted a figure that he would not have blinked at if she were redoing his living room. A great silence and then a resigned, "All right, I'll look into it."

So Stevie went to live with his father and his father's new girlfriend, and Janie, in the worst way, was happy. She couldn't admit this even to herself without acknowledging that a terrible fault resided inside her. Stevie was now enrolled in a school for the retarded outside Oxford. And Janie felt terrible because her life was made easier, because the very first emotion that washed through her was relief. It was not a feeling she trusted. Relief was a spitefully mixed blessing. Those nights she couldn't sleep she went down the hall to Nikki's room. Nikki smelled of just-washed hair. Janie resisted the temptation to slide into bed beside her daughter. It was enough to sniff the child-skin about her neck, to sniff the wet strands of hair still scented with shampoo. It was enough to remind her that her daughter was still there, still alive, still whole.

9

Sometimes the clouds look like they're big gray swatches of fabric that have been sliced with pinking shears. Other times like they've been ripped right across a straight edge. A tall slate mass of clouds edged sharply, blue sky trailing. Or that high pale blue with the perfect wall-cloud behind. Bad storms—sheet lightning, torrential downpours, tornadoes, landfall hurricanes—always, always, always with the wall trailing. The professor from the apartment above says it's because they live at the end of a trough where cold fronts from the north meet the leading edge of stationary fronts that bubble over the Gulf. The systems meet smack over the Mississippi. Hence the dramatic, changeable weather.

He repeats the usual joke: "If you don't like the weather in Memphis, wait fifteen minutes. It'll change." He's new to Memphis; he has to know the reason for everything.

10

The last week of the trial there are no clouds. High ceilings, unlimited visibility day after day. Not even humidity. The weatherman is glowing. It's February and it isn't raining and the daytime highs are nearing seventy. To unwind each day everyone goes back to Janie's place. It's a big brick house on Russelford and Janie keeps painting supplies—a ladder, dropcloths, wood crates filled with stains and turpentine, and paint brushes soaking inside coffee cans—behind the porch's long brick wall. She hasn't touched this particular cache in months and spiders have spun webs over everything. Her mother takes a broom to clean places for people to sit. "Janie, really—" her mother says, then stops. Nikki and her boyfriend Louis sit on the porch smoking cigarettes, Janie and her mother on white cushioned wire backs. Louis has the soft handsome features of the genetically wealthy—soft sculptured cheeks, very dark eyebrows, long sandy hair he keeps in a ponytail. He's wearing cuffed chinos and no socks, boat moccasins taped with silver duct tape, and a loose-fitting tweed coat over an equally loose-fitting turtleneck. Nikki met Louis at Rolling Meadows, the Episcopal boarding school for the recalcitrant but recovering well-to-do that Stephen had picked out for her.

Stephen has come to the house. It's the start of the last week and he feels obligated to be there. First days and last days—there's a gravity to these occasions that needs upholding and he is there to uphold it. Solidarity, he says, making it sound like he's sympathetic with Poland. He's the same way about everything. When the children started school he'd insist on driving them there on day one, and on the last day he'd collect them as well. He liked graduations, too. First days and last days rolled into one. Gravity. In art he always wanted the first or last in a series of prints or etchings. Anything in between, no thank you. The other numbers in the series exist only to establish distance between the items of real worth.

He stays in his car now. The secretary girlfriend (the first secretary is three? five? girlfriends ago by now) pouts in the front seat. She has lips specially made for pouting. They form a bright red cherry when she sucks in her cheeks. The car is a white Caddy with Mississippi plates. He has a Sunbird registered in Arkansas, and a 4X4 registered in Tennessee. Janie has no idea what his Alabama car is, and for all she knows he might have a western Kentucky car, too. He likes to keep cars in each state he does business. None are over two years old. After Peter, she told Stephen she didn't want him buying cars for the children, but he bought Stevie a maroon and blue pickup, which Stevie promptly totalled, and a Nissan 300 ZX for Nikki, on the grounds she'd repeat her senior year at Rolling Meadows, thereby qualifying her for Vandy, or at least Alabama or Ole Miss. He doesn't want her going to Memphis State or the community college, like her mother. All they know how to do there, he says, is play basketball.

Stephen's window vanishes into the door frame. From where they sit on the porch they can hear the cool exhaust of the air conditioner. "Janie," he calls, perfunctorily waving, "we'll see you tomorrow."

Nobody says anything. Nikki blows at a fly that's inspecting her knuckle.

11

Janie is thirty-eight but she used to be forty-one. She started subtracting three months ago, one month equalling one year. Now she's holding. She goes every evening at five-thirty to an aerobics class, and her body is hard and lean. Sometimes Nikki joins her. Nikki is a little soft, the way teenagers get when they drink beer and diet soda and don't exercise, but Janie has biceps that jump when she paints. Her forearms look like knotted rope, and the slight bulge of muscle on her upper arms shapes her back like a wedge. Her waist is small, and she has the hard thighs and tapered legs of a swimmer. If her mornings were freer she'd take up cycling; stationary bikes lack vista. Small women usually go soft, their behinds widening like plush pillows. Janie is taut as a bowstring.

It's her skin that worries her. After Stephen left, she made a point of acquiring, and keeping always, a deep mahogany tan—he hated that—and the effects are showing up now. Fine, tightly woven wrinkles pucker her arms and legs and face. She looks wiry but unstrung, a little haphazard. Her origins betray her. Working class. The ladies of the homes she works on say that to themselves, to each other. "Pretty once but . . . working class. You see how that turns out? They don't last. They're like those pretty Negro girls. Or *Indians*."

These women are friendly to her. They are pleased they have somebody handy with whom they compare favorably. And since she charges a hard wage but still less than an interior designer would, they speak to her with a candor they usually reserve for their hairdressers. Rolling salmon-colored paint onto somebody's living room walls, or marbling those walls pink or rose or white magenta, or sponging trompe l'oeil with a wrinkled baggy, she hears about divorces, infidelities, addictions, and neurotic obsessions. They make it sound like staying is obviously preferable to leaving, but they sound so sad in relating this that Janie wonders. All that forced brightness, all that levity. It's obviously a great strain for them. They have voices that go higher up the register with each fabrication, they crane their necks forward with the earnestness of those who want you to believe, until Janie has to shut her eyes to drive out the pictures of these shrill, contorted ladies protesting their happiness.

You don't know, Janie wants to say, having never left. And yet they want Janie, the one who has, to comfort them about staying. They have vested interests, they explain, they can't leave. Can't Janie see? And doesn't she feel awful about leaving? They are wearing navy wool dresses with pearls. Diamonds as big as pearls adorn their fingers. Clusters of pearls are set about their ears. Janie wears no rings; she takes off her turquoise when she's painting, and her brown fingers are stained and dried and stink of paint thinner and Elmer's Glue-All. A trade secret: Elmer's, when painted, makes new woodwork look antique.

What Janie wants to say to these ladies is, The diamond's never big enough.

But they've already decided it is.

What they want, it seems to Janie, are the spiritual benefits of leaving—freedom, release, privacy, space—with all the material comforts of staying. She understands completely their desires. She'd like for them to be true, too. But she wants to shout at each and every one of them, *It can't be done! Do you hear me? It can't be done!* THE DIAMOND IS NEVER BIG ENOUGH!

It's from their neurotic obsessions, though, that she derives her business. These women can't leave well enough alone. The furniture's all in place, the paintings, the candlesticks from the aunts in Carolina, the antique picture frames, the Oriental carpeting, it's all in place, but rose, not salmon, is the color sweeping through the formal dining rooms and living rooms of Germantown and Central Gardens and Collierville this spring. No, wait. It's teal. Teal for the dining room, rose for the parlor. They are conservatives of radical conformity. Which is fine with Janie, since during the slow months her business is mostly furniture work: faux antiquing, marbling, coordinating window treatments with caned radiator covers. Labor intensive and low margin. She'd rather be doing walls, big spaces she can feel her muscles stretching to accommodate. Territory, walls she can gallop across. Antiquing or marbling a mirror frame is like doing miniatures. Her business really depends on people changing wholesale. New homes, new walls, new looks. "We want to give the place a face lift," her clients tell her, believing that a certain attention to cosmetics can make everything new, everything better, everything wonderfully, inexplicably alive.

It can't, she wants to tell them. Look at me. Her face is a web of fine brown wrinkles, her arms shriveling berries. And Peter! Peter looked so preposterously perfect in his makeup. You could really believe he'd only fallen asleep in this oddly formal, static pose. A child mumming death. And everyone with the veils and black capes and condolences because this was a mummer's ball, a celebration people took too seriously. They had assumed too completely their roles. Really, it was starting to get on her nerves; it was really in very bad taste to continue dissembling like this.

At the private showing she lost it. Something gave way completely and she lost it. Nikki kept telling her this later, while getting her to drink water and holding tissues to her face. "You lost it, Mama. You really lost it." Janie had shaken Peter, slapped his face, tried pulling him free of the coffin by his lapels. All the while screaming, "Peter, wake up! Wake up, Peter! Wake up! You'll be late for school! *Pe-ter! Pe-ter!*" And then she collapsed, sobbing "Oh, my baby! Oh, my baby! Oh, my baby!" until they pulled her away from him.

She spent three days driving nails into a piece of clay. She made misshappened hands with stubby arms and drove nails into the palmy lumps. She fashioned a head, a torso. Nails went into the skull, the cheeks, into the chest, the back of the neck where the spine rose humplike into the shoulders. She took bits of plaster of paris and jammed them into the eye sockets, and wounded the clay further with twigs and bits of stick, with gravel, with green glass. When she was finished it looked like something from a fifteenth-century Polish church. Medieval, full of nudity and power. She worshipped it. Then she painted wildly in oil for three weeks, drunk on bourbon, coke, wine, codeine, coffee, iced tea, and tranquilizers. She painted almost exclusively in dark yellow, forest green, blood red, and black. Each square canvas featured a line of rectangular boxlike bodies with wide shoulders and stick-like limbs. Small rectangles for the heads. The teeth a row of tiny yellow boxes.

Recovering now, she wonders how many of these women lose it every day and never tell a soul, never say a word to anyone. Or if they do, make it seem all right even as they relate it to their friends over coffee in the sunroom: Oh, I had myself a good cry yesterday, you know. And the other women nod, and that's all that's said about it. A good cry, it's over now, it's just sometimes it gets to be too much, you know?

If a housewife screams in a suburb and there's no one there to hear her fall—?

12

Nikki has been kicked out of some of the finest Catholic and Episcopal boarding schools in the South. St. Catherine's, St. Lucia's, Pennywhistle, Argus, and now Rolling Meadows. Stephen should never have given her that car. There she is, tooling about the Mississippi Delta with a carload of kids doing whippets. That's what nailed them at the school's check-in gate. The clink of metal from spent whippets. Nikki claims she wasn't doing any. She was only driving home people who'd partied too much. "What am I supposed to do, Mama? Let them kill themselves?" That always gets to Janie. That plea. She believes everything Nikki tells her. She has to. Nikki is the last real child.

The last time this happened, the previous spring, Janie told Nikki, "I just don't know what to do with you. Why are you doing this? You're a fine student when you apply yourself. Why are you pulling these stunts?"

"I don't know, Mama."

"Well, find out, dammit. The trouble with you, young lady, is you listen to every fool who comes along with an idea that might be fun but isn't."

That was what Janie had decided about Nikki originally. When her grades plummeted and she started getting in trouble and St. Kate's asked her to leave and later St. Lucia's: it wasn't that she wasn't smart or wasn't good, it was just she listened to the wrong people. She allowed herself to be persuaded into doing foolish things by bad people, and all the time she thought she was doing them some good. Saving them in a way she couldn't save Peter. That drinking episode at St. Kate's, for example. Nikki knew that boy was going to get his liquor one way or another, and he'd most likely drive himself home later and kill himself. So she bought the liquor for him—she looked older, it was only when she opened her mouth that she sounded seventeen—and took the wheel, and she was the one arrested at St. Kate's gate for being underage in a car with open liquor. Nikki swore she hadn't been drinking herself. And only one boy, the boy Nikki was trying to protect, had tested intoxicated. The other two boys and the girl Nikki was with had tested only "impaired."

It was so silly it was stupid. The girl just didn't think.

Stephen blamed the Catholics. "It's the school itself. It's lax. I don't care what they say about discipline. The fact is Catholics are soft. That's why there're so many of them. Lord knows, I've had two Catholic women in the office, and they seem very nice and all, but—"

"But what, Stephen?" They had been through all this before. Janie had been a Catholic before she married Stephen. She converted before the engagement. They never breathed a word to Stephen's mother, for whom the word "former" or "lapsed" just meant you were biding your time. And given what transpired, perhaps it did.

"Let me handle this, Janie. Some things simply need to be taken care of." Stephen called his friend Hollister, whose own daughter went to Rolling Meadows, and the arrangements were made. Nikki would start the spring semester late, take summer term, stay the next fall and spring, and the following fall be at Vanderbilt or Ole Miss, her grades finally high enough to justify placing her there. The extra year of school wouldn't hurt and being a nineteen-year-old freshman might even give her a leg up on things.

"Stephen, let's just get her through the first spring, all right?"

Janie wished she could send Nikki farther away to school—something in Connecticut or New Hampshire or Vermont, where Janie had gone several times on vacation. But Stephen bought a hair transplant and started poor-mouthing himself. "Besides," he wanted to know, "what was so terrible about a Mississippi prep school?"

"Nothing," Janie said, "only Nikki might do better someplace else."

"She's going to do fine," Stephen said.

In celebration of her anticipated graduation the following spring Stephen sprang for the ZX. It was fire engine red with a red leather interior and a CD player with Bose speakers. Stephen was very proud of the speakers.

"Stephen, how could you? A car! She hasn't even graduated yet!"

"She will," Stephen said. "You know she will. She just has to be among the right sort of people."

In July Janie went to collect her. The car was being impounded. Janie would have to collect that later. Janie's only satisfaction in the whole business was that this time it happened at Stephen's school. "With Catholics it's drink," Janie told Stephen over the phone. "With Protestants it's whippets. I'm not sure I see the difference."

Now Nikki runs around town with her girlfriends and whatever boys are in that pack. Janie can't keep track of them all. There's Stacy and Jules and Amanda and Tricia and Beth and Winnie and Joleen and Diedre and Dixie and Sue Anne and God knows who else. Janie can't remember ever having that many female friends. Nikki buys beer for those younger and gets beer bought for her by those older. Her face has settled into that "Oh, yeah?" sullenness common among teenagers but never present before in Nikki. They hang out at the Antenna Club and the doughnut shop across the street they call Heavy Metal Doughnuts. The Antenna patrons head over there after closing for a sugar fix. Janie herself prefers Huey's. The burgers there are held together with cocktail tooth-picks and the acoustic-tile ceiling is studded with red and green cellophane-tailed toothpicks driven ceilingward through drinking straws. "It's sort of a tradition," she explains to Nikki, though she's been here before with Nikki and didn't feel the need to explain anything. "At the home of the best burger in Memphis," Janie says, feeling like a TV commercial, "you shoot your toothpick at the ceiling to see if you can get it to stick."

"*Mo-ther!*" Nikki says, rolling her eyes. "You're ruining my life. Huey's used to be cute, but it's bourgeois now, bogus. Don't you see? It's filled with old people."

Janie wonders when exactly she became old people.

Louis, although he seems like a nice young man, is evidently at least partly responsible for Nikki's new attitudes. Louis has come to dinner with Nikki, and it's obviously from Louis that Nikki learned her eye-rolling. He also says "Bogus!" quite often while studying his fingernails. Janie has an image of Louis in ten years saying "Objection!" with the same practiced boredom.

But that doesn't matter right now. What matters is that Nikki is sleeping at various friends' apartments, Diedre's and Jules's especially, but maybe also at Louis's and she's just eighteen. And Janie can't say anything against her, can't raise her hand though she's raised her voice plenty. But Nikki knows it's meaningless, knows that whatever Janie says now she'll relent on later.

"Don't you come back in my house if you do this! Don't you dare set foot in my house!" And a week later Nikki's back, raiding the refrigerator with her friends, taking Janie's books and cassettes, even Janie's sweaters. Janie's missing two silver picture frames and thinks maybe one of Nikki's friends stole them. "That's it!" Janie screams. "Never again do your friends set foot in my house!" But her alarm system is broken and though she threatens to change the locks she doesn't.

If Nikki were really to stay away Janie wouldn't be able to bear it. Over Christmas Nikki goes to Biloxi with Jules and Diedre, and comes back talking about Eddie. "Eddie's serious, Mom," Nikki says. "He wants to call me Nicole."

Eddie is a lifeguard. Nikki met him on the beach (Where else? Janie would like to ask, but she bites her lip), and he's real dreamy. "Dreamy," she says, like it's 1963. Isn't dreamy bogus? Janie wants to ask, but she doesn't say that, either. And she can't simply say, That's nice, because "that's nice" doesn't cover any territory at all. Neither does, What about Louis? All she'd get in reply to that is Aw, mom! as though the question were beyond belief. So instead Janie risks the one question that matters. "Are you using anything?" she whispers, as conspiratorially as Jules or Diedre might ask her, only without the giggles, and all she gets for her trouble is "Oh, mother!" as though she's asked her daughter to wear a sweater on a chilly morning when it might be nice later.

Janie's working on a house at Carr and Willett now, a big brick foursquare with a two-story clapboard addition in back. They call the addition a hang-on, after the way these homes were built— four huge rooms to a floor, no attic to speak of, and forty years later came the addition once eight gigantic rooms simply weren't enough for the way these families lived. Some people have even blown the roof off the attic, built in dormers, and use the extra space for the maids or as a family entertainment center. Before air conditioning, attics were of no use except as a place where the heat could escape to, and even now some people leave their attic windows open so the heat doesn't pent itself into an explosion. In other attics, though, window air-conditioning units have blossomed like mushrooms. Janie's seen some of these attics because she's been asked to decorate them. Often they're a room for the eldest son, soon off to or just back from college. To paint these walls, Janie pries off the thumbtacked posters of models in thong bikinis and crotch-hugging jean shorts and thinks, My daughter's sleeping with a lifeguard in Biloxi, Mississippi brought up on posters like these. She wishes she could tell Nikki she understands, because she does, really, but Nikki is not going to want to hear it. Oh, mother—! Janie can already hear that, can hear Peter's never-voiced Aw, mom! as she orders him to take down the thong ladies, posters he never put up, would never put up, and she comes to with a start when she realizes that the wall she's speckling has nearly dried. The tacky tsch-tsch-tsch of her baggie on the paint finally wakes her.

So how does she wake up Nikki? She can barely wake herself. For years now she has gone off with men she didn't trust. With Kenneth to the Outer Banks, and to Cape Cod with Stan. She went a couple of times with Stan to Wellfleet and Provincetown, and once even to Martha's Vineyard. They rented bikes and went looking for Kennedies. Stan was a tall man, thin and athletic. The word ropey comes to mind recalling him, and the hair on his head— black, oddly kinked curls going gray—was vaguely pubic. She liked to rub his bald spot, a point on his crown where baby fine hair grew like lawn seedlings doomed to frost. She met him on vacation. It isn't hard meeting men on the beach. You simply lay there and wait for them to talk to you. And they always, always would. Stan was a photographer. He wanted her to relocate, talked of marriage, said he could get her started in her own gallery, or if she wanted to keep doing walls she could do that, too. He knew a lot of people, artists and craftspeople all up and down the coast. He assured her she wouldn't be hurting for work.

His friends couldn't hold their liquor. Janie suspected they waited till they got drunk to say the things they wanted to. Or at least things they oughtn't. Janie couldn't tell if it was maliciousness or just bad manners. Every time she opened her mouth to speak—she usually waited until the evening was well along before she said anything—they stared at her as though she were from Mars. "Ah do declahre," one of them said with great quilty breathing, "a reg-u-lahr southern belle!"

"That's a phone company," Janie said, but she was already outside the circle. The moment she opened her mouth, she had become Stanley's Memphis belle. Stanley protested but Janie knew it was the same as if he were seeing a colored woman or a Jew. They were the open-minded sort who closed ranks on anyone not from the tribe. You could be different, but only in a limited way. Say as a liberal Republican. One had to stay with one's own sort, after all, at least in marriage. Until then it didn't matter who you slept with.

Janie found this out after she said she would stay with Stanley another three weeks in August. She had misgivings but pooh-poohed them. She could postpone her jobs in Memphis, and the two of them would go to Wellfleet, where Stanley knew some gallery people he'd like her to meet. Ditto people in Boston. She really shouldn't pass up this kind of opportunity. Cleaning the Boston apartment one day, she came upon a cache of ladies' underwear behind the bureau and hotel receipts mixed in with his correspondence for days she was in Wellfleet and he'd gone back to Boston on business. "But I was captivated by you," Stanley said.

"It's your own fault, really. You shouldn't look if you don't want to find."

So she was merely an oddity, a Memphis belle he could make promises to and cheat on. Among themselves they would put it cutely: *So Stanley's been fucking the maid again. How perfectly (choose one) awful/charming.*

So how can Janie blame her daughter for a fault they share? She wants to call Nikki and tell her, Don't trust anyone possessing both a smile and a penis, but instead she calls Nikki and reminds her that succumbing is not hope, that submission is not salvation, and that it's not easy, but you can maintain distance and skepticism even in the most rapturous of positions.

"Mother," Nikki says, "what in tarnation are you talking about?"

13

The boy who killed Peter was a quarterback for Presbyterian Country Day. That's how she thinks of the blond boy in the blue suit and the blue and maroon foulard. When they pulled him from the car he had long strings of blond hair hanging in his eyes and a chin beard of black and blond and rust-colored wires. He reeked of alcohol. She knows this because Peter was struck by a car going sixty-three in a thirty-five zone. And he was not alone. William, a friend, was with Peter when it happened. They were trying to cross Poplar Pike. They were on the curb chatting and there seemed to be a gap in traffic and Peter stepped off the curb. William started, then stopped, then made a grab for Peter's shoulder. The car—a '59 candy-apple red Plymouth convertible, boat sized, with a white interior and fins—spun Peter over the front grillwork and up the windshield and spun him off to one side the way you might send a penny spinning off a table. Only this penny—these were the words her attorney used in court—only this penny ended up dead.

William said he couldn't remember anything. Pieces only. He remembered the car, its looming grillwork, its shriek of brakes, the thud, like the sound of cars colliding, you know? Only it wasn't cars colliding. It was Peter. Peter and the boat. Peter with his cheek bruised and scratched, his legs bent up under him in a way that didn't seem natural unless you were a little kid playing Army and pretending you were dead. Kids die in poses like that. When Janie paints in her sunroom she sees the children across the street with their sticks and toy guns. Their elaborate death throes are appalling. They clutch their chests, stagger, throw wrist to forehead as though in a faint, then collapse to the ground, knees first, then shoulders, then their bellies slump, they twitch once, twice, an arm gets thrown out, they lie still, they jerk, they roll over, they fake electric shock, they throw out the other arm, and then finally, finally they lie still, crucified on their parents' front lawn, their heads tipped to one side.

Peter just had a little dirt on him. His T-shirt and pants were stained and smudged, his cheek was scraped and there was some grit in his hair. He'd come in sometimes looking worse than that after working on the car. Surely—

Janie doesn't want to talk about it, but she can't not. Every day she goes to the trial and watches a parade of human beings she doesn't know or only vaguely recognizes all claiming to know her son or the boy who killed him. There are photographs, diagrams, calculations that remind her of high school trigonometry problems. If Fig. A is traveling from East Memphis at fifty-nine miles per hour, and Fig. B is a stationary object on a curb near Sound Warehouse, what will the velocity of impact be at 3:38 P.M., Central Standard Time, given dry road conditions, a clear day, and six empties clinking about the floorboards behind the front seat?

Each day she goes home with her mother and Nikki and sometimes Louis and they sit on the porch swing or the metal deck chairs in the mild February air and talk about bulbs maybe breaking free of the ground soon and the first flair of forsythia—how soon? how soon?—until she can't take it anymore and runs inside crying.

Some nights on her walks with Rufus she rolls in the oak leaves and shows up later at Huey's or the P&H Cafe with bits of oak leaf and other detritus in her hair. She has three or four or five Lite beers, then goes home and showers obsessively.

Her attorney tries explaining due process to her. He is a serious young man with tortoise shell granny glasses and a neatly trimmed mustache and only the hint of second chin forming underneath an otherwise handsome face. He is married with two children and lives in her neighborhood. She sees him sometimes tossing an orange Nerf ball at his three-year-old son, who tries batting it with a monstrously huge banana yellow Nerf bat with an outsized blue handle. The swings are clumsy, the father relentlessly encouraging. The ball travels maybe three feet. In his offices he tries explaining reasonable doubt and jury of your peers and she's screaming, "Jury of your peers? Jury of your peers? How about Peter's peers? How about a jury of people hit by automobiles? How about a row of bloody corpses, huh? Huh? Huh?" And her attorney, the mild young man with the round face and the tortoise shell spectacles calmly lets his blue-suited chest and shoulders absorb her beating.

14

There is a problem with the boy who struck and killed her son. (She can't think of him any other way.) He's the son of an appellate court judge and is a star quarterback. The policeman at the scene recognized this. Eight hours elapsed before they gave him a breathalizer test. There seems to be an unspoken agreement among all present—judge, jury, spectators, courtroom personnel—that this was a terrible accident but not, repeat not, a criminal offense. The defense attorney, a florid man with iron-gray wavy hair and a propensity for double-breasted suits, fosters this view, repeating over and over that the freshly barbered boy in front of them should not pay a lifetime's worth of guilt and sorrow—he is already sorry—and certainly should not be criminally liable for a single moment's lapse of concentration, especially since that stretch of Poplar Pike—a commercial street of strip malls and dry cleaners and florists and restaurants with funny names like the Halfway House, Ben's Lobster Supreme, and the Normal Barbecue—has neither a consistent sidewalk nor a crosswalk.

"It could," the defense attorney concludes, "have happened to anybody."

Janie cannot believe what she's hearing. Why hasn't her attorney leapt to his feet? Why isn't he riddling that flimsy argument full of the holes it's so easy to poke? Why does he seem to be cooperating, even acquiescing in this clean, clinical discussion of what this one boy has so carelessly, remorselessly done to her son? And to talk of that barbered boy's suffering! Twisted, grievous mess—that's what her attorney said in his opening arguments, and after that Janie could barely bear listening, but she did, and now it's come down to this calm reasoning, this weighing and sorting of testimonials and pitches for leniency. It could *not* have happened to anybody. Even the way he says the word is a lie. He says *any*body, not any*body*. Body body body body! Don't they see? Don't they feel it? The cold rush of metal into one's abdomen, the whoof! of air dispersing, disappearing? The internal blossoming of organs loosed in blood?

It's a conspiracy of concern for the living body over the lifeless one. The boy in question is a prettified drunken quarterback who had the good fortune of being born into an appellate court judge's household. What matters most, it seems, is how to dispose of the evidence and not muck up the future for the guilty when what's done is done for the innocent.

That night Janie feels something biting her under the covers. Her legs, her feet, her thighs, it's even chewing into her pubes. Something is biting her legs or crawling on them while she sleeps.

She gets a flashlight and shines it down the length of her torso—nothing. Examines every inch of the bed covers—still nothing.

And yet that morning she has a rash. Red pustules as though an army of something was eating her alive while she slept. Ointment, a hot shower, more ointments help. She still has the rash but it feels less like fire.

She makes a notation on the phone pad, "Call dermatologist. Call exterminating company," then rushes off to court, tearing another mud flap free from her car as she backs down the driveway. There's a clunk and a scrape and after she pulls forward and backs out again, she can see the mud flap in the driveway. It looks like a roofing shingle. She gets out, picks it up, and tosses it into the back seat on top of some magazines and McDonald's wrappers. The car is filled with the fumes of thinners and paint.

Something is going to happen to me, she says once she's moving. The window is down and the sun is streaming across her face and the yellow dust motes flutter like leaves. There is a tickling inside her stomach and about her waist. The car smells now of warm dash and upholstery, and the air of wet mold.

Something is going to happen to me. She can feel it in the way her knuckles curl over the steering wheel.

The rash is spreading.

15

After the trial is like the first day of the trial. Her husband Stephen is there, but he stays out on the street in his white coupe with his new black hair and his red wool and silk mini-skirted girlfriend. All he can say when Janie comes up to say goodbye is, "If he'd have stayed with me—"

And then he drives off, the engine roaring.

Janie's eyes sting and she thinks it might be from the way the dying sunlight lands on her hands, her cheeks, her eyelids. She looks up through the bare trees and there are high cirrus clouds, brightly white against the palest blue imaginable. They are as thin as fish vertebrae. Is this the something? she asks herself. Is this the something?

16

In the morning she stands in her nightgown in front of her dry sink. The dry sink has been in her family for ages. It is high backed and mirrored. She keeps a speckled enamel bowl and a pitcher on the table, but she showers like anyone else. The bowl is for letters, the pitcher contains dried flowers. She wonders when it was that her arms started to wrinkle, and has her face always seemed this weblike? Her hair is the color and texture of spun cocoa.

Every night for the next week she is visited by the vermin. The dermatologist can't help her; neither can the exterminator. He checked the mattress, box spring, mattress pad, bolsters, bed frame, sheets, blankets, pillowcases, wardrobe, everything. She has to leave the house for an entire morning while he sprays and pokes at holes. When he's done he says she can't go back in the house for another couple of hours, then she should air the house thoroughly. "And what was it?" she asks. The exterminator man shakes his head. "Negative, ma'am. It all came up negative." Dr. Polanchard tells her the same thing. Whom should she believe, these experts or her own skin?

She tells the history professor upstairs about it. The poured cement and brick porch is the only covered place outside, and they have an arrangement that allows them both to use it. Janie is out there now refinishing somebody's furniture—a bedroom set for a five-year-old with a painted border of leaves and fairies on the bureau's sides and headboard. Or maybe they wanted bunnies and mushrooms. It's hard to remember. Blue and white, pink and green. It's so pastel Janie can't stand it. But she's trying to get herself back into some kind of normalcy. Dr. Polanchard says her painting will help. He says throwing herself into her work will help. But that's a guy thing. She's too distracted to concentrate.

She's drawing the stencils while waiting for the apartment to air. The history professor listens sympathetically when she tells him about these things that keep biting her, but nobody can find anything. She gets going and going about it until she's telling him that it's spread to her buttocks and the small of her back. At aerobics the raised hives show through her tights; her legs have the look and feel of a pebbled basketball. Even the undersides of her breasts are affected. I thought it was prickly heat but it's not, she says, and lifts up her arm. She's wearing a tank top, and the hives run like an army of marching rats into her armpit. The history professor says maybe it's stress. He's preparing a paper on the divorce rates of Nebraskan homesteaders in the 1840s and 1880s. Women were more likely to bring these suits than men were, and that establishes his assertion that emancipation on the Plains began a lot sooner than people generally think it did. It coincides, he says, with the rise of mental hospitals for the female insane. Surely, he says, this is not without significance. Janie wipes her hands with a rag and nods. She knows he's in the middle of an affair with one of his soon-to-be-divorced graduate students. It's just like a man, she thinks, to be writing lectures, papers, even whole books about the emancipation of women while doing that. Dead women, she thinks. Safely emancipated. Dead, free. She throws the rag down, suddenly enraged. Then she discards the notion of telling his wife as soon as it occurs to her. What business is it of hers? She has problems aplenty without alienating the neighbors.

"Can I make you some tea?" the history professor asks. He's going inside and he'd be happy to bring her a glass. Janie says thank you and then feels his eyes lingering on the sway of her breasts and the jump of her biceps as she rubs stencils onto the bureau top. She allows herself a brief crinkling of smile. After his graduate assistant, she's next. It will be a silly business, her telling him she's not even remotely interested while he's saving face by saying he thought it was her idea, something she wanted. After all, she lifted up her arm to show him her hives.

And something is still eating at her. In the mirror she sees bite marks. It's not just itching; there are pinpoints of blood from the teeth.

She wonders, *In this the something that's going to happen to me? Is this the something?*

She paints walls now with a special fury. The marbleized cornices and trompe l'oeil buffets have a finished, angry look to them. The customers never notice, except for one woman who asks if maybe she isn't working too hard?

Janie promises she'll slow down. This is not a business where you can afford word of mouth containing qualifying "buts—." So she practices being calm, wiping her fingers as though she might be dusting, moving her crates of material about with an intensity of professional purpose. Her own work takes on the frenzy instead. A surviving victim of Francis Bacon meets feminization. That's what she wants to title her latest. An inverted V of boxlike figures with stick hands and red bloblike heads flank the familiar elongated hexagon, the painting's monolithic center. The brushwork is frenzied, the figures hideous, as though, like the clay figure in the living room, they were made of cardboard, plaster, pieces of earth, and branches. Everything beckons to her, the turkeylike flesh and the sticklike arms, the blood black and red bodies, the sickly green eyes. They are androids from hell, and her nipples are itching. Her flecking breasts are on fire, and she wants to feed them, she wants to feed them. She throws down her brushes and screams.

17

Months pass. Janie still goes every night to see the military payloads rattle through the switching yard, listing like somnolent bulls. Half-tracks and troop carriers and tanks and jeeps on flat-beds, each machine in camouflage colors or Army green with the white bars and stars and lettering. And the chemical tanks and boxcars, each stenciled DANGER RADIOACTIVE.

She just folds her arms across her chest and watches them clank and rattle through. Her attorney says if not the criminal case, then the civil. They can at least get something. Janie pinches her muscular biceps with her thumb and four fingers and watches the veins jump in her forearms. Corded mahogany. There's a wrinkled sadness to every bit of flesh she touches these days. It's even true of her new boyfriend, with whom she already knows she won't stay long. It's as though every bit of moisture has been wicked clean away from her life, leaving her nothing but wrinkled sacking.

Four jets from the Naval Air Station at Millington make matching razor slices across the sky, unfurling themselves into bleached asparagus tips.

"Janie?" her attorney asks.

Janie comes to with a start. "I don't think so," she says. Then, more definitively, "No, absolutely not."

"But we can win this one," he says. "We have a real chance."

"No," Janie repeats. "Absolutely not. Please, don't ask me again."

Nikki has moved in with Louis, though she still writes Eddie. Maybe she'll marry them both. Or neither. The world is so full of possibilities, and who's to say polygamy might not come back into fashion?

Janie's beginning to believe that what she's received from life are only some of its possibilities.

Nikki's friend Jules has become Janie's confidant. It is from Jules, not Nikki, that Janie hears Nikki's quit Louis and gone to see Eddie, who lives in Nashville, and it's Jules who later tells Janie that Nikki's moved in with her. Janie sees that as a good sign.

Nikki is worse off in some ways than Janie. Janie at least knows something's happening. Nikki hasn't a clue. She's spent the last year being social, or whatever it is they say now when they mean a girl is sleeping around to keep from being alone with herself.

By October, Nikki's moved at least partway back home, leaving off books and laundry, though officially she's still staying with Jules. When she and Jules come back from their dates or wherever they've been, they won't go inside the house. They sit on the poured cement railing instead, their backs against two square brick columns, and toss cigarette butts and Lifesaver wrappers and Diet Coke cans and Corona bottles over the railing and into the box hedging. A little trash heap gathers beneath the porch. Outside where Nikki parks her car, there's another. She just drops her wrappers out the window. God or the city sweeping crew will eventually whisk everything clean away.

Some nights Janie finds Jules and Nikki sitting there when she comes back from her walk, and Janie thinks of joining them, of saying, Make room, y'all, but she doesn't for the same reason she didn't climb into bed with Nikki years ago. Rufus nosing their hands is intrusion enough, though Nikki leaves her hand where Rufus can lick it and wag his tail happily.

When they want her, they'll ask her.

18

Nearly eight months after the trial Janie is wondering if she should mark the second anniversary of Peter's death. Not if, rather, but how. How do you celebrate an event like that? A party? Call up Peter's friends—Jules would know, she used to date Peter once upon a time—and invite them for a cookout? Ask everyone to come in dark suits, black velveteen dresses, and dance to Halloween organ music? Give people those purple funeral flags with the white cross and the magnetic bases and drive Central Gardens into a panic? (The dead of Central Gardens are discreetly buried elsewhere.) Janie doesn't know where to begin. She's driving past the Maryland Arms on Mansfield and Central, however, when it hits her. The Maryland Arms is an exclusive condominium. It's red brick with green- and pumpkin-colored awnings. Each unit has its own brick and stone balcony and underground parking. Out front, there's a wrought iron fence with brick pilasters and a circular drive. Out on the lawn they've having a party. They're still setting things out. There's a large yellow-and-white striped tent. Yellow napkins, tridents of candles, white lawn chairs, and tables. Wine goblets, water glasses, silver place settings, aluminum canisters of soda, and great troughs of ice. What Janie can do is get everyone to come over just after this party has broken up. They'll sit among the rumpled napkins, spilled wine, half-full water glasses, discarded finger sandwiches, melting sherbet, drying fruit slices, and crumbs. The breeze will ruffle their hair and they will all think of long ago, when Peter was alive and the bright yellow leaves of the ginkgo trees did not seem to mock them.

Janie feels the nape of her neck, then signals for a right turn into the drive. A curious thing has happened: since late summer the rash has subsided. It is only a rash now, and it's centered just beneath her neck, an inverted triangle of raised dots that spreads across her thorax and funnels like water between her breasts. Sometimes she feels it beneath the bra she wears while working out, but that's just sweat.

Janie does a slow turn around the drive. Her car labors in third gear, bucks even, but she's watching the white-jacketed waiters too closely to pay attention to her driving. Even her rash gets brief attention; she scratches absently, downshifts absently. The waiters set out butter dishes and mint trays and linen-wrapped bread baskets and bowls of grapes. Tiki torches are being set, bug coils lit. They are below the gnat line. Even in October no-see-ums and mosquitoes can pepper your limbs with bites.

Bites. Janie is scratching her neck harder as she completes her circuit. She's still looking over her shoulder as she prepares to pull from the drive into traffic. From behind the building, three black men are pushing a shiny black 300 ZX into the drive. It's wrapped like a Christmas present. Foot-wide red ribbons run the entire length and width of the car. On the Z's hood sits a huge red bow. She's watching as this car creeps up in her rear- and sideview mirrors—objects are closer than they appear—so she doesn't see the larger vehicle from her left that she's rolling into as she exits the drive. She doesn't even see it's a truck until it's two-thirds of the way past her. There's the single eeeeeehhhh! of the horn and then her car is shuddering several feet to the right. Her bumper flies off beneath the truck and a headlight skitters and slides and jumps like a dropped head of cabbage.

It's a dry ice truck. Janie sits with her hands at ten and two o'clock, the crushed front of her car pointing at Archer Hall across the street. A Victorian stone mansion with crenelated towers, high arched gables, and coppery green gutters and flashings, Archer Hall has been empty since the last owners tried and failed at turning it into a restaurant. The Rotary Club has their House of Horrors there each Halloween. Janie is sure the Archers, when they built this monstrosity, never intended for their front lawn to be an asphalt parking lot with fading yellow parking lines, the lot roped off by a cankered chain looped like cartoon ocean waves between short yellow fence posts. Nor did they intend for their house itself to be a joke ghost house, a fundraising gimmick for a men's drinking club. But it is, and suddenly for Janie everything is very clear. She sees things in a way she doesn't believe she ever has before. In a way she didn't think before was even possible. She starts to laugh and cry all at the same time, the tears running down her cheeks and dropping like snowflakes into her mouth and onto her chin and fingers.

"Are you okay, lady?" the driver's asking. He's not from around here, his voice is too nasal. Janie keeps staring straight ahead, her hands at ten and two o'clock. The driver is offering her his license. She should reply, do the same. But she simply cannot take her hands off the wheel. She holds on tight; it feels like Play-Do when you can't squeeze it any tighter and it's a cool snake inside your fingers. Janie can't feel anything but that cool inanimate snaking just beneath and outside her grasp.

Amazing, simply amazing. She leans her head forward until her forehead touches the top of the steering wheel.

"Lady, are you all right? Lady? LADY!?"

She lifts her head, smiles weakly, then bites the steering wheel, gets it like a dog might a favorite stick between her teeth. She tongues the warm plastic and she is amazed at its rigidity and texture inside her mouth.

"LADY? Lady!?"

She lets the steering wheel go. "It's all right," she says. "I'm fine. I'm going to be fine, really."

"Jesus, lady, you gave me a fright." He starts going on about her going into the street like that, just rolling like a trike as he was lumbering toward the interstate. Janie again shakes her head and smiles weakly.

"Yes," she says. "Yes. I guess I gave us all a fright."

The Last Great Dream
of My Father

The last great dream of my father was having his fields cut and manicured into the likeness of a bottle for a liquor company. I call it the last great dream of my father because surely there had to have been others, though I never knew about them, except for the unspoken one: that one day I would succeed him, which I didn't. I have often wondered what my father's other great dreams might have been. Or if he had any. It's not that I can't imagine him not having them, but it seems as though his dreams were marked chiefly by their betrayal, and he nurtured himself from betrayal to betrayal rather than from dream to dream. And perhaps after I betrayed him twice, and the liquor company had betrayed him once, he'd had enough.

The liquor company needed about sixty acres of uninterrupted field in which to grow their bottle and toward this purpose my father tore out what fences there were, and allowed them to bulldoze a lane his grandfather had cut, which ran to a back hill where once, his and Norm Jenz's and Ronnie Theobold's fields all met at a single maple on the crest. Most of my parents' land was rolling, but he had managed to stitch together these adjacent thirty-three acre fields which, though near the river, nearly never flooded and were flat as anything you'd see in Iowa.

He told me of his dream over the phone. Or rather, Mom told me this. My father and I didn't speak on the phone. There was no animosity behind this, though there was reason enough if he'd wanted any. But he just didn't like phones. Not seeing the person he was speaking to tended to freeze up his tongue. He could answer easily enough, but then the machinery of his speech would seize up, there'd be this long silence, and then my father would say, "Here's your mother," or "You want to speak to your mother?" and we'd communicate that way, with my mother relaying the news, which mostly had to do with people I no longer knew or had never met and didn't care to.

My father was in his third year of chemo. They'd taken out part of one lung and his hair loss was stabilizing but it did not appear to be in remission. Like its host, his was a patient cancer, slow and inexorable.

"How did this happen?" I asked my mother. "About the liquor ad, I mean."

"He saw an ad they had done in snow on a frozen lake in some magazine and opposite it was something about those Indian designs in Ohio—you know, the things that look like snakes and monkeys, turtles, maybe, I don't know—anyway, he took it into his head to write these people and he told them that their bottle would look better in green. He pitched the whole idea to them, saying he had the right land for it and everything, and although he'd planned to put in corn this year, it already being in alfalfa they could cut a design in it easy as pie. He got a phone call back saying they were already working on that very thing, but they were wondering if they couldn't use different crops to get different tones—you know, so it'd have, what did they call it? Oh yes, texture. Your father said certainly, it'd just take a little more work plowing and planting and laying it out, but certainly it could be done. He could do it. They said fine. When he got off the phone with them he said he should have gone into advertising."

"Had he been drinking, Mom?"

A pause. "I'm not going to fight him on this, Matthew. He says it helps with the nausea. If he believes that, then fine. I'm not going to get into a knock-down drag-out fight with him over this. Not now. Not over this."

"Fine, Mom. Just tell him to lock in a good price."

"Oh, he's done that, honey. A lot more than if he'd planted and harvested it himself. Even Milo Ayres says so. You remember Milo, don't you? Lives over the hill? Never married, not even when Ernie Bremmerman's daughter showed all that interest. She was in Fred's class, but I think it was her cousin Frieda that was in yours. Or was she in your sister's? Anyway—" and she launches into the history of the Bremmermans as it might coincide on a time line with our history, and I nod and say yes yes, and wait a decent interval before I say I have to go now, the kids need to be put to bed.

The liquor company didn't use my father's fields, of course. They went to Iowa instead, or had fields like my father's contracted in twenty-seven different places figuring one would come in right. This was in the days before computer graphics really took off, so an ad like this would still be done on an actual field somewhere. But I don't know the real story, I only know his. My father, of course, considered it a betrayal. It wasn't a betrayal. It was a contract, and he failed to read the fine print, the cancellation and kill fee clause, which provided for a payment fifteen thousand dollars less than what he'd have earned, had he planted it in corn like he'd originally intended.

He must have known, though, that something like this was happening from the beginning. He was used to betrayals. Abandonments. I moved to another state and made a decent living selling land for developers, land a lot like what he was working and losing his shirt on. That was one of my betrayals. The other was Rita Sabo, the woman I didn't marry, a woman he didn't like because she was part Indian. He warmed up to her once she was pregnant— he liked the idea of fertility and its eminent demonstration in a real live grandchild—but I abandoned her like I abandoned my father, the two of them knowing this would happen but wishing otherwise. I married neither the land nor the woman, and if we didn't talk on the phone much it may have been as much my not wanting to speak with him as it was his being uncomfortable with phones in the first place. A practical man, I am uncomfortable around people who should know better—who do know better—but who wish to believe otherwise. Cynical saps, pessimistic romantics—they creep me out. All that belief they wear in their eyes, all that hurt trust, all that wounded pride. They creep the bejesus out of me. The last time I saw Rita she was getting ready to marry somebody else, but the look in her eyes was the same as when I told her I was leaving Augsbury. I'd been saying it often enough that she had probably stopped believing it was so. And even as I was taking leave of her, promising her things about the checks, she probably believed it was still going to work out okay. Even as she was working up her hate of me, even as she knew all her future dealings with me would be done out of spite for me and what I'd done, she still probably believed—hoped against hope, really—that it was going to work out okay.

It's the same with this liquor ad: my father had to have seen it coming, yet he also had to have hoped otherwise. It's what keeps people like him and Rita Sabo going, like visualizing the numbers of the lottery just before you pick them. The numbers turn out all wrong, of course, but just before you write them down, and again before you read the actual numbers in the paper, you have this mystical moment of connection and believe that everything's going to line up for you. The crosshairs of the universe are going to sight true for you and you alone.

And afterwards you have an equally strong feeling that you picked the right numbers, but for the wrong day, and which day was it going to be anyway? Maybe the day those numbers lined up has already past, and even though there's this sick feeling in the bottom of your heart about lost chances, missed opportunities, the next time your feeling is equally strong for some other combination of numbers, bound each to each by a force as elemental as fate, as immutable as the laws of physics, as mystical as any religion.

And they turn out wrong, too. And the one day you don't buy a ticket there they are, the numbers you would have picked, you're sure you remember thinking this combination, only you didn't buy a ticket, and there they are, vibrating in black ink in the newspaper's lower right hand corner.

It must be something in the machinery. A glitch. Somebody monkeyed with it, interfering with the workings of fate. These are not accidents. There is a logic to these things, and if the order is upset, if when you look at the numbers they seem completely random, or they look suspiciously like the numbers you picked for the drawing before this one, or suspiciously like the ones you were *going* to pick for the lottery after, then the conspiracy of people working to deprive you of what is rightfully yours is at it again.

Rita Sabo believes that, I'm sure. And not without reason.

But maybe it's not people conspiring. Maybe it's a conspiracy of fate. Fate is its own conspiracy. It's like fate seeks out volunteers, people willing to believe, and if you volunteer to believe, fate's willing to lead you on. And then laugh at you. Not at everybody, but at you in particular. Could anything be crueler than that?

I imagine my father's betrayal running along lines like these:

He gives those advertising people everything they want. They fly out to the Appleton airport, complaining all the while what a pissant little town this is, rent a car, complain of nothing but dust and the smell of manure and how the local restaurants give them La Croix water at lunch rather than Perrier or Evian, then they have the gall to say to my father, "We see things a little different than how we agreed on the phone. We wonder if we couldn't get two fields, one in variations of green and one as we already discussed. We think some variation in color will show up better from above than just varying shades of green, but we'd really like to be sure. Could you spare two fields like this? We'd pay you extra, of course."

My father would chew his lip for a while and then say, "Okay." The men would nod to each other. There would be two of them.

My father is a great haggler one-on-one with anybody, but these two suits, one talking, one silent, had it all worked out already, which one would do the talking, which one would stand silently by, like an executioner just waiting for the word to pull the plug on the whole deal. My father would swing his head between the two of them and know he had a snowball's chance in hell of getting them to agree to anything they didn't already see as being to their advantage.

He grew his crops on those fields just the way the advertising people asked. They brought in some of their own people as well. Dad planted whole sections by hand while two or three techies sat hunched over clunky "portable" computers punching up numbers on a screen like the whole thing was paint-by-numbers.

"We need yellow for the lettering. Can you do that, Mr. K?" They would have already forgotten his name.

"Wheat," my father would say. "Spring wheat."

"And a kind of border, paler," they said.

"Oats," my father would tell them.

And so on and so forth. They worked it out from there. Timothy for the main parts of the bottle, alfalfa for the shading, more wheat for the proof business on the bottle's bottom. They wanted diagonals off to the side for the bottle's shape to play off against. "Geometric designs give us a strong contrast, Mr. K,"—they remembered it started with a K—"like the patterns you see in baseball diamonds on TV. Cross-mowing, it's called. A strong visual. It looks very nice."

"I don't watch baseball on TV."

He wound up giving them everything. "Eighty thousand dollars," they told him. "For two fields, each with a bottle design on it, we'll give you eighty thousand dollars." Eighty thousand. It seemed like a fabulous amount right then. Eighty thousand, though, less my father's time, less his hired labor, less his seed and fertilizer. Less the feed he'd have to buy to feed his dairy herd that normally he'd grow himself. They printed out these schemes, like the old four-color map problem you used to work on in eighth grade, and my father and these techies colored them in. They surveyed each field and drove stakes and strung string. My father took another field, one he usually rented for feed corn, and staked it out, too. This they'd do in alfalfa and timothy just to see what they'd get. My father wasn't thinking when he agreed to all this. Or he was always thinking, but it was drinking thinking, as reliable as a five-cylindered Chevy. Who knows what the chemo was doing to him, too. His hair was still falling out in tufts. What was left looked like alfalfa sprouts scattered and wilting across his head.

"Corn might be good for that lettering," my father told them. "Maybe even nicer than wheat. There'd be more space for the sunlight to shine into the depths of the lettering. I'd furrow deep around each letter, too, and around the label and the entire bottle, just for the sake of contrast."

He got to thinking like them. Or at least he thought he was. He thought he knew his business and theirs besides.

"Remember, Mr. K," they kept saying. "Remember we need a strong visual. We need to see this from an airplane."

The label was the hardest. Tiny lettering—"State of Tennessee." He had to stagger the planting to keep the quality of the lettering intact, and then there was the face of that bearded fellow, winner of the Nobel prize for whiskey or some such thing, taking up the label's center. It must have driven him crazy. Pruning these letters and the figure as though he were a gardener, only the garden was now one hundred and twenty acres in size. Toward the end Mom said his hands were shaking. He'd come home at night, filthy, beat, done in. It'd already be dark. He'd drink the advertiser's product— he'd switched, out of faith, out of loyalty—and hope that he hadn't blown the face or the lettering, which in turn might blow the whole deal.

It was the only time she saw him, she said, anxious not for the weather or the crops or the animals, but for himself. Like his goddamn reputation as a farmer was at stake with these idiots. "His confidence has gone out of him," my mother told me over the phone. "I'm not sure what's replacing it."

Once the techies were through planning, of course, they left. Flew back to New York and left him to his own devices. Then, periodically throughout the summer, they'd fly over in light planes, never telling him they were coming, to see how it was progressing. That must have driven him crazy as well. Big Brother is watching, but he's not telling you he's watching, you just notice he's there, and anyway, there's nothing you can do to keep him from watching even if you wanted to make him stop.

About this time my father started remembering the Polish he'd learned as a boy from his maternal grandfather. Whether this was drink or chemo or just plain old age (he was only fifty-eight at the time) I don't know, but circuits were misfiring, or connecting in ways they hadn't in decades. "He goes around the house in the evening," my mother told me, "muttering '*Gdzie jest butelka? Gdzie jest moje buty? Daj mi buzi,*' and then he tries to kiss me."

I wrote everything down, looked them up in a Polish phrasebook. Where is my bottle? Where are my shoes? Give me face, which the phrasebook says means 'Give me a kiss.' "Relax, Mom," I told her over the phone. "He just wants to kiss you." But I could see my addled father in his stocking feet, his boots already shrugged off in the mudroom, looking for his bottle and his house slippers, and having found and utilized both, suddenly getting amorous with my mother.

It was not a pretty picture.

I could imagine other things as well, though I don't like to think about them. I'm a solid citizen now, a responsible Republican, liberal enough to have married a Democrat. Not so conservative I don't feel guilt over what I have or haven't done, not so much guilt that it stops me from doing or not doing. How Rita Sabo is getting on in the sixteen years since I didn't agree to marry her is none of my business. How Garrett, that child we made, is getting on—that

neither. I mail them the checks. They cas[...]
thing comes out even. You want to get al[...]
and Garrett understand this, as much as th[...]
wife maybe doesn't, but she knows it's n[...]
either. I don't suspect I learned any of [...]
then we stopped speaking to each other long before [...]
the phone line between us. I could say it was my fault, bu[...]
wouldn't change what has already happened. Like my brother always says, shit happens. And sometimes it happens more to some
people than to others. Sometimes it goes looking for volunteers to
happen to.

Case closed. Adios, amigo.

Years later, though, driving out to Wisconsin when my mother
remarried, I imagined my father out in that field as he must have
been that last summer he was alive, working on that face by hand,
planting it meticulously, hoeing it religiously, reseeding the bare
patches so there'd be no embarrassing nicks or cuts in the beard.
His whole life reduced to this tender, patient growing of grains for
a faux bottle of grain alcohol. How it must have eaten at him. How
he must have believed. *If you grow this,* I can hear him saying to
himself as he knelt, the outlines of the face dribbled into the dirt
with white paint, *if you grow this, the check will come.*

A year and a half after that summer he was dead. I didn't go to
see him till he was already in the box. But in my mind's eye he's
still out there. I think sometimes what it must have been like
for him—what it would have been like for me had I stayed—the
sun high, beating down on his sparsely populated head, his face
flushed and sweaty, his eyes stinging and blinking, his balance un-
steady from the chemo and the alcohol, his brain clear one minute,
hopelessly fogged the next. Shot through with disappointment,
riddled with despair, and yet his chest cavity aching (still! still!)
with hope—it must have seemed to him sometimes as though he
were working on the face of God.

And God's lips, mute with timothy, refusing to part.

Consent

Porter Atwood's Chevy Blazer screeches to a halt behind Clayton Jones's police cruiser and a county ambulance. He hears somebody say the county sheriff is on his way. The cars are lined up one two three on Atwood Lane, one of six serpentine roads in Atwood Acres that bear his or his family's name. Porter wipes his face with his handkerchief and makes a mental note to have Leo Puhl at the dealership check his brakes. They might be due. Porter doesn't want to hear any screeches or squeaks when he brakes, just the shower of stones and the slurred crush of gravel. A cloud of gravel dust drifts off behind him, mingling with the white haze of a clean and hot blue day.

He mops his face again, then puts the handkerchief in his pocket. He's here in Atwood Acres because on this very day it has become a real and true subdivision, a place distinct from the fields it used to be. There are enough of these new people to make it so. They've achieved a kind of critical mass, outnumbering the farmers and the townies, and what they call things is what things will come to be called. And nobody's going to call it Matty Keillor's anymore, or you-know-that-subdivision-Porter-cobbled-together-from-Matty's-eighty-and-the-Brudecki's-and-the-old-Schniederbaum-place. From now on it's going to be called by its proper, true and real name.

Atwood Acres has had its first drowning.

Porter mops his face again quickly. He's florid. All his weight seems to be going to the balls of his feet and his cheeks. He used to be tight-bodied. The woman he used to sleep with before he was married to his wife, Deniece, used to lick ice cream off his washboard stomach with her tongue. But now Porter is awash in excess flesh, and grease oozes out of him every time the mercury climbs above sixty. The machine of his body labors, tries to keep up with the demands made by the loose folds of flesh on his belly, the dewlaps on his throat, the soft ripplings of fat that dip down his rib cage as though he were melting. He has become the ice-cream cone itself. He thinks of that woman again, the woman who liked him before Deniece. He recalls the bright pink blob of her tongue making its way up and down his belly hair, but for the life of him he can't remember her name.

Straightening his string tie as he heads toward the knot of people gathered behind the Surhoff place (dentist from Neenah, upset that the two-and-a-half acre lots on Atwood Cove were already taken), Porter hopes it happened in a pool. Personally he finds pools an abomination. Deniece forced him to install one for their kids, but both the girls go skinny-dipping with their boyfriends in the quarry, same as everybody else. It's the one thing about Augsbury he wouldn't change: the quarry.

That pool went in what? three years ago? It's amazing how much he's let himself go since then. He would almost be embarrassed about the weight gain except that it seems like an outward sign of his success. Girth equals greatness. Though not so great that he can throw his weight around in his own home. Deniece makes him swim in the pool, has at first curtailed and then forbidden Porter's quarry visits. She knows, she says, what goes on down there. Porter mops his face again and thinks, Pools. Medallions of stupidity.

He goes over to the knot of people around the Surhoff's above ground pool, but it turns out these are the squeamish onlookers, moms with kids who've corralled their youngsters and won't let them get any closer. The more serious gathering of the morbidly curious is by the ravine. Clayton Jones is there, as are the para-medics with their gurney and lockboxes.

When this was fields that ravine was a bit of a problem. Cows grazed right to the edge and the spring run-off carved deep crum-bling erosion channels in its scoured, plum-colored banks. When he first bought this field he let it sit a few years before he had it lotted. He needed that ravine as a selling point. A creek, good drainage—that field needed time to restore itself. The erosion cuts needed time to heal themselves, the crumbling banks time to acquire some cattails, the scrub trees along the banks time to look less like Halloween scarecrows—that haunted, lonely look people like in landscape paintings but not in their own backyard. Never mind that their lawnmowers would eat things right down to the nubbins again and the erosion would start all over. What he needed was picturesque weeds.

He got them, and the lots sold nicely. Better than he hoped, really. Feeling pleased, Porter has to remind himself to wipe the smile off his face when he clamps a solicitous hand on Clayton Jones' shoulder and asks, "What's happened here, Clay?"

Jones indicates the gurney. "You got eyes. See for yourself."

Porter steals a quick glance. It's not a Surhoff kid. This boy is older. Eight, eleven? As he's gotten older he's lost his ability to distinguish kids by their ages. They all look so big. This kid, though, doesn't. He's thin and his ribs show. He's one of those kids whose limbs look like match sticks; their scapulas stick out like wings when they reach behind themselves to scratch their backs. It would have been years before the flesh on this kid's body caught up with those willowy limbs.

Nobody knows the boy who's drowned. He's a playmate of some-body else's kid, drawn here by the newness of the big houses and his friend telling him that after yesterday's thunderstorm the ra-vine is running thick and brown, a good day for sending radio con-trolled boats, plastic boats, construction paper boats, pieces of bark, anything that floats down the newly revived current. Bikes are clumped or dumped all along the bank. The grass at the top is matted and muddy, trampled under bare and sneakered feet. It was a regular field day. Whole regattas were launched and disappeared.

Porter peers down the bank. The water's running fast, but it's only a foot deep, maybe two or three at the channel's deepest. It's amazing how little water you need to drown in. He's heard of six-month-olds drowning in three inches of water in the bathtub when the parent looks away for just a moment. Ten-month-olds drowning in a toilet. He's even heard of infants drowning without getting wet. Placed on unbaffled water beds, the child sleeps in the warmth of the receiving plastic which eventually conforms to the shape of the baby's mouth. Surrounded by water, dreaming of the womb, the child returns there. It's too tiny to lift its head to save itself.

Usually these ravine and river drownings, though, happen in springtime. The creek's swollen with run off, sometimes four or five or eight feet deep, and the kids, not knowing this, dare each other, or sometimes a single kid, alone, will dare itself to cross the turgid water, will lose its footing, and be swept away. Sometimes the kids will string a rope across a ravine or creek and ford the creek that way. The current is surprisingly strong, however, and young hands weak. They find the body miles away sometimes, usually amid a collection of branches where some municipality has screened its culverts. The child looks like something you find in drain traps. Wet, matted, limp, greasy.

This kid, though, nobody knows what happened to this kid. But edging over the ravine, conscious of where his feet meet the ravine's crumbling muddy edge and conscious, too, of the child's drowned body a few feet behind him, Porter can guess. These kids were playing with their boats. It was a lazy summer day, kids were scattered up and down the ravine, and there was the constant huzzing of crickets and the voices of children. This kid, or maybe a kid he knew, or maybe a kid he wanted to know, owned one of these radio controlled boats. It got away from him. Maybe the transmitter was weak, maybe the surging of the current was able to overpower the boat's tiny motor, maybe it got tangled in a floating branch and wouldn't heed the call of its owner. Most of these kids wouldn't care that much about losing a boat. They can afford to lose just about anything. Some screeching, a heaved sigh from their parents, a quick trip to Toys R Us, and everything is back to the way it was before, maybe even better if they were able to cajole their parents into something bigger. But this kid couldn't do that. This was it; it was his only boat and if he lost it there wouldn't be another. Or maybe, not having the money for a radio controlled anything, the kid thought that about the boat's owner as well—that if he lost it there would be the inconsolable grief over the loss plus the yelling of the parents. So whether to reclaim what was his, or to impress the boat's owner, maybe get a turn at operating it himself, the kid slogs out the ten or fifteen feet to where the boat is hung up in the branches. The branches themselves are hung up. Maybe they're caught against a rock, or maybe against some other branches growing close to the water's edge and the boat's mired someplace inside them. The boat has a white hull and blue gunwales. Its tiny motor is whirring and can be heard over the intermittent gurgle and rush of the creek. The kid has volunteered to get his friend's boat. At first, the water's only ankle deep. It gets knee deep when he gets to the branches. There's more branch than he thought. He can't simply reach into the tangle and retrieve his friend's boat. A spider walks a tightroped filament of web from one leaf to another, quavering as the leaf does in the light breeze. A mosquito buzzes in the boy's ear. He slaps at it, the buzzing resumes at the base of his neck, by his other ear. His jeans are rolled to his knees but the cuffs are soaking wet. Something drifts past his calf. Instinctively he reaches down to scratch, panicking a little. Recently he's seen for the first time *The African Queen*. His parents rented it. Leech! he thinks, his heart racing, but it's only a leaf. He brushes it aside, knocks the spider off its tightrope just out of spite. The spider spins away on the current, he loses sight of it.

Maybe it found a new leaf or twig, maybe not. He forgets about it. The sun's hot on the back of his neck but his legs feel cool. The creek bottom is muddy and rocky both and his shoes are filling with silt. His feet feel squishy. He stands there wriggling his toes inside his canvas sneakers until he's called back to his task by his impatient, lordly friend. The friend with the boat who will be the kid's friend only if he retrieves the boat.

But it's not that easy. The boat is trapped in a nest of branches, tucked between them in such a way he can't just reach in and grab it. He has to penetrate the nest. At the same time he has to be careful. If he just pushes himself inside there he could set the whole mess moving and the boat might swamp or get away. So he eases himself between the branches. It's an oak tree these branches came from. They still have last year's leaves on them. They're russet and the twigs break easily. Must have been a lightning kill. He can almost feel the residual electricity. His feet, his fingers are tingling. Perhaps it's because he knows now what he must do. The oak branches, always gnarly, have formed a kind of dome, and to retrieve his friend's boat he must submerge himself and then resurface inside the dome. There are too many branches to simply throw it aside. How did that thing get in there, anyway?

Perhaps at this point the boy turned to shout something at his better-heeled companion. Perhaps he told him what he was planning on doing—the quick duck, the resurfacing inside the dome of brown leaves. He would be a hero to all of them.

There were other boys in the creek or on the banks, surely, Porter thinks. There was a scattering of bikes there when he came down, and he saw one or two boys with wet jeans and muddy feet and plastered hair. Towels over their heads like monk cowls. Porter recalls seeing these things. He remembers them shivering in the heat.

What next? he wonders. Did he go under, get a belt loop caught on a branch, did he struggle, lose his footing, panic? If he thrashed, would the boy who owned the boat, or any of the other boys notice? And noticing, would they do anything or simply stand there, horrified and fascinated? Maybe where those branches form a dome there's a sinkhole, and stepping into it he lost contact with the surface and face up, sliding, he wound up underneath the dome of branches and was held in place by them. It would be as though he were being pulled by his feet. Pinned, held in place by branches and current, his thrashings lost under the many branches that held him. Even if he screamed it would only hasten his drowning.

Another thought occurs to Porter, and it has to do with Porter's knowledge of the male species in adolescence. Those boys gathered at the top of the ravine or standing on rocks where the current meets the bank—what's to prevent them from doing what they usually do when boys gather?

Pick on the most vulnerable. The new kid from one of those cracker-box ranch houses in the cheesier section of the subdivision. The white trash ghetto, you've heard your parents say.

There are plenty of rocks. Nice hefty granite ones, rocks as big as your fist. You're up high, you've got the numbers, he's down below, disoriented from ducking under those branches and trying to find his way through the fertilizer-laced water. You wait till he surfaces, spluttering, unsure of his footing, and then you start raining rocks down upon him. KaCHUSH! KaCHUSH! The geysers and spray are magnificent. Sometimes the rocks come down next to each other and you can hear the clack of their meeting just a second before the geyser. Hey! he yells. Quit it! Stop it! Stop it, hey, quit it! Ouch!

Somebody catches him on the shoulder. Everybody laughs. Then somebody has the bright idea of going with whole handfuls of rocks—clumps of mud and gravel and pebbles, whatever your fist closes around—and flinging them shotgun style at the now cowering, weeping kid. Then it's a mixture—gravel and clumps of mud from some kids, the bigger rocks from those higher up. The kid is spluttering, confused, crying, bent over, humiliated, ducking beneath the water and resurfacing to fresh fusillades. Sometimes he's bent over with his face in the water, his back taking the blows; other times he's upright, imploring them, begging them to stop, his arms raised to ward off blows and to surrender. Finally— this is the part that now seems inevitable—one catches him on the crown or by his temple just as he's surfacing. Got 'im! somebody yells. Got 'im a good one! Did you see that?

They throw stones for maybe ten or fifteen more seconds. They're waiting, poised, for him to resurface. He's staying under longer this time. Maybe he's hoping to wait them out, the silly dink. Another scattering of plips, plooshes, thlupps and clacks. One kid rolls down the biggest boulder he can move. It tumbles lazily down the embankment, then gathers speed just as it reaches the bottom, and seemingly catapults itself several feet out into the creek a yard away from where that new boy is hiding in his nest of oaks. The KaCHUSH! this time is tremendous. That oughta make him pee his pants!

Then nothing for a long time. No movement. Two or three minutes elapse. Some pebbles trickle down the embankment and plop into the water. In the general silence they sound ominous.

"Maybe he's hiding," somebody says.

"Yeah, maybe he cut one of them reed things. I saw a movie on Nickelodeon where a guy did that. These guys were shooting arrows at him so he ducked into these reeds and breathed through them till the king's horsemen and these arrow guys went away. Arrow Flynn, my mom said it was. The reed guy, I mean."

"Maybe he got away," somebody else says. "Maybe he got out from underneath those branches and he swam away."

"Dummy! We'd see him if he swam away. He's still there. He's just hiding." And the speaker of this remark throws another handful of gravel at the kid's bower. Some stones hit branches, others plop directly into the water.

Everyone becomes immediately aware of how hot the day seems. And how irritating it is to be kept waiting. And how uncomfortable it is to fight off what is suddenly an inchoate but nagging sense of blame, responsibility, and guilt.

What happens next Porter's not sure about. Maybe one of the boys screams out, "I see him! I see him!" and they gather around and they do see him, a ghost in the water. Or maybe they look at each other for a few moments of panicked silence and then they scatter, gathering here again only when they hear the sirens.

One of them had to have called. He checks this with Clayton. Yes, it was a child's voice, very excited, saying that they could see somebody on the bottom of the creek in Atwood Acres. They didn't stay on the line long enough to identify themselves. They were shouting, nearly hysterical. Then they hung up. No way to trace who it might have been, and upon arriving, Clayton makes one half-hearted attempt to determine who it was—"It would be really helpful if one of you boys, whoever it was called, would step forward"—and gives up on that for now. Porter eyes the kids who stand in clutches near enough the body to be a part of what's going on. A few mothers are with them, their hands protectively on their kid's shoulders.

They find the boy up under the branches almost as if he'd been sleeping there. The blue and white boat is still bobbing in the tangle. Now we have something. The boy whose boat it is—he's still clutching the remote as though he could get everything going again if he just keeps turning the dial, pulling the trigger—steps forward under Clayton's prodding. "Just tell me what you saw, son." And the boy says that he saw the kid go under the branches trying to retrieve his boat and they waited and then he didn't come out again. He speaks haltingly, but what he says, to Porter's ear, which is used to hearing lies, sounds rehearsed, insincerely apologetic. "We waited," the boy says. "We waited and waited and waited and we waited but Kenny—" Somebody nudges this kid.

"Danny," the nudger says, "the kid said his name was Danny."

"—Danny," the boat boy continues, "Danny didn't show up again."

"Who called me?" Clayton asks. "Who called the ambulance?"

"I did," the boat boy says.

"And why didn't you try getting your friend out right away?"

"I was freaking, sir. I was really afraid. I was afraid the same thing was going to happen to me." He shivers involuntarily.

"Please, officer," the boy's mother says. "I'm sure you can see they're scared out of their minds. Can't you leave well enough alone?"

Up until now Porter hasn't been able to—hasn't really wanted to—take a close look at the drowned boy. Just that first cursory glance trying to determine if it was anybody he knew. He looks now. The boy has a spider webbing of hair over his forehead and his lips are blue. His cheeks and eyelids have that bloated quality, and there is the tiniest suggestion of baby fat around his hips, that puffing of very pale flesh over his pant loops. His arms are skinny but his belly's full. That could be from the water, though. Or maybe he was recently a chubby kid and was just now hitting puberty, the baby fat stretching itself over willowy bone.

He looks like a child on ice, sleeping.

Then he sees what confirms everything he's previously imagined: a bruise the size and color of a pomegranate on his shoulder. An abrasion on his cheek—that could be from the branches—and a bruised spot, quarter-sized, above his right temple. There's the slightest inkling of an indentation where the forehead and the hairline meet.

The kid was wearing jeans and underwear, socks and sneakers.

Such a pitifully easy target.

For the briefest of moments Porter Atwood wants to see justice done. Check out that bruise, he wants to say to the paramedics, who are already packing up. The one on the shoulder, there, and the one by the temple. Clayton, check these kids for dirt under their fingernails, for gravel dust on their palms. Put the screws to them. Drill them for the truth. A boy died here. The least we can give him is honesty.

The boy's mother doesn't even know he's dead yet.

But Porter knows these boys. Knows them in the sense that they look familiar. He sold their parents these houses or the lots they were built on. These kids were the bored ones kicking at the wall boards in the models, leaving scuff marks. These were the boys he had to keep his eyes on. Not that there was anything to steal, but if there was, he knew they'd steal it. He has a sense about these things. He knows what happened, he knows what's been done. It would have happened like this, the way he imagined. He has learned to trust his gut feelings on these things, the same as he does when he's calculating to himself how much a farmer's willing to give up to get off the land that feeds him, and how much a buyer's willing to spend for that same piece of earth. His success depends on appearing absolutely disinterested to both.

So Porter satisfies himself by nodding and saying in his mind only, Yes, it would have happened like this. And out loud he says, to the boys and their mothers, to Clayton and the paramedics and all the interested bystanders, to all these people who've bought from him and who want their tranquility restored, who want this unreasonable chaos put into a box, out loud he says, "What a tragedy. What a horrible, horrible tragedy. What a horrible accident. Really, we must take up a collection for the boy's family. I'll personally see that this is taken care of."

There, he's done it. He's done what he could. He walks back to his car conscious of his weight, his blubber, really, all that acquired flesh, and puts a new cigar between his teeth. On the way he runs into the mother, a wan woman of thirty, maybe thirty-five, it's hard to tell once these women start having children, especially a woman like this, short and slightly-boned. She comes toward him, but her focus is clearly on what's behind him. She's wringing her hands, clutching her elbows, not willing to believe what she already knows. No, Porter Atwood thinks as she flutters past him, No. She will not get the truth from me. Kenny's or Danny's or whoever that kid's mother is will have to find out her own truth. He's not helping. Porter Atwood has already done what he could.

And That's the Name
of That Tune

1 · Loose Lips

"Okay, you kids, get in the car."

Trips started like that. Our father acting like a traffic cop, a May-flower mover, a warehouse worker stuffing us all in. It didn't matter whether we were headed to church, to the IGA, to Great Grandma Hluberstead's, or to northern Wisconsin on vacation. Our father stacked the five of us like cordwood. Big kids—sometimes that included me—in the wayback if the middle seat was up. Our father had convinced Dinkwater-Adams that his company car should be a station wagon. Easy to haul around samples. So he got one, a Chevy Bel Air, with what felt like real panels of wood on the side. Only it wasn't wood, it was something better. Plastic. Anything really good was being made out of plastic—plates, silverware, hula hoops, yo-yos, telephones. It was only a matter of time before the cars themselves were made out of this superior material.

The only provision the company put on the car's use, which our father said was for insurance purposes, was that the sole driver had to be our father. Our mother, who grew up on public transportation, had no trouble with that. She was probably the last woman in America who believed it wasn't necessary for her to learn how to drive. There were times when we weren't sure our father knew how to, either. He had a penchant for coming home and running over our bicycles and tricycles, for crunching our Radio Flyer into the gravel of the drive, pinning it underneath his car, or squeezing it up against the concrete stoop outside the kitchen door. "You kids shouldn't leave your stuff in the drive," he'd say. He'd have a bemused look on his face, like he was puzzled being home at all.

"Been to The Office?" our mom would ask.

"I stopped for a few with the boys," our father would say.

"More than a few, if your parking's any indication."

"The kids shouldn't leave their stuff in the drive," our father repeated. "How many times have I told them? How many times do I have to tell them?"

"How many times have I asked you not to go to The Office?" said our mother.

Our father not going into work—was she crazy? Everybody's father left in the morning. Didn't they all go to work in the morning and come home from The Office? The only exception was Ollie Cicerelli, who didn't have a father that we knew about, and whose mother was a waitress at the Woolworth's on York Road, which was downtown, not too far from the candy store and novelty shop where every Saturday morning we blew our allowance.

When we weren't envying him his freedom—he was frequently left alone until seven or eight P.M. and had the run of the neighborhood—we felt sorry for Ollie Cicerelli. He had only himself to keep himself company, and we had a wealth of relatives who, it seemed, we were always running to see.

We even had a relative living with us—Grandma Nomi, which meant Grandpa Artu was living with us as well. Artu kept up their apartment in downtown Chicago while Nomi recovered from hip surgery, but most nights he slept at our house and in the mornings, our father dropped him off at the train station before making his calls. No question, this made for a crowded house, and that might explain why our father spent so much time at The Office.

That's what we wanted to believe, anyway—that there was a

correlation between Nomi and Artu being in the house and our father's being at The Office. The other explanation—that he was getting away from us kids—we didn't want to believe. According to our mother, all he had talked about while he was aboard ship in Korea was how, if he lived, he wanted to be the father of a big family. So now he was—there were five of us kids and another was on its way. How could he not want to be around what he had engendered? Could it be the idea was easier than its execution? That his time aboard ship had made him unable to deal with the squabblings of a growing family? That he liked his privacy, and there were now simply too many of us in the house for him to have any? That the democracy of our disorder undid his belief in a hierarchy, with him at the top of it?

It was easier to explain the friction between him and Nomi. Nomi and our grandfather Artu were urban Democrats, and our father was a budding suburban Republican. Artu usually held his tongue on matters of politics, and outside the house our father did, too, but inside it he was lord of his castle, and the idea that this chain-smoking, bed-ridden woman upstairs was spouting off pieties about Jack Kennedy and what an evil man Richard Nixon was, was simply too much to bear. We didn't understand the politics of it but there had been arguments ever since our mother had gotten a letter that made her cry. It was 1962, and after our mother composed herself she explained to us that our father might have to go away because of a bad man in Cuba. He ended up not having to go, but he seemed to bear a personal grudge against President Kennedy in the same way that Nomi bore one against Richard Nixon, whoever he was. Although Nomi and our father liked each other, all that fall and continuing through the winter and spring they argued, and it always seemed to be about politics:

"Eisenhower was just lucky. Anybody could have overseen a post-war boom. Even Nixon could have done that."

"Well, nobody gave Nixon a chance because they stole the election from him! The Tri-Lateral Commission had it out for anybody who'd stand up to them! Them and Daly. They crucified Nixon for telling the truth just like they crucified McCarthy!"

"McCarthy hung himself."

"They crucified him! Crucified him!"

Stealing an election? Couldn't they make them give it back? Crucifying a man, in this day and age? We had pictures in our heads of Roman soldiers in their helmets and little skirts nailing a corpulent man in a suit to a rough-hewn cross. The soldiers looked like John Wayne. So did the man in the suit, only pudgier.

And there was, of course, the fact that Kennedy nearly got our father sent away. "I had my marching orders!" our father thundered at Nomi. "My G—D— marching orders! And then where would we be? I ask you, where would we be?"

"I won't say we weren't worried, Walter, but it didn't come to pass, did it?"

"Easy for you to say! You weren't on alert, were you?"

"Oh, wasn't I? And just who would be helping Susan with the children in the event you did march off to Florida? Who helps you now? The fact is, Walter, that somebody needed to remain calm in that situation, and that somebody wasn't you."

We noticed in these arguments that our father was the only one shouting. Nomi spoke very calmly and smoked her cigarettes, rolling the tip around the inside edge of her ashtray to get the ash to drop. Then she would hoist the cigarette up by the side of her face and cross her other arm under her chest. "Your problem, Walter," she'd say to our father, "is you believe the crap they're telling you."

Our father would storm off, complaining that no one allowed him a chance to think. Later we'd find out he went to The Office. He wouldn't be back till late. Nomi would keep her cigarette circling her ashtray. She'd sigh. "His problem," she'd repeat, "is he believes the crap they're telling him."

For the longest time, where our father's Office was and what he did there was a mystery to us. He did his salesman's reports at the kitchen table on Sunday and Thursday nights. Did he sometimes do his paperwork at The Office then, too? We knew he worked hard. He must work even harder at The Office, because whenever he came back from there he seemed addled, as though he'd been thinking too hard.

It was only by chance that I was able to clear up the mystery for myself, and even then, I could not help my siblings with my knowledge. It had happened in the middle of the summer, before our mother had gotten the letter that made her cry. Nomi's hip was doing better—the cast was off—but she still slept upstairs, and the steel- and chrome-armed pulley and brick whatchamacallit—the traction device—was still at the foot of her bed. Hers would be a long convalescence.

One Friday evening our father mowed the yard front and back—a job he usually reserved for Saturday mornings—so we knew something was up. He stopped every few turns for a good long pull at his bottle of Pabst, then put the empty in the case nestled up against the Weber grill and rotisserie. There were more there waiting to be consumed. We were already in our pajamas, running around the yard, in the new mown grass, catching lightning bugs, and putting them in a jar with freshly cut grass. Our father did not like an audience that moved. "Hey, you kids," he shouted, "sit on the stoop. And stay there!" We listened for maybe fifteen seconds, then we were dancing around the lawn again, the grass cool on our ankles.

"You keep that up, I'm not doing what I'm doing tomorrow."

What are you doing tomorrow? we asked, but he was already heading the other way, and our question was lost to the bark of the mower. Besides, it was dark, and if we trailed after him with our questions he was liable to cut off our feet. Then our mother came out and said, "Off to bed with you, tomorrow is a big day." We asked our mother, but she remained her enigmatic self. "You'll see tomorrow," she said. She was obviously pleased about something.

"We shall see what we shall see," said our father, who'd come in while we were wiping the grass off our toes. He was finishing his beer. He, too, seemed pleased.

"What are we gonna see? What? What?"

"I see, said the blind man, as he picked up his hammer and saw," said our father. "Loose lips sink ships," he added.

We pretended to puzzle over this one for a few moments. If you answered him it only encouraged him to say something about the hair between your toes. Or the hair on your chest. Or how you were a day late and a dollar short. Our father was full of these sayings, none of which we understood.

Our father held up our jar of lightning bugs. "I'm going to let these go outside," he said. "They make lousy night-lights."

How did he know that's why we had brought them inside? "You think you're the only ones who were young once?" he asked. Our father was once as young as us? Every time we heard this we found it impossible to believe.

Then he sat on the edge of Robert Aaron's bed and told us again about how when he was a young boy he used to watch Al Capone's cars run down his alley, and how he used to catch lightning bugs in a jar, and go to sleep watching their irregular flarings on his bedside table, and how that gave him an idea: to build balsa wood airplanes with tissue paper skins, with rubber bands attached to the propeller for the engine. He went into loving detail about this, how he would spend hours making these things, cutting the struts and gluing the wings, all the bracing and infrastructure, and how he would paint British circles on the wings, carefully, carefully, or the tissue paper would rip, and how he'd then take his just-finished airplane to his attic, wind it up, stick a lit match up by the nose, and sail it out the window, the whole thing catching fire, bursting into flame before it hit the trees across the street. "Magnificent," our father breathed at us in the dark, his bottle of Pabst squeezed between his thighs. "The whole thing was magnificent!"

"You did all that work, and then you burned it up?" Our heads were filled with the image of that balsa wood and tissue paper airplane burning as it glided into the trees.

"It was mine. I could do with it what I wanted. Lights out now."

In the hallway we could hear our mother tell our father, "I wish you wouldn't tell them stories when you've been drinking. You always make things seem better than they are."

The next morning the family wrestle was cut short because our father said he had "big things cooking for you kids," and we should let him sleep. We kept bouncing on his belly, and when he rolled over to get away from us we continued on his back. "What big things? What big things?" we shrieked as we kept bouncing.

"Go look in the car," said our father, groaning as he rolled into our mother, and we dashed out of their bedroom to look.

In the back of the Bel Air—all the seats were down—was a box, large, rectangular, deep. "SAMUELSON'S ABOVE GROUND POOL" it read, "48 in. tall."

"All right!!!" Robert Aaron and Sarah screamed. An above ground pool! We weren't naive. We knew that the box was too short for it to include a diving board. But there would probably be a deck we could dive off of, a shallow and a deep end, and a rope of red-and-white colored floats. On hot and humid days, the whole neighborhood could cool off in our above ground pool! People would come over from blocks all around just to see.

We went inside and asked our father when he was going to put the pool up. And how long would it take to fill? And how soon could we go in? And could we invite our friends over right away? Could we help? Did it come with a diving board or could we get one? How deep would it be—over our heads? How deep was deep, anyway? Could we drown? Would we need life preservers? Would it be big enough for a boat? Could we go sailing on it? Would we have lights on it at night? Would it have its own alligators? Could we leave it up in the winter and use it as an ice rink?

Our mother, coming up from the basement with an armload

of laundry she dumped on the bed and her husband, said, "Let Daddy sleep. Daddy's very tired. Daddy had too much to drink last night, didn't Daddy?"

Too much to drink?"

"Pool water," said our mother, separating the staticky sheets from each other. She always separated them first to find the socks hidden within their folds, then folded them last. "He was testing it."

We were starting to sound like that Sam-I-Am. "Could we, would we—"

"Let me be, goddamnit!!"

"Pool water makes Daddy cranky," said our mother, who started folding underwear and dropping them on the bulge in the blanket that indicated where our father's belly was. "Still, he shouldn't use language like that, especially in front of his own children."

Actually, he was using that language *on* his own children, but it didn't seem like the right time to point that out. No use starting the day off with him screaming at us, not if we wanted that pool in by lunchtime. So in a rare display of family unity, we helped our mother fold laundry, making neat, if wobbly piles down the length of our father's body, stacking each pile on its own separate bulge of flesh, our father snoring all the while. Ike carried the stacks to our beds, which we hadn't made, but promised we would—later. We swept the kitchen, washed our breakfast dishes, dusted, put away the National Geographics we'd been looking at, refrained from asking for our allowance, and didn't dare leave the immediate area of the driveway.

Our father came outside by nine-thirty, still rubbing his eyes. Artu had gone off and come back with a trunkful of sand. Our father got plastic sheeting and his toolbox from the basement. "I see, said the blind man, as he picked up his hammer and saw," said our father. He unloaded the pool box from the station wagon, and then drove off to get more sand. We stared at the box, trying to imagine it unpacked, set up, the water glistening. When our father came back, he and Artu first unloaded the sand from the trunk of

Artu's car into the wheelbarrow and then dumped the wheelbarrow out onto the stretched out plastic sheeting. During a break, when they switched cars in the drive, Artu opened up the pool box and took out the instruction sheet. "I see here we're supposed to cut a circle in the sod for the base," Artu said. "Wouldn't it be easier, Walter, if we cut that first, then dumped the sand right where we wanted it to go?"

"I see, said the blind man, as he picked up his hammer and saw," said our father. Our father said this every step of the way. He said it less frequently as the day wore on. In fact, by the end of that day he was using a lot worse language than he used on us when we'd tried waking him that morning.

It was getting hot. Robert Aaron and I stood on the sand pile while Artu and Dad cut the sod. Ike tried getting onto the pile with us, but it was too small for three and we kept pushing him off. Sarah was off somewhere, pouting over not owning a Barbie doll, and Wally Jr. stood at the bottom of the sand pile with a bottle hanging from his mouth.

"Hey, you kids, stop that," said our father. "We won't have any sand left for the pool bottom if you keep kicking it around like that."

It was hot work, we could tell, cutting the sod in a circle, chopping it out, hauling it in the wheelbarrow to our compost heap along the back hedge-line. Too hot even for the T-shirt our father had been wearing. Artu had stripped down to his athletic T and an old pair of his elevator operator's pants, which were slate-colored and had a dusty-blue stripe up the sides. Our dad had gone inside and came out wearing his Christmas present from our mom, a fishnet T-shirt he'd seen advertised in a magazine as the latest thing from Sweden to keep warm in the winter and cool in the summer.

They finished removing the sod from the circle they'd cut and started hauling sand. Our mother called us in, no doubt just so we would stop bugging our father and grandfather as they toiled under the hot, hot sun. Our mother served them lunch in the shade on the north side of the house while we were eating inside. Artu had put on one of his old elevator operator's shirts, leaving it unbuttoned but covering up his arms and shoulders. "You should put a shirt on, too, Walter. Sun's bad today. It'll fry you."

"I've seen tougher suns than this aboard ship," said our father, for whom his time in the Navy had become the reference point for all experience. He was taking things out of the box and lining them up on the grass. The big curl of the pool's frame looked as though someone had taken shears to the sky and cut out a goofy rectangle. The lining was the same color, and there were yards and yards, it seemed, of curlicued white rim to keep the lining in place. Now came the hard part: stretching the lining, getting it to stay on the frame, keeping it smooth on the bottom and sides, getting the trim in place without the lining slipping away. They worked on it for hours. We got bored watching them, despite even our father's bad language. Our mother kept coming to the kitchen window and yelling, "Walter, the children!" as though we were meat he had forgotten on the rotisserie, and he'd yell back, "I know, I know," and then quieter, under his breath, "Jesus H. Christ, you'd think they never heard the words before."

"At least not from you," said Artu, which is as close as he ever got to reproving our father.

We rode our bikes around the neighborhood for a while, then went home and there it was, our oasis, with an aluminum-and-white plastic ladder on the side and a green garden hose looped over the railing. Water was gurgling into the bottom. There was already an inch or two, enough to cover the tip of the hose, and you could watch the turbulence of the new water coming in, clear and cold, against the bright blue bottom. We went inside and drank about a gallon of Tang and begged our mother to let us sit in the pool while it filled up.

"Your bellies will burst," said our mother.

"Where's Dad?" asked Robert Aaron.

"Your father," said our mother both loftily and with pity, "is in a world of hurt."

Indeed he was. We found him in his bedroom lying belly-down on the bed, a thick smear of orange jelly across his back. He was moaning. It sounded worse than his morning moan. Threaded through his morning moan was a certain good-naturedness; we knew it would eventually stop and he'd get up. The underpinning of this moan, however, was a pitiful whine, the sound dogs make after you've kicked them. And underneath that smear of orange jelly you could make out the source of his whine: a diamond plate pattern of boiled skin. It stood out even more because each diamond was separated from its neighbors by a white border formed by the netting of the shirt he'd been wearing. His back looked as though a white window-well cover had been laid over a slab of hot meat. As though the grill had left its marks on his back in negative.

Our mother joined us in looking in on him. "When he took his shirt off all I could think of was that scene in *The African Queen* when Humphrey Bogart takes his shirt off and he's covered with leeches and he knows he has to go back into that water."

"What did Nomi say?"

Our mother hadn't taken her eyes off our whimpering father. "'Good God.' That's what Nomi said. 'Good God.' Just like that. That's just what she said. Oh, God, he does look pitiful, doesn't he? At least Dinkwater-Adams makes an unguent." Dinkwater-Adams—that was the pharmaceutical company our father worked for. We had drawers and shelves full of free samples.

Robert Aaron raised his opened palm. "I see, said the blind man, as he picked up his hammer and saw." He was about to bring his hand down flat against our father's back but our mother caught his wrist while it was still in the air. I do not think Robert Aaron was simply being mean. It was that, in part, but I also think he wanted to see what it would feel like to land his hand in the middle of that jelly. I think we were all curious about that.

It wasn't that we were callous, either. After our mother said, "I think you better leave," each of us went up to our father to tentatively touch him and tell him we hoped he was feeling better. "Don't touch me," our father said through gritted teeth as each of us came near.

We went back outside to watch the pool fill up. When it was about half full we reported this fact to our mother, who let us change into our swimsuits and splash about in the pool. "No diving," said our mother. "It's not deep enough. And wipe your feet before you climb in."

The water was freezing cold despite the heat, and it didn't get any better the longer we tried to stay in. We kept getting out, shivering, then felt hot again and climbed right back in. We quickly forgot about the plastic washtub we were supposed to use as a footbath, and the pool surface was soon covered with a scum of dirt and grass clippings, and the pool bottom was gritty with sand. We were quite a picture: five shivering kids, the water barely up to our waists, huddled like refugees in scummy, grass-littered water.

We were still like that when our father emerged from the house. It must have been about five P.M. The shadows had been lengthening for a while, and while it wasn't evening yet you could feel that the tenor of the afternoon had changed. It was the time when all games become possessed of a certain fury and intensity born of the desperate knowledge that soon you would be called in for supper, and even if you had nothing at all going on, even if you were shivering in a half-filled pool, you still didn't want to go inside.

Where was our father going in his weakened condition? The hardware store? The Office? The grocery store? The pharmacy? It didn't matter. We all started shouting, "Take me with you! Take me with you!" as though he were abandoning a deserted island and whoever was left behind would be marooned.

Our father was moving gingerly. His face looked like a Christmas ornament, beet-red behind his green-lensed aviator sunglasses, his crew cut a bit of fringe on top. He was wearing a pair of khakis and a light blue sportshirt made of very thin cotton. I had gotten colder quicker than anybody else, and had already changed into a pair of blue pedal pushers. I had a towel draped over my skinny shoulders and I was still shivering, but my T-shirt was draped over a lawn chair, within easy reach.

"You got shoes?" my father asked.

I nodded vigorously. They were right under the lawn chair.

"Okay, you get in the car, Emmie. The rest of you—it'd take too long for you to get ready, sorry." This was our father's excuse when he didn't want to wait for us. We knew the drill. He didn't like going anywhere with more than one of us, and less than that, if he could help it. I think our mother talked him into this—the idea of making us feel sequentially special. Our turn would come, if we were patient and waited. Of course, it had the opposite effect, all of us vying for position, trying for it to be our turn, always keeping score, who'd gone most recently, who got to go the most often, who seemed to be on the outs with Dad when he did his errands. It was all random, but we tried to make it a science.

"I can be ready before Emmie even gets his shoes on," shouted Robert Aaron.

"I'm only taking one of you," said our father. "You went last time." He meant to the York Liquor Store, which was in a little shopping center just down from our church. He went to the York Liquor Store about once a week, usually for a six-pack or maybe some scotch for Nomi. It was a short trip—up eight blocks on Madison to York, then a right past our church and school, then another three or four blocks. Only this time, at the corner of Madison and York he turned left, not right.

"Where are we going?"

"We shall see what we shall see," said our father. He put his finger over his mouth. "Loose lips sink ships," he added.

I sat forward in my seat. When you were the only one in the car with Dad you got to sit up front. Place of honor. Usually only our mother sat there. If there were two or more of us we rode in back, or even asked to sit in the wayback so we could see everyplace we'd just been.

Our father was sitting forward in his seat, too. The orange burn cream—what our mother called an unguent—was staining the back of his shirt. Above the collar, his neck was orange and bright lobster red. It looked like it was on fire.

"Does it hurt?"

"Like hell." He winced as he moved the steering wheel. "Don't tell your mother I said that."

I didn't say anything. We kalumphed over the railroad tracks and then we were in the old part of town. The houses here were bigger. Some of them even looked like mansions. It was always special crossing St. Charles Road; it was like you were visiting royalty. You knew you didn't belong, but they let you in anyway as long as you promised not to get out of your car and not to stay long, which you wouldn't because it made you uncomfortable just being there. We crossed another set of train tracks and we were downtown. This is where the York Theater was, and the Yorkhurst Family Restaurant and the Elmhurst Coin Shop and Mazgar's Furniture Store and Lowell's Jewelry and several appliance stores—RCA and General Electric and Zenith. The storefronts were old and mostly brick and glass. The York Theater was done up in neon and curved chrome. We went past all that, then turned on a little side street and found a parking space right away. It was a Saturday so the commuters hadn't filled up all the angle parking flanking the train tracks. We walked down Addison and midblock came to an alley. "Here," said our father, turning down the alley, which opened up into an asphalt courtyard. I had always wondered about the backsides of buildings. But it was not so mysterious. Even in late afternoon the sun shined hot and bright, washing everything of its color, and the backs of the buildings either had loading docks or little wood huts, or brown or sunbleached forest-green awnings covering their back entrances. We went up to one of

the green awnings—it was labeled "131 N. York Rd.," and my father said, "This must be the place." He winced when he pulled
open the back door. Everything that required movement seemed to
cause him pain. I felt sorry for him. He had worked hard for us all
day and now here he was taking me on an outing to the magical
world of downtown Elmhurst.

Once we were under the awning and inside the building, the
sun, which had been so brittle and harsh I was squinting, dimin-
ished. Now it was dark, and the contrast between the harshness of
the hot outside light and the cool, mute darkness inside made my
eyes swim. It was like I had entered a cave. Then I could see light
up ahead, some of it green, some of it yellowish, some of it red. All
muted and distant and a little washed out by the brighter white
light behind it—that must have been the front window. It seemed
like a long way away right then. We were in a paneled corridor.
Near the bathrooms, if my sense of smell was accurate. Then I
could see the name-plates: MEN, WOMEN. It had always scared
me, what went on inside the women's bathroom. It must be something mysterious, or why would they need a separate bathroom in
the first place?

Beyond the bathrooms, the corridor was still dark, only now
something was crunching under my feet. I felt like I was stepping
on beetles and tried to walk very carefully, but the floor was strewn
with them. The corridor opened to a big room. There seemed to be
four or five round tables in the room, each surrounded by barrel-
backed chairs. Everything was wood and looked heavy. There was
a long, long table to the right, and behind it a long mirror, and a
whole wall softly glittery with bottles arranged on shelves that
went up higher than you could reach. On the top shelf there was an
old radio and a long row of beer cans, and above that even was a
moose's head sporting a Cubs cap. I couldn't not think of Rocky and
Bullwinkle. Now that my eyes had adjusted to the half-darkness,
the light from the front window seemed a lot stronger, almost
blinding if you looked out at it. There was a neon sign hanging in

the window. The side I was looking at had the tubing painted black and you couldn't read it. Men were spaced erratically down the length of the long dark table in front of us; two sat together at one end, just before it curved back to the wall. I couldn't see them very clearly—the light from the window they sat up against washed out their features. My father had us sit on stools right at the curve. His body blocked the sun but when I leaned forward I caught it full in the face. A beefy man with a striped shirt and a crew cut cropped so tight his head looked like a bowling ball with stubble—which is to say he looked like my father—was leaning against the back shelving where all the bottles were.

"What'll it be, Walter?"

This man knew my father! Somehow I knew what this meant. We must be at The Office! So this was it—where my father got all his work done, where he went to be alone, to think, to get away from Nomi's serenity and the pandemonium caused by us kids. "I can't even hear myself think!" our father would sometimes shout when he was at home. "I'm going where I can think, away from these kids. I'll be back later." "When?" our mother would ask. "When I'm through thinking!" our father would thunder.

My father boosted me up on the black stool with the chrome legs, then hunkered down beside me. "We're here to unwind," he said to me. "Don't tell your mother. She'd kill me." Then he said to the man in the striped shirt, "The usual, Bobo."

"Your kid wants a boilermaker?"

My father grinned. "Shut up and pour. A soft drink for the little guy."

"You know what a boilermaker is, kid?" He poured something amber colored into what looked like an eggcup and then drew a draft for my father. He put those side-by-side in front of my father. Then he made the same thing for the two guys sitting just down the bar. Only they dropped the little glass inside the fluted big one and drank it down like that. "That's a boilermaker, kid, only your dad can't seem to get the hang of it."

"That's because you don't stock tomato juice."

"That's because nobody in here drinks bloody fucking Mary's."

"Hey, my kid."

"What, he's got virgin ears?" said Bobo. "Sorry, kid. The way your old man talks in here, I figured you already got an earful. Forget what I said. It don't mean nuthin'."

Bobo had a big gut and he looked pretty serious, but the gut was hard as a rock and you could tell he liked to look serious just so he wasn't grinning all the time. He liked to move the ashtrays around, too, especially when somebody was about to flick the ash off the end of their cigarette, and then he'd make a big deal of wiping down the countertop, loudly complaining about what slobs we all were. He also liked to turn the bottles every so often so their labels all faced front. He made me a coke decorated with a swizzle stick and a maraschino cherry—what I knew as a Shirley Temple—and whenever he saw my glass was low he refilled it.

Bobo set a wooden bowlful of peanuts in front of me. "Go ahead, kid," he said, "knock yourself out. It helps polish the floor." I looked at the floor. It was covered in peanut shells.

"The oils," my father said. "That Bobo, he's a smart man for a dummy."

"Takes one to know one," said Bobo.

"Hey, Bobo, you lettin' us die of thirst here or what?" said one of the men under the window.

Bobo said, "Yeah, yeah, it's a regular frickin' Sahara in here is what it is. I want people to find your bones bleaching in the sun come next spring." But he was already making their drinks. He had a glass of coke with a swizzle stick in it, too, which he sipped from while working a toothpick around in his mouth. He seemed to like to wait until somebody insulted him before he poured them another drink. Then he wiped down the bar again. He seemed to like everything just so, which was funny, given how the floor was littered with peanut shells. I was fascinated by that. Nobody paid me much attention except Bobo, who from time to time offered me maraschino cherries straight from the jar. "I gotta get rid of these," he said, like he wasn't doing me a favor.

My father was distracted by his boilermakers. Or maybe I should say he was intent on them. He would throw back the shot and say Ah! like my brothers and I did after we guzzled a full glass of milk in one long, deep draught. Then he'd sip his beer and say, Ah! again. He and the two men at the end of the bar and Bobo got to talking about the Cubs—what a rotten team they were, but that Banks kid was something, and so was Santo and Billie Williams. If they ever got some pitching, the men agreed, they could do some damage. Then they started talking about what branch of the service they'd been in, and where they'd served, and what a swell group of guys they'd served with. It went on like that for quite a while. When his beer got low my father would make little dancing motions with his index finger, as though he were trying to point to both glasses simultaneously, which is what I suppose he was doing, and Bobo would fill 'em up. That's what my Dad said to Bobo, "Fill 'em up, Bobo, fill 'em up." Like we were at the Sinclair gas station and my Dad was speaking to the attendant just before the attendant sprawled himself across our windshield wiping it clean. He did this for the other guy a couple of times, too, the little finger dance—he even did it to Bobo—and they drank to his health.

"May you be in heaven half an hour before the devil knows you're dead," said my father.

I looked out the window at the people going past. Men in hats, women in skirts with boxy yokes, their arms bare, kids on bicycles. I made out what the sign in the window said despite the electrician's tape or black paint or whatever it was. Pabst, it said. I looked at the moose, who seemed to regard everything under its massive chin with benign amusement.

My father turned to me. "These are men," my father said. "These are *men*. Never forget that."

I had no idea what he was talking about, but there was something about my father's intentness that scared me. I asked to be excused. By this time I'd drunk three or four sodas and my father had had four or five boilermakers. I don't know about him but I was really feeling it. My father excused me and I gingerly made my way across the peanut shells on the floor, not sure if I was allowed to stomp on them or not. In the bathroom everything felt better. The urinal was a wall model shaped and sized like a bathtub and it gave me great pleasure to relieve myself into its curved porcelain immenseness. I wrote my name, broke up cigarette butts in the bottom, chased flakes of the sanitary cake around the drain. It even came to me what my father was talking about in the bar: All these men had served in the military. That's what made them men. Although I was also pretty sure he was alluding to some other quality as well, something intangible that he could just *feel* about them, but for the life of me I didn't know what that was. Maybe I would have to join the military to find out. I decided not to let it bother me. My father said a lot of things I couldn't figure out.

It was always a strange experience going into a public toilet, more so this time because I wasn't accompanied by anyone—but it was also liberating. I felt like I was my own boy; I belonged here, peeing hard, feeling droplets of backspray land on my hands, avoiding the faux pas of pissing on my pants leg or shoes. Maybe this is what my father meant about being men—a steady hand, a sure aim. Women, I knew, sat down for this. I shuddered, shook myself, zipped. I washed my hands and dried them on the revolving towel, yanking down hard on the green striped edges to leave a dry spot for the next guy, the way my father always did. Then I left, empty of bladder but very full of myself, ready to take on the world. I crunched peanut shells to my heart's content, and back at the bar I started opening peanut shells, popping their contents into my mouth, and discarding the husks with gay abandon.

The men were talking now about where they lived and the new highway spur and what it was like getting around Chicago these days. "Me, I wouldn't go in if you paid me," said one of the men. "I have to," said my father. "I got a lot of clients there." "Condolences," said the other man.

"I hear you," said my father. I knew what was coming next so I started to tune out again. Whatever the other men said our father would answer with one of his thousands of one-size-fits-all comments: "You can't keep a good man down," our father would say. Or "There she goes," or "You're up the creek without a paddle." "Sure as shootin'," he'd say. "You betcha. You can't squeeze blood out of turnip." I wondered sometimes what it would be like to have an actual conversation with him. I wondered sometimes what it was he was thinking, what he was feeling. When he got started like this you never knew.

My eyes started looking for something to latch onto again. The moose was interesting but its range of expression was limited. Then I saw something behind Bobo that I hadn't noticed before. It was an advertisement for Hamm's beer. The Hamm's bear cartoon figure was on the left side of the sign, and in red script letters at the bottom was the Hamm's beer slogan: "From the land of sky-blue waters . . ." That made me hear the theme song itself, a drum going and a kind of Indian chant: "From the land of sky-ey blue-ue wa-a-ters . . . Comes the beer refreshing . . . HAMM'S the beer refreshing . . . HAMM'S the beer refreshing . . . HAAAAMMMMMMMS," the drums hitting really hard on the word Hamm's. But it was the sign itself that held me. It was a lake scene, only it seemed to be on a scroll, and as you watched, the sky-blue water and sky-blue sky and the evergreen trees slowly scrolled out of the frame, the sun twinkling, twinkling on water and rocks alike until you came to a couple of canoes pulled up on shore, and then you panned down the stream—it was a stream now, all pebbly with rocks—and the lake started over again. A circular universe, amazing. I got lost in it, in the shimmering of the water, the slow pan, the trees . . . it was beautiful. And I kept watching and listening in my head,

"HAMM'S the beer refreshing . . . HAMM'S the beer refreshing . . ."
until the front door jingled and heads turned, including mine.

It was a woman, and from the reaction of the men at the bar this
was unusual. It was hard to make her out at first, and we squinted
as though we had resided too long in the dark and she was made of
the light from outside and had brought it in with her. She was
wearing a broad-brimmed straw sun hat and had on Jackie Kennedy sunglasses and a lightweight cotton sundress with a rose
pattern—big roses—scattered all over it. She seemed a little heavy-
set, but she carried it well. For some reason I expected her to be
wearing gloves, white kid gloves up to her elbow or at least mid-
forearm, but she wasn't. She sat on the opposite side of my father,
between him and the two men closest to us.

"Can a body get a drink?" she asked Bobo, and Bobo rolled the
toothpick around in his mouth. "A body like that can, sure," said
Bobo.

"Sure as shootin'," said my father. I think he just wanted to say
something to be polite—our father often said meaningless things
just to break the ice—but this woman seemed to regard my father
seriously.

"Well," said the woman lighting a cigarette, "aren't you the eager
beaver."

I thought she was talking to me. In school I was often described
as "an eager beaver," so it seemed natural for her to call me that,
but seeing as how I was sitting on the opposite side of my father,
and he was massive, it seemed rather amazing that she had noticed
me at all.

"Fill 'er up, Bobo," said my father. And we were back at the
Sinclair station. I always felt excited at the Sinclair station. There
was plenty to watch—the dinosaur on the sign, for example, whom
we named Dino, and the attendants who scurried about our father's car, filling it with gas, checking its oil, cleaning the windshield, the headlights, wiping down the side windows, even the

triangular vent window that we loved to have open—but we never felt we were part of the proceedings except as an audience inside the car's bubble. Things went on around us and we watched. It was like that now with the three men at the bar, and Bobo behind it, and the woman sitting among them. Things went on between the five of them and it was like I was now in the bubble, sealed off from the proceedings but watching.

The woman's name was Shirley. I found that out because one of the men sitting at the end of the bar, the one who had earlier said he wouldn't want to go into Chicago, had said, "What's your name, Sugar? I'm Roy and this here's Charlie," indicating the man sitting next to him.

"That's a very nice name, Roy," the woman said. "I think I'll have one of those," she said to Bobo.

"One of what?" said Bobo.

"A Rob Roy," said the woman. She hadn't given her name yet. Everybody was still looking at her, especially Roy. My father was either smiling or grimacing, I couldn't tell which.

"I asked you what's your name, Sugar," Roy said. He was a burly looking man with a big forehead on account of there being almost no hair on his head. He had a round face and long strands of hair that came from just above his ears and were greased onto the top of his head like colonists forced to live in a barren new country. The few indigenous strands stood up short and wild and were highlighted white by the window behind him.

"I heard you, Roy," said the woman, waving her hand at him. She had the reddest nails I'd ever seen. It was like the tips of her fingers were still dripping after being dipped in the blood-red model paint Robert Aaron used on the mouths of his Flying Tigers. She turned to my father just as Bobo was setting her drink down in front of her and taking the singles from the small stack sitting in front of my Dad. She lifted her Rob Roy and made a little toasting gesture. "Thank you," she said to my father. "My name's Shirley. And who might my benefactor be?"

"Walt," said my father, still smiling and grimacing. He looked embarrassed, pained and pleased to boot.

"Walt," said Shirley. "I like that name, too. Walt, Walter. Do you mind if I call you Walter?" She was already taking another cigarette out of her pack. She kept them in a little green purse with a clasp, and when she opened the clasp the purse looked like a frog opening its mouth. "I never liked my name," said Shirley. "You know who I was named for, Walter? Shirley Temple. I hate that." She had the cigarette in the corner of her mouth but before she could light it herself my father had taken out his lighter and lit it for her. He didn't smoke anymore but he still carried around his lighter, a silver Zippo with his ship etched in the side. She bent her head for the flame and when she straightened up she was already blowing out smoke.

"Shirley," said Roy. "I always kinda liked that name."

"Me, too," said Charlie. "I known a lotta Shirleys and I liked 'em all."

My father dipped his head and whispered to me for the second time, "These are men. Never forget that." He was creeping me out again. I knew they were men. What else could they be? Except for Shirley, of course, who looked a little like our neighbor Mrs. Duckwa, unhappy and hungry. My father sat back. "And this," said my father a little louder, indicating Shirley, "this is a lady."

"Why thank you, Walter. For the light and the compliment."

Then there was silence for a few moments when nobody knew what to say. It was like they were waiting for the conversation to get going again after all the small talk had been completed. I could tell Roy and Charlie would have liked for her to talk to them; they were even trying to get her attention, leaning forward on the bar with the same hungry looks on their faces, but Shirley had turned herself so she was mostly facing my father. She'd crossed her legs, too—she had thick ankles—and was holding her cigarette at an angle in a way that years later I learned was called a "studied" pose. She looked like somebody from a 1940s movie, sort of glamorous and sad all at the same time. She smoked for a while and just sat there, regarding my father with what I guessed was curiosity and interest, which she confirmed when she leaned forward with a look of concern on her face. "What happened to you, Walter? You look incinerated."

"I was putting up a pool for my kids," our father answered, a little sheepishly.

"A family man, I like that," said Shirley. She let out a great lungful of smoke and sighed. "I have always depended upon the kindness of family men," she said in a fake Southern accent. I don't know why she did that but my father gave a pained little laugh, heh-heh-heh, which was unusual for him because he usually had a big booming laugh that you could hear clear across a room. You heard that laugh at parties (when our parents gave parties we often snuck down the stairs after we'd been put to bed and listened in) and invariably you would hear somebody near us say, "What's Walter think is so funny?" And somebody else would say, "Walter thinks everything's funny," which was news to us, seeing as how we lived with him and the laughs didn't seem all that continuous—though they were right about him finding a lot of things funny.

My father straightened up and that let her see me behind him. Her face lit up in a sickly sort of way. I thought it might be the smoke. She was going through cigarettes pretty fast. "Oh, and I see you brought your little boy with you. How sweet." She brought her cigarette up to her lips again. "Maybe your little boy could meet my little girl sometime."

Now I didn't like her. The idea of meeting somebody's little girl, with its attendant "make nice" requirements sickened me. What sickened me even more was she had called me a little boy. No boy who thinks of himself as big—and to Ike and Wally Jr. and to the baby still inside our mother's tummy I was a big brother—likes being called a little boy, and certainly not when he's out on an adventure with his father, an adventure you were sworn not to tell

Mom about. There was something guilty and delicious about playing hooky from Mom. If she'd said, "little man," that would have been all right. But she hadn't. She'd said "little boy" and that riled me. She kept saying it, too. It sounded like she was talking to my father through me, or about me, although after she took notice of me the one time, it was like she was the attendant at the Sinclair station and I was in the station wagon's wayback. "I like little boys," Shirley said to my father, paying me no attention. "Does your little boy like to come out and play sometimes? At night, I mean. I like the little boys who come out 'round midnight. In the late afternoon with the sun streaming in is beautiful, too, but maybe your little boy has chores to do before he can come out and play."

While she was saying this about me she was getting off her stool. She'd come to stand beside my Dad and she was checking out the burn on my father's neck and shoulders. The way she lifted up my father's shirt I thought of nurses in a burn ward in the war movies, how they were so gentle with the men swathed in bandages, only their eyes showing, and how they cooed and ahed as they gave the men sponge baths, and the look that came over their faces when they saw the horrible burns themselves, this look of pained sympathy they got.

"You don't tan well, do you?" She seemed nicer now, and my antipathy toward her lessened. She had arms like my mother, a little soft beneath her bicep.

My father allowed that he did not.

"Somebody is going to have to be gentle with you," Shirley said, peeking inside my father's shirt collar. She curled all her fingers except her index finger into her fist, and with the tip of her blood-red fingernail started writing in the unguent smeared on the back of my father's neck. I craned my own neck to see. "S-h-i-r" she'd written in cursive. She wasn't finished yet. Her fingernail kept going. " . . . l-e-y." She was done. She rearranged my father's collar, pinching it between her thumb and forefinger, then wiped her fingers on a cocktail napkin. She was smiling at my father with intense interest. My father was still smiling sheepishly into his drink. I wanted to tell him she'd written her name on the back of his neck in unguent, but I didn't know if I was allowed to. Usually in the wayback you kept your mouth shut and let your Dad deal with the attendant.

"Tell me, did your little boy get burned, too?"

"I'm right here," I said, waving. "I'm fine. Just a little red on my face." Something about the way she'd written her name on my father's neck wanted me to speak up, to receive the same attention my father'd received. I wanted her fingernail to write across my neck in cursive. I bet it tickled. Or maybe it felt different if you were covered in unguent. I wanted to find out.

"That's sweet," said Shirley. "You must be pleased," she said to my Dad, "having a little boy who's so well-mannered. So polite. I bet he'd stand at attention if we asked him. Or does he only take orders from one drill sergeant?"

I was about to leap off my stool and stand perfectly still, my arms at my sides, just to prove to her I could do it, but my Dad put a hand on my shoulder and squeezed. I was to stay put.

"He only takes orders from one drill sergeant," said my father.

"I'm disappointed to hear that," said Shirley. "I thought maybe we could do a little close order drilling tonight, after the other little soldiers have all been put to bed."

"Some other time," said my father. "I need to be getting back to the base now."

"Well," said Shirley, getting back on her stool and lifting her Rob Roy again, "you give your commandant my best regards. She must be quite the commander."

"I will," said my father. "And she is," he added, picking up his singles and putting them back in his pocket.

Shirley reached into her little frog of a pocketbook. "Here," she said, and she gave my father a card. I couldn't see anything except it had flowers on it. My father put it into his wallet, a wallet thick

with gas cards and business cards and prayer cards and held together with rubber bands.

"Dad," I whispered as we were leaving. "You left one. On the bar.
One of your dollar bills."

"That's called a tip," said my father. "And I'll give you one, too.
Loose lips sink ships."

I had no idea what he was talking about, but I nodded like I
knew, like I'd just been given a valuable piece of knowledge that
would last me for the rest of my life.

2 · And That's the Name of That Tune

Afterwards, I thought I had something special with our father,
but I was mistaken in that belief. Our trip to The Office was an
aberration. He took us—me—on many of his other errands around
town, but after my one special trip I became another of "you kids"
again, and The Office reverted to being a mysterious place, a place
to which our father disappeared, and from which he returned a
different person altogether. I could not enlighten my siblings as to
what went on at The Office because I felt sworn to secrecy—"Loose
lips sink ships"—and because I was reasonably sure our mother
would take a dim view of my having been there at all. Also, I was
hoping against hope that eventually I would be singled out again
to be our father's companion on one of his forays there. I did not
understand what had happened that one time, but I had the feeling our father, when tested, had acted nobly. This was not our
mother's interpretation of his behavior, though it wasn't clear
whether her response was to this one incident (how could she
know, unless Shirley's name was still there, written in unguent on
the back of our father's neck when he came home), or to the fact
that The Office never failed to wreak some kind of change on him,
a change our mother vociferously protested when she thought we
were asleep. When he got in late at night there would be talking,

screaming, tears. Our mother shouted one night, "You're not the man I married!", which made us wonder who it was she thought she'd married, since our father had been like this as long as we could remember. Still, it was obvious to us, upstairs in our beds listening, that the world of adults was a hard place to live, strange and dark, and that our father's long hours at The Office were taking a toll on him, and the best thing we could do was steer a wide path around him, and step quietly. Our task was made easier by the fact that our father was gone so frequently, and did not much like taking us with him anywhere when he was home, unless it was all of us, and we were visiting our relatives, where we were expected. It did not seem, though, that our father much wanted to visit our relatives, either.

Perhaps this was because the relatives we saw most often were our mother's. Nomi and Artu, of course, were already living with us, and the contrast with our father's parents was striking. When we went to see our father's parents—Grandma and Grandpa Cza-cza—it felt a little like we were being put under glass. Grandma Cza-cza, despite her bouncy name, was a serious woman, and she sat in her house knitting afghans and throws for her couches and chairs, as if she were one of those babushkas ensconced in Eastern European museums who eke out a pittance guarding the galleries while knitting scarves and mittens and balaclavas for the coming winter. Her own furniture needed the afghans and throws. They had gotten rid of everything old when they moved to Morton Grove and replaced it with light, almost peach-colored furniture. It was fifties furniture through and through: soft corners, boomerang shaped end-tables, stuff that looked bulky and fragile at the same time. It was all encased in plastic, too—"To protect it," she said—and she really didn't want you sitting on the plastic either, as it was liable to split under the weight of our skinny, eight-year-old butts. We could sit on the carpeted floor watching Lawrence Welk, play shuffleboard in the basement, eat some cookies in the kitchen, or escape to the park that their backyard bordered on at the corner hedge. We blasted through that hedge like rockets were strapped to our shoulders.

It was better visiting our Great Grandma Hluberstead, Artu's mother, even though that house was stocked with old people. For one thing, we could entertain them by showing we remembered how Hluberstead was spelled by singing it to the Mickey Mouse Club theme song: H-L-U-B-E-R-S-T-E-A-D! For another, while it horrified our mother, the old folks didn't mind us kids crawling all over their furniture, which was equally old and heavy and solid, nubbly in texture and draped in antimacassars. For still another, though she was old and wrinkled and looked like the Pillsbury Dough Boy at age ninety-seven, Great Grandma Hluberstead encouraged us to call her Hubie. Our mother insisted we say Grandma Hubie, at least.

Great Grandma Hluberstead—Hubie—lived on Chicago's South Side, on 101st and Bell, just south of Evergreen Park. This was as far out toward the edge of the city as you could be and still be in the city, which was something Hubie insisted on. She didn't say she lived in Chicago, however. She lived in Beverly, which was the name for her neighborhood, Beverly Park being just a few blocks over. This greatly reassured her sisters, Tillie and Eunice, who'd moved in with her after their own husbands had died, too. Taking care of the three widows and stealing money from them was Artu's younger sister, Gwen, and her ne'er-do-well husband, Bruno Goelz. For a long time that's what I thought Bruno's title was: Gwen's ne'er-do-well husband. Other people were Aunt this, Grandma or Great Grandma that. Bruno was Gwen's ne'er-do-well husband. He looked the part, too, something of a cross between a heavy-set Nazi mad-scientist and the evil banker in Frank Capra movies, all jowls and wire-rim glasses behind which his eyes lurked as he contemplated doing bad things. Bruno didn't dress like a banker or a Nazi, however. He wore white socks and black shoes and grey pants and washed-out urine-colored short-sleeve shirts with greyish-white T-shirts underneath. He favored suspenders, which allowed his belly to bulge over his pants like a sack of cement being pushed off a ledge. His head got bigger as it rose up his forehead toward his grey, receding brush-cut hair, and with his heavy jowls and perpetually pouty expression, his lower lip always thrust forward, it looked as though his head narrowed in the middle. We called him Deputy Dog, after the cartoon character. Our father, who had to suffer through these visits as "that Bohunk that Susan Marie married"—Deputy Dog's favorite occupation being ethnic and racial slurs directed at whoever was visiting—called him Gulch, which is how our father pronounced his last name.

"It's pronounced Gelch," said our mother.

"Hey, you call him the ne'er-do-well husband," said our father. "At least I give him the dignity of a last name."

"What is it with men and calling people by their last names?" wondered our mother.

"I have no idea," said our father. "Okay, you kids, get in the car."

"Where are we going?" asked Sarah, our designated asker.

"To Gwen and Gulch's," said our father.

"To Grandma Hubie's," said our mother. "Her house isn't theirs yet."

"No," said our father, "but it's going to be." This idea chafed our father, who thought a fine old house like Hubie's—a big brick Prairie foursquare built in the late teens for Hubie and her husband—would have been just right for us, and that it was a shame Gwen and Gulch, the vultures, were going to get it, and meanwhile they were robbing these little old ladies blind while ostensibly taking care of them.

"They're not robbing them blind," said our mother, who cocked her head back to indicate all of us. We knew her protestation was for our benefit, since on other occasions she'd voiced the same opinion herself.

"Little pitchers," said Artu, who sometimes drove his own car and who sometimes came with us. That seemed to be Artu's phrase for us: little pitchers. Sarah and Robert Aaron once had a debate about this, whether he was saying "little pitchers," or "little pictures." To me, "little pictures" made more sense, especially since our father got the Polaroid and was forever dragging that chemical-saturated sponge over the pictures he took of us to keep the images from fading. "Little pitchers"—did that mean little pouring vases, which made no sense whatsoever, or a reference to our playing baseball? This wasn't resolved until years later, when our mother actually uttered the whole phrase while she and our father were discussing the young man Sarah was seeing and "no doubt sleeping with," according to our father, which in itself didn't seem like that big a deal—what could happen while you were asleep? Rather than focus on the possible meanings of "sleeping with," I was struck by the fact that "little pitchers" *did* refer to what I thought it did, and it still made no sense whatsoever.

"I see, said the blind man, as he picked up his hammer and saw," said our father, working the shift on the steering column.

We braced ourselves. Ike and Wally Jr. were oblivious, of course, but Sarah and Robert Aaron and I knew that whenever our father said either, "And that's the name of that tune," or "I see, said the blind man, as he picked up his hammer and saw," he was either in a good mood, chipper (and possibly about to build something), or he was faking it, and about to become surly, which would end up with him and our mother having an argument in the kitchen, which most often would terminate with his saying, "Jesus Christ, Susan, I can't take this. I'll be at The Office," and putting on his jacket and slamming the kitchen door. When he said it on a trip it usually meant he'd grin his way through the evening, have a beer or three too many, and just before it was time to go home our mother would whisper to him, "Are you all right, Walter? Are you going to be okay?" and our father, bemused, with a grainy look in his eye, would wave her off. He would drive home very slowly, however, and from the stupefied, contrite look on his face and the green glare in our mother's eyes, it was obvious we should make ourselves scarce and get right to bed once we got home.

I don't think our father ever felt comfortable at Grandma Hubie's house, which was a shame—and a problem—because we drove down there a lot now that Nomi and Artu were living with us.

Our mom was pregnant with what would prove to be her penultimate child, Ernie. Artu still kept up his and Nomi's apartment at Wilson and Malden, a mile north of Wrigley Field, which pained him, being a White Sox fan—but it was quiet there, with cemeteries at both ends of Malden, and the lake was not too far away. Artu would stay at the apartment when he was pulling a late shift as an elevator operator, but mostly he worked days, and during the week he would stay with us. Although he owned a car he usually took the train into the Loop and our father would either pick him up at the Lowell-Wackstein building or on Erie between Wells and Franklin at one of the coin shops he liked to frequent. Then he and our father would drive out to Elmhurst along with everyone else heading out to the booming western suburbs. Nomi had broken her hip falling down the wooden back-stairs of their apartment. She'd just wanted to put out the milk bottles, but it was March and icy. With Artu gone all day it wasn't a good idea for Nomi to be laid up all by herself. Dad and Artu had set up a bed in our upstairs front bedroom—the room that was supposed to be our mother's sewing room and I-need-my-privacy get-away room. The back bedroom was for us boys. There were four of us at the time—Robert Aaron, myself, Ike, and Wally Jr.—and we were very curious about this contraption that Artu and our father had built to help Nomi's recovery. It looked like a huge steel fishing pole with a pulley and a rope for the line. They baited it with house bricks left over from when they built our house. They were sand-colored with flecks in them like freckles. "Iron-spotted," said our mother, "the best kind." She believed ours was the house that God built, all evidence to the contrary. We touched the bricks—they were textured on the sides—and wondered what they were trying to catch at the foot of Nomi's bed with this. A closet-monster or something that lived under the floorboards? Traction, Artu told us. The bricks provided traction for the cast on Nomi's hip, which was heavy and uncomfortable. The bricks provided some relief by being a counterweight.

"I see, said the blind man, as he picked up his hammer and saw," said our father as he and Artu adjusted the tension.

"Can we see it?" asked Robert Aaron. "The hip, I mean."

"It hurts her to move," said Artu. "We have to be very careful."

What did it look like, a smashed hip? Was the bone showing? Was there a scar? We didn't know. Nomi was pretty open with us about everything, forthright and plainspoken, so her reticence in this matter puzzled us.

"Why won't Nomi let us see her hip?" we had asked our mother after Nomi had been living with us for a while. We were downstairs eating lunch.

"It's the first time she's ever been really hurt," said our mother. "I think it pains her to be getting old." Our mother was washing dishes.

"Will they shoot her?" Ike asked. He was a year-and-a-half younger than me, which made him not quite four.

"Shoot her? Why on earth would anybody shoot her?"

Ike said, "Daddy says it's what they do with horses."

Robert Aaron said, "Dad says, 'You know what they do with horses?' whenever we get hurt. Then he makes his finger into a gun"—Robert Aaron demonstrated, his forefinger extended, his thumb up in the air—"and pulls the trigger, Pkew!" He did this right at Ike, who started crying.

"Nobody's shooting anybody!" shouted our mother. She wiped her hands on a dishtowel. "Your father, really. Sometimes I wonder why I married him."

Statements like this, of course, made us wonder, too. What if she'd married the Italian, the other man she dated in college, whom she sometimes told us about? Would we look the same, only with black hair? We were all blonds, except for Ike, who had auburn hair, like our mother. We didn't wonder for long, however. Your parents were your parents. That seemed pretty much irrevocable. What we did wonder about was that traction business. Those bricks suspended by a rope held a pretty strong allure for us, so we were in there constantly. We'd arrange ourselves around Nomi's pillows while she read to us in the evenings, but during the day we'd sneak in while she was dozing just to study the bricks, the rope, the steel arm—a bright chrome—and the pulley. We'd touch it—the rope—and Nomi would say, "Don't. Don't mess with that," and we'd jump. We thought she'd been sleeping. "Eyes in the back of her head," said our father. "Just like her daughter." We were alarmed that there seemed to be a symbiotic relationship between this contraption and our grandmother.

We got a glimpse of Nomi's hip only once, when our mother was giving Nomi a sponge-bath just before our Friday evening trip to Grandma Hubie's. Our mom wanted Nomi to be clean and comfortable before we left, and we were leaving as soon as Artu and our father returned from work. Our father's work consisted of calling on doctors' offices all over greater Chicagoland and trying to get them to buy something from his sample cases, two big brown valises that he carried into the house each evening. Like Nomi's cast, we weren't allowed to examine their contents.

Our mother needed all our help rolling Nomi up on her side. Nomi kept herself covered in blankets and when we pushed it was like trying to get a boulder to roll uphill. It was easier pulling her towards us, which we did. Our mother washed her back while we stared at a mass of blankets and didn't see her hip at all except for the crazy railroad spur of the scar-end, a railroad spur spun by drunken spiders. It was purple and scared us. It looked like something was living beneath her skin and sending out tendrils, a vine's fingers, to see if it could spread.

Nomi said, "I could use a beer before you leave."

"You want anything with that?"

"Sausages. Them little bitty breakfast sausages and some eggs and a nice glass of beer." Nomi was staring up at the ceiling. I thought maybe she was imagining herself back at the diner she and Artu had owned and lost during the Depression. Beer, sausage, and eggs sounded like something you ate for dinner at a diner. We had heard those stories. Our father loved to hear about them. In fact, except for politics, Nomi and our father got on well. They shared the same tastes, greasy breakfast sausage with beer for dinner being only one of them. At Grandma Hubie's, Nomi would not be the only woman over fifty drinking beer. She hated not going.

While our mother made the sausages and eggs, I was dispatched upstairs with the beer.

"You want a sip?" asked Nomi, pouring her beer into the short glass she always used. "It bites," she said when my face scrunched at the taste of it.

"How can you drink that?"

"It's an acquired taste," said Nomi. "Some people acquire it, some don't."

"I'm never going to acquire it."

"Don't be so sure you won't. Your father thought he wouldn't acquire a taste, either, God bless him, and you see how much he likes it now." Nomi looked out the window. She had a long thin face with high cheek bones and heavily lidded eyes that reminded me a little of a frog's eyes. I didn't realize it at the time, but once she had been very pretty.

"How do you acquire a taste, Nomi?"

"Lots of ways," said Nomi. "Out of hope, out of disappointment, out of other people's example or expectations. Mostly, though, you just keep on drinking the stuff until you like it. Me, I'm half Irish; I was born with a taste for it. And that makes you an eighth Irish, so you better watch out, or you'll acquire a taste for it, too." She poked me in the tummy with her finger. I laughed and held on to her index finger. She ran her other hand up my forearm. "You're rail thin," she said, "like me. You have to be careful. Spirits will go straight to your head. You see how big your father is now? He used to be rail thin, too, you know. But then he acquired a taste. Too great a taste instead of 'just a taste.' I like your father . . ." She trailed off and looked out the window again. She looked sad, but when she turned to me again she was smiling. "You be careful you don't be acquiring too great a taste," she said in what I recognized was an Irish brogue. She kept it up. "Now scoot wit' ya, and bring your old granny her sausages."

I wondered about that all that afternoon and evening at Grandma Hubie's house in Beverly. They drank their beer in short glasses at Grandma Hubie's, the same as Nomi did, so it was hard to tell whether they were having too great a taste or not. I didn't know what the limits were anyway. And could special events allow you to supersede the limits? That was our father's reasoning. "No drinking before five," our father would say, pouring himself another glassful, "and fortunately, it is always after five someplace."

That day at Grandma Hubie's was a special event, as it turned out. Our Great Uncle Harold had brought his fiancée home to meet the family. Nancy was a skinny redhead with her hair done up in a low beehive and a swoop of bangs over her forehead. She had plucked out her eyebrows, then drawn in new ones that looked like the way I drew crows at a distance, had the crows been flying upside down. Her skirt was too short, showing a good four inches of thigh above her knees, which endeared her to no one but Grandma Hubie. "Sit down, my dear, sit down," Grandma Hubie cried, and Nancy was left to her fate while everyone else went about their business. Even Harold eventually removed his hand from hers and went to have a cigarette in the backyard. Hubie and Tillie and Eunice took turns reminiscing to the girl about their own families, then she was released (or rescued) by the other women, who had their own inquiries to make.

It was spring, but there was still snow on the ground and the air was chilly, especially on the sunporch behind the kitchen, which is where the men sat engaged in a poker game of mammoth proportions. Harold joined them there after his cigarette was finished. He knew better than to interfere with Nancy's being welcomed into the family by the other women. This was a test, really, and if you were polite and made an effort you passed. Nancy had displayed her patience with the ramblings of Tillie and Eunice so she was already halfway home free.

When we played poker at home we always used the plastic chips our father kept in a wooden carousel, but here, on the sunporch, the men were using money. Real money, not Monopoly money as we sometimes used to spice up the games: I see your five hundred and I raise you Park Place. There were piles of nickels and dimes and quarters, stacks of ones and even five-dollar bills. Everything was bathed in that yellow light of late afternoon that seems warmer than it is. It was like the men were sitting in a halo, drinking their beer out of short glasses, pouring themselves a second glass, calling for more bottles. We kids were kept running. Sandwiches— ham and Swiss on pumpernickel bread smeared with butter and mustard—dill pickles, potato chips, radishes with salt, onion spears, apples, tomato slices, mayonnaise (Hellman's, not the Miracle Whip we used at home), cucumbers, peanut butter, bananas, oranges, cheddar cheese cubes, Limburger on rye, olives (both black and green), pearl onions, three bean salad, potato salad (both sour and sweet), roast beef on platters, sliced summer sausage and pastrami, blood sausage and ring bologna—you name it, we fetched it. And beer! There must have been a dozen different kinds of beer: Carling's Black Label, Adler Brau, Old Milwaukee, Schlitz, Pabst, Budweiser, Chief Oshkosh, Blatz, Red, White and Blue, Miller's High Life, "The champagne of bottled beer" (in bottles you could see through!), and some I've no doubt forgotten.

The beer bottles were crammed into a spare refrigerator in one corner of the sunporch and there were more in an ice chest next to that. The empties went into cardboard cases stacked in the basement. Besides delivering sandwich fixings, our job was to run the empties into the basement and to keep the players supplied with their favorite beer. We were also to collect the bottle caps and used napkins for the trash and sweep the sandwich crumbs off the oilcloth and into the napkins, the way we'd seen our mother and Nomi do at home.

Although this was family, everything seemed foreign and wonderful to us. Strange in a good way. It was like our immigrant forebears had come back to life even though these old people (Uncle Harold was already twenty) were descended from people who came over from Germany and Ireland a generation or two (or three) earlier. Our own family—our mom and dad and us—was American; we were just born under a funny name, a name you could dance to: cha-cha-czabek. But everything about *them* was foreign. The sandwiches were not Oscar Meyer bologna and Kraft singles on Wonder Bread with Miracle Whip. Their meats came wrapped in butcher paper, their pickles from jars that had funny writing on the label ("Polish dills," explained our mother), their cheese came in rounds and bricks you had to slice, or if it came sliced, the slices were separated by waxed tissue paper and wrapped in that same ubiquitous butcher paper. Their house smelled old and seemed heavy. Even the air seemed heavy, heated as it was by monstrous cast-iron radiators with screened covers. On cold days, after playing outside, we'd sit on the radiator to warm our bottoms. Even that seemed foreign and wonderful. We'd put our snow-encrusted mittens and hats under the radiators after we came in, and when it was time to leave they'd be toasty and dry: marvelous! And if it weren't for Harold, who insisted the game be poker because he was getting married, and "condemned men always get a last request," the men would be playing pinochle and euchre, games Artu loved to play, games whose very syllables seemed to belong to another century. Nomi, had her hip allowed her to come, would be at the table, too, betting and drinking, telling stories and laughing, tapping her cigarette in the ashtray with a nonchalance I thought only Humphrey Bogart possessed. Nomi also would have left Nancy alone except to give her a quick hug and a kiss and to say if she was marrying into this family she had her work cut out for her.

It was a big house neatly divided into four zones: front room, kitchen (with the dining room between), sunporch, and upstairs, where the teenagers (Sarah and our cousins Cicely and Katie) held sway, listening to Beatles songs on a hand-held transistor radio. Grandma Hubie, Tillie, and Eunice always sat in nubbly easy-chairs in the living room, and they were attended to by the other women and whoever wandered into their vicinity. If we brought them tea we were expected to sit down and "pleasantly spend time with them," as our mother ordered. This was not that hard since they loved nothing better than a silent audience, and we were rendered silent staring at their bulbous knuckles and the liver spots on their hands, and the wattles of flesh on their necks that swung back and forth like a turkey's as they talked. We were not willing to comprehend that eventually we would all look like that, that our mother would become like Nomi, that Nomi would be-come like Tillie, and that we would pass through these same phases ourselves, perhaps someday becoming as fat as our father. These thoughts never occurred to us. We simply couldn't believe people could get this old. It was a marvel to us. It was as though they had distinguished themselves chiefly by the shrunken state their bodies had obtained. This made them seem both benign and scary at the same time. We focused on absolutely the wrong things: the wrinkles around the mouth, the rheumy eyes with the soft, wrinkled bags of flesh beneath; the very skinny, delicate glasses; the short, soft, and wavy platinum hair; and the wattles, the wat-tles!, that swayed ever so slightly as they prattled (we thought) on and on. They were obviously pleased to be in the company of young people, and if they noticed we were in awe of them, and slightly scared, and that our ears were stopped up, and our mouths were shut, or hanging open like fish, they paid no notice. Conse-quently, we didn't hear a word they said about our family's his-tory: about our mother as a little girl; about Hubie, Tillie, and

Eunice as little girls; about what it was like growing up in the latter years of the previous century or the early years of this one. We were rocks in a stream of stories. It all rushed over us, rendering us smooth and small. We could feel the current of words rushing by, but we didn't hear a word. Like Nancy, we simply waited, fidgeting, and hoped we passed muster and would soon be released from our duty.

That meant that besides Artu, the only people who really paid attention to these repositories of the family history were the women: our mother, Irene, Margaret, and Gwen. And although Gwen lived there, she was an impatient caretaker. You could tell that she and Bruno were just waiting for Hubie to die so Tillie and Eunice could be put in a home, and then Bruno and Gwen could have the house all to themselves. Watching the two of them move around the house was like watching fat versions of Cruella De Ville hustling after the dalmatian pups. We stayed out of their way. As the only kids at these gatherings, we stayed out of everyone's way even though Aunt Irene, who was Nomi's sister, and Aunt Margie, who was Gwen and Artu's older sister, were very nice to us. When they weren't sitting with Hubie, Tillie, and Eunice you could find them in the kitchen, unwrapping strange goodies like head cheese from their butcher paper cocoons and talking about their families. With our mother being pregnant with Ernie, and Nancy being new to the family, the talk this time was mostly about the upcoming wedding and about pregnancies past and present. Yucky stuff. Irene and Margie, like Nomi, drank beer. Irene looked exactly like Nomi except she had brilliant yellow hair, like flax. It wasn't a color that appeared in nature, but that just made her Aunt Irene. Gwen was drinking coffee out of the good china. Our mother drank something she called a Sidecar, which she had our father mix up for her special. She also had Wally Jr. on her shrunken lap. Wally Jr. was there because if you left him on the floor he put everything that fell onto the floor—coins, bottlecaps, crusts of bread, olives, bits of cheese—into his mouth.

The men, of course, were on the sunporch: Artu, our father, Bruno, Irene's husband Frank, Aunt Margie's husband Alvin, and two of her three sons, Harold and Howard. Howard was older, probably our father's age. Aunt Margie had had him with her first husband, whose name and whereabouts we weren't told. What we were told was that Aunt Margie was lucky to have found someone who "treated her right," who accepted Howard as his own, and who was, in general, a nice man. And Alvin was a nice man. His face, though, looked like he used it to stop trucks for a living. He had a bullet shaped head and a gash for a mouth and bad teeth, which was alright because it looked like he only possessed seven or eight of them. He loved to laugh, though, exposing those horrible teeth, and after a while you got used to it. You especially got used to it because he had the most amazing habit of elbowing his stack of winnings—the coins anyway—onto the floor. "Get that, would you?" he'd ask us, and we've dive to the linoleum. Retrieving fistfuls, we'd proffer our gleanings to him. "Keep it," he'd say, and we'd snug in close to his elbows, sentries to his needs, fetching him another braunschweiger-and-onion sandwich, or another of the pickles he liked to gnaw on for his poor sore gums. The others would do it, too, of course—knock their change on the floor—so eventually we would spread out, each of us picking a great uncle or grandfather whose elbow movements we shadowed. Sometimes Sarah, Cicely, and Katie joined us, but being teenagers, they usually kept to themselves upstairs, away from "the children." So there were just the three of us, Robert Aaron, myself, and Ike. Wally Jr. hardly counted. He tried to swallow pennies, which was bad, but he couldn't move fast enough to gather much in. To keep him from crying, we'd give him a fistful of nickels. That would usually put an end to his screeching.

Bruno, of course, never knocked his money to the floor. He kept this sour, surly look on his face like every coin on the floor rightfully belonged to him, seeing as how it was in "his" house where they were playing, and why should these tow-headed vermin be allowed anything? And our father didn't do well at cards usually, so his piles of coins were disappointingly small when he did knock them over, and Harold—well, Harold was getting married so they wanted him to win, or at least not lose too much, so whenever his elbow got close to his coins Artu or Alvin would send a rainy waterfall of jingling coins floorward. We had one other favorite uncle, Stephen, Harold's and Howard's younger brother, but he only played a few hands before he said he had to get back to school. He was a sophomore at Notre Dame. "Mid-terms," he explained before he put on his jacket and left. "Major parties," said Aunt Margie sighing once he'd left. She'd come into the sunroom with a warm glass of milk for Alvin, who loved to eat the food he ate but suffered from heartburn. "You'd think he'd stay to chat with Nancy."

"Why?" Harold asked. "He's not marrying her. I am."

Margie cuffed Harold gently on the back of his head.

"It's okay, Ma. We already agreed, he's going to be my best man."

"All the more reason he should be visiting with Nancy."

"Mom, give him a break. It's Friday night. I'd be out partying with my friends, too, if I wasn't here."

"The point is you are here."

"If you ask me, he should be in the service," said our father, shuffling the cards in his hand. "Stephen, I mean. It'd do him a world of good."

"Nobody asked you, Wally," said our mother. The women had come into the sunroom. It was growing dark and with Stephen's quick departure you could feel the day closing in on itself.

"Last fall they had me on call-up duty, you know that?" said our father. "The Cuban missile thing, and they had everybody in the Reserves all charged up and ready to go."

"They could have sent Wally-bear back to San Diego and then to Florida," our mother said. "And me, big as a house here with our sixth."

"It seems crazy," Margie said.

"Frightful," said our mother. It sounded like our mother was confessing something, which indeed she was. This was our mother's way: something horrible would happen, and you would only find out about it later, when she had surmounted it enough to make light of it. You could tell she had been cut, but the wound was healing. That, anyway, was the image our mother wished to present to the world, an attitude no doubt ingrained in her by Nomi, whose motto could have been, "Never let 'em see you cryin', girl, never let 'em see you cryin'." Inside her own home, however, was another matter. And even then it was more a matter of our eavesdropping than her giving vent to her emotions in front of us.

That whole fall had been a tense time in our household. There had been a letter from the government, and our mother had cried when she opened it. Our parents spent a lot of time in front of the TV watching the news, which they didn't usually do, and ushered us out of the room whenever the outlined map of Cuba appeared over Walter Cronkite's shoulder. Our father often didn't come home until we were nearly ready for bed, and then he and our mother would talk in hushed, plaintive voices. Or at least that would be our mother's voice. Our father's was calm and accepting, as though a balance of power had shifted in the family back toward him. One evening we heard our mother wail, "But they can't make you go, Wally, they can't make you go!" and our father answered, "I'd have to, Susan. I have a commission. I'd have to report." "You can't leave me!" our mother wailed, and then we heard her weeping. We peeked over the railing to see our father comforting her. She sat on his lap, folded into his shoulder, her just barely pregnant belly bumping into his. Our father had his arms around her, and he was kissing her hair saying, "There, there. There, there," while our mother cried, "I can't do this again, Wally, I can't, I can't. Don't leave me, please, please don't leave me."

It scared us. Usually our mother was the indomitable one, putting up with our father's absences—even when he was home he was gone—but here she was weeping on our father's shoulder like a little girl who had skinned her knee. Without a word passing among us we agreed not to speak of this. It just settled into our consciousness, that everything could change at a moment's notice, the world turned upside down. Your parents were your parents, sure, but evidently one of them could leave and that was called duty. We didn't understand this. That evening, behind the closed door of their bedroom, there was a desperate furtiveness to their noises, a plaintive urgency, as though they felt they had to use up everything inside them before their world fell apart. That knowledge seeped into us as well.

"It would have been my third war," said our father. "All under Democratic presidents, if you get my drift." He winked at everybody around the table. I hadn't been counting how many beers he'd had, but it had been a lot. Our father drank beer in short glasses quickly and refilled them often. He had acquired the taste.

"Wally, don't be bringing up politics. You know how I hate that," said our mother.

"Facts are facts," said our father. "You want peace and prosperity you get a Republican. You get a recession under a Democrat, and the first thing after that you got a war on your hands to balance the budget."

"World War II was about balancing the budget?" Artu asked.

"It got us out of the Depression," said our father. "Don't think Roosevelt didn't know that. He let Pearl Harbor happen just so he'd have an incident to get us involved."

"Don't answer him," said our mother. "It'll just keep him going."

"I thought this one was about keeping the communists out of Asia," Harold said.

"It is. But you watch. If the economy takes a tumble it won't just be advisers going over there. That's why Stephen should enlist now. ROTC. Life's a lot better for you as an officer, and that's the name of that tune."

"It's not okay as a civilian?" Harold asked.

"It's okay if you got a job. Once Kennedy runs out of jobs to give away he's going to start putting people in uniform come hell or high water."

"I already got a job." Harold had a Borden route. He delivered dairy products and bread from a van with Elsie the Cow painted on both sides.

"Stephen doesn't."

"Stephen is in school," said Artu. Stephen was Artu's favorite nephew.

"They'd make him get a haircut." Stephen's hair was "shaggy," according to our mother, which meant it touched his ears and hung a little bit over his collar. Our own hair was allowed to grow over the winter, at least on top, so we had bangs, but it was close-cropped on the sides and in back. Come summer our father took out the clippers and gave us all "Indianapolis 500" haircuts: he tucked our heads into his armpit and shaved our heads down to the nubbins, accompanying each stroke over our skulls with "VVVRROOOOM! VVVRROOOOM!" You stepped away from him when he was done with you, dazed from the strangeness of being in his armpit, smelling that acridy smell from flesh rubbing wetly on flesh, and feeling, yes, love.

Humiliation and intimacy: in our family these were two sides of the same coin.

"Enough, Wally-bear, I mean it," said our mother.

"Real men serve in the military," said our father. He looked around the table. Bruno had had a bad knee that kept him out of the Big One, and Artu had come of age between the wars. That left Harold, who had a soft, serious look on his face I could identify with. Harold was a watcher and a listener. He cleared his throat.

"I'm getting married," Harold said.

"Real men—" said our father. He poured himself another beer. As though he were speaking to the glass he was filling he said, "And that's the name of that tune." Then he put his fist to his mouth and quacked like a duck, his fingers opening as he did so to let the noise increase in volume. He had this tight, befuddled little smile on his face as though he wasn't quite sure what line had been crossed, but he was pleased one had. This was different from how he had acted at The Office. I was puzzled. I wanted him to act noble and large and kind-hearted, and here he was being small and mean and aggressive. And he had been acting this way for a while now—at Thanksgiving, at Christmas. What was going on? It got even stranger when Artu, who usually ignored our father when he got like this, got into it with him.

"You fought the Battle of Lake Michigan in World War II, didn't you, Walter?" said Artu.

"I served my country in her hour of need," said our father.

"In the Coast Guard, wasn't it? Stateside?"

"I served my country," our father repeated.

"And in Korea, you hauled troops and ferried refugees around, right? You didn't see any real action, did you?"

"I could hear the guns," said our father.

"But you didn't see any action, did you?"

"I fucking served my country, you son of a bitch!" our father roared. He was standing now, swaying forward on his fingertips. He refilled his glass again. "And that . . . that is the name of that tune." He sat down again.

Nobody had knocked their coins to the floor in some time. This was how family gatherings with our father ended these days. Our mother stoic but near tears. Her eyes glistening as she got our coats. Artu said Irene and Frank would give him a ride home. Our mother said she understood.

"Are you coming, Walter?" Our father hadn't moved while our mother got our coats. He sipped from his glass, then refilled it. He held up the bottle and toggled it back and forth, meaning one of us should get him another. We didn't move. Our mother would yell at us if we did. Our father shrugged, put the bottle down. In the dining room we heard Sarah complaining. Why did we have to leave so early? Why couldn't she stay? Katie and Cicely's parents would see her home. Our mother explained icily that nobody was driving out of their way for us. And Sarah Lucinda was old enough to help with getting Wally Jr.'s coat on. Did she need to be reminded that she was part of this family, too? "I hate this family," said Sarah Lucinda. This was followed by a loud smack.

Our mother reappeared in the sunporch's doorway. She was furious and resplendent, her green eyes blazing, her pregnant belly lending her a power she didn't usually have. "Walter," she said, in clipped syllables that made it sound as though she were cutting them off her tongue with a knife. "Are you coming home with us or not?"

Our father studied his cards. "I believe I'll let you play this hand out," he said, tossing his cards into the pot and rising heavily to his feet.

A pall filled our car on the way home. "I have never been so humiliated—" said our mother, but she didn't say anything more. It was a phrase we had not yet gotten used to hearing, although eventually we would. Our mother would repeat it whenever we came home from any event our father had drunk too much at, exclusive of his many trips to The Office, which is where he would go this evening once we got home.

We knew what he would say as we trooped out of the car and reluctantly entered our dark and empty house: "And that's the name of that tune," he'd say, and roll up his window, and put the car into reverse and wobbly back out the drive. And our mother would want to say something to him, but wouldn't, except maybe to thinly press her lips together and breathe, "You shit," once he was already into the street, too far away to hear her or to see the fear and determination that lit up her face. "Come on inside, you kids," she'd say, and usher us upstairs and make us ready for bed. Then she'd make herself tea and bring it and a beer-and-sandwich platter up to Nomi, who would listen as our mother poured out her grief.

That was the rest of our evening—the rest of our childhood— already spread out silently before us. For now, our parents sat in the front seat, and we sat in the middle and the wayback, and the air itself seemed permeated with silence, a silence that insinuated itself like a vapor, like a wraith. We kids—we all looked out the windows. Brick houses, ranches mostly, filled our view. We wondered—would life be any different for us if we lived there, or there, or there? We came to the conclusion it wouldn't.

War Babies

If God was going to watch over us
you'd think He'd be less haphazard about it.
—Rita Sabo

What you can't explain you don't.
What you can explain nobody listens to
or believes in anyway.
—Betty Sabo

1 · The Cooling Tank

The woman they pulled out of the cooling tank should not have been there.

But she is, and as they haul her out, there is the click and whir of a hydraulic winch, an industrial winch with its yellow arm decaled KASCO. This is the same winch they use for lowering the baskets of #8 and #16 cans into the water after they come out of the cooker. The block and tackle with its enormous hook is swung out over the cooling tank, which is a uniform orange-brown from decades of rust. It looks like a watering trough, only scaled for Babe, the Blue Ox. It's long—maybe fifty yards—and the water inside is maybe four feet deep. There are huge wrought-iron baskets of layered cans half-submerged farther down the tank, as though they had been dipped and then somebody forgot about them. Standing in the chest-deep water under the winch is a man dressed like a fireman, with that distinctive hat and a blue-black shirt with red suspenders, and those school-bus-yellow waders. Other firemen are milling about outside the tank like high-tech honeybees in their black-and-fluorescent-yellow jackets. They guide the hydraulic winch with its chain and hook to the fireman inside the tank and he attaches the grommeted end of a sling to it, and it's when he bends down with the sling that you see what he's attaching it to. It's only a flash—white skin, white belly, arms out in surrender or supplication—but it's enough. He's flipped the body onto its back so he can get the sling under it; you glimpse her torso and what you fixate on are details—bare shoulders, the hair floating around the open eyes like seaweed, the merest suggestion of a breast. You are struck by the marbleized, slightly bloated bluish-green skin, the purple lips, the blue and red lights of the police and fire cars outside twirling against the factory's corrugated tin walls, against the flesh itself. The woman is still just beneath the water's surface, and the lights are spangling everything into watery rhomboids.

Then they get the sling under her. The second grommet gets attached to the winch-hook and the fireman nods. The honeybees look grim. Red and blue and orange lights wash over everything. The lights, too, look like they're underwater. The winch whines and ratchets. The chain drips water as it moves. The first thing you see emerging is her knee. Then the rest of her. There's a collective gasp at the awesomeness of that much flesh on display.

At first the woman comes out of the water and she looks almost lovely, like she's one of those Playboy models splayed back in midair on a swing set. But then you notice how stiff she is, how the sling under her buttocks makes her dangle backwards, like somebody shot her midswing. In rigor mortis she looks more grotesque than erotic. They get a second sling, only they can't fit it around her easily. They try a couple of times and give up. She's still dangling while they try this, her body turning this way and that, her arms splayed out.

Finally the fireman in the water shifts the sling to the small of her back, drapes the other sling over the tank's side and the woman comes out of the tank the rest of the way, her hair streaming water.

2 · Quonset Love

Until Betty Sabo was killed, there hadn't been a killing in Augsbury, Wisconsin—not one of passion, anyway—since the '40s. Not since the German prisoner of war camp was housed in the Quonset huts over by what later became Hawley's Kountry Klub. Fourteen hundred POWs were stationed there, farmed out as field and factory labor. Despite the hard work, the Germans had been amazed at their treatment. Three squares and sturdy clothes. But then, this part of Wisconsin had been taken over by German immigrants after they'd driven out the Indians. The triumph of the beefy-faced and thick-ankled. Sauerkraut *über alles*. Anyway, one POW, Ernst Tschnauble—Ernie Schnauzer, he was called, with his graying brush-cut hair spewing off in all directions and his tenacious wooing of women he shouldn't even have been speaking to—married and settled down here after the war. Ernie was old for a private, thirty-eight or so, and he had no intention of going back to Germany after the war. Not if he could help it, anyway. They were going to repatriate him at war's end, same as everybody else, but then he and Ellie Frodert announced their intentions. And then Ellie announced she was pregnant. It took a great deal of courage for Ellie to say that, and she was shunned for it, but with concerns for the child's welfare foremost in people's minds (the baby, after all, would be an American citizen), they arranged, God knows how, for Ernie to stay. That a baby girl, Marcella, wasn't born until nearly sixteen months after Ellie and Ernie wed was attributed to wartime rationing. Ellie said, "They take longer to develop when it's foreign babies inside you," but she was smiling when she said it.

One of Ernie's POW friends wasn't so lucky. He took a liking to a woman named Francine Sabo and they used to meet in the woods behind the barracks. His name was Hans Robert Proser and he and Francine worked in the toy factory, which during the war was turning out gun stocks for Thompson machine guns, in addition to toilet seats and foot lockers. (The POWs were paid for turning out the toilet seats, but at a fraction of the regular wage.) Security was surprisingly lax at the camp, and any time Francine wanted to, she could visit Hans over the back wire. Or if she decided not to eat lunch in the factory break room, but instead have a picnic on the railroad embankment that ran behind the toy factory (a mile down the railway line was the canning factory, Augsbury's other major wartime industry), her POW beau didn't find it that difficult to join her.

Francine Sabo, unlike Ellie Frodert, did not announce that she was carrying a German soldier's child. That fact eventually announced itself. And when the facts were unmistakable, it was only a matter of a few weeks—it was December, 1944, and a fresh eight inches of wet snow was bunching the tree limbs—before they found Proser's body on the railway embankment near the canning company's settling ponds, just a few miles from the glade behind the Quonset huts where Francine Sabo and Proser used to meet.

Proser was found with a double-edged hunting knife buried to the hilt where his left eye used to be. The knife had been driven with such force into his eye that his cheekbone was chipped where the fingerguard hit home.

That was how they ruled out Francine Sabo as her child's father's killer. They figured that kind of blow had to have been delivered by a man. Suspicion fell on her immediate family, which was large and extensive. Francine had eighteen brothers, cousins, or uncles of various proximities who'd all have had access to such a knife. So did about twenty-five hundred other people in the county, if anybody had cared to think a second, and Proser was known to be a ladies man, tall, blond, good-looking. Rumors were that Francine Sabo was not his only lover, just his only pregnant one.

Anti-German feeling was also running pretty high right then, even among people named Schmidt and Hemmelberger. The Germans had smashed through in the Ardennes Forest, and for a little while, at least, what looked to be a whole new war was starting up. And here was this smiling Kraut—boy, oh, boy, did he have it good or what?—making time with our women.

But nobody was going to follow it up any further. The Sabos were Indians, or mostly Indian—a few of them still lived on the reservation. Francine Sabo got what she deserved for being promiscuous, and that Kraut POW, he shoulda thunk twice before messing with a bunch of Indians. Even just one, if the Indian was a woman.

Unsolved crime of passion, case closed.

Ernie Tschnauble and Ellie Frodert and little Marcella benefited some from what happened to Francine Sabo and Hans Robert Proser. Maybe it was revulsion over what had happened with Proser. Maybe it was guilt. Maybe it was that Ellie was Gene Frodert's daughter, and he was the village board president and ran the Volunteer Fire Department, was in charge of the war bonds drive and owned Frodert Chevrolet. And Francine was a no-account Indian, no matter how well she kept up that trailer of hers over by the river. So it was that the town took leniency on Ernie Schnauzer and Ellie Frodert in a way they never did on Francine Sabo and Hans Robert Proser.

I know that because Francine was my mother. And my older sister Betty was that child. Eight years later my mother had me. My father was away in Korea. When he came back it wasn't to live with us. "He's a leaver," my mother said. Then she fixed her eyes on me. "And you're one of his leavings."

3 · War Babies

Our mother often used to speak ironically of Betty's father as the only guy she knew who stuck around after he was through with her. He was buried in Mosquito Hill Cemetery, tucked off to one side in a small section separated from the rest of the cemetery by a road and a line of bushes. It was where they buried the POWs who had fallen ill and died while in Augsbury's care. There were eight of them, all pneumonia and influenza victims if you didn't count Proser.

I don't know if our mother loved Proser or not. It was wartime, all the regular men were away, and Robert Proser might just have been a delicious lark. He was supposed to be our enemy (though so were most Anglos, if you thought about it), yet he was caged inside that Quonset hut. It may have been she took pity on him, his skull close-shaven, the broken blue eyes, the lips hard and chapped, yet wanting. It may even have been romantic to be in love with him. Then again, maybe not. Having grown up on the reservation, our mother was used to the smell of man-sweat and corrugated tin. Maybe she didn't feel the illicit thrill some other woman might have. Still, she was eighteen, nineteen—the right age for stupidity and romance and daring-do.

But if she had loved—even briefly and incompletely—Betty's

father, she certainly hadn't loved mine. Or she left that feeling pretty quickly. And for a while there, Betty and I weren't even sure she loved us. She talked for a time about scraping together enough money and flying to Germany and meeting Proser's family. Betty was fifteen and I was seven. Francine was afraid that if we arrived and something untoward happened—my mother liked to use phrases like "untoward" and then say, by way of clarification, "if they nabbed us"—if something untoward happened to us and we were held for ransom, the federal government would not go out of its way to rescue a bunch of half-breed Indians. The way she talked about it later, though, our getting nabbed would have made her life a whole lot easier. I think, in fact, her original plan was to drop us both off with Betty's father's family and then leave for the States herself, free of her encumbrances. Once she was back she could cry "My babies!" safe in the knowledge that nobody in authority would do anything about us. If my mother had had anything to say about it, it would probably not even have come to their attention.

It didn't happen. By the time Francine had saved enough money for us to go, the Berlin Wall had gone up. If our mother had hoped to rid herself of the products of her wildness, it was too late. And taking our cue from her, as we got older we got wilder and wilder ourselves. And when she wanted to reproach us for our wildness she'd recall that trip that didn't happen. "I should have dropped you both off in Germany when I had the chance," she'd say. As though she'd actually made the trip. As though we'd actually accompanied her and an opportunity had actually presented itself, and she'd thought better of it, and was now rethinking, or had already rethought and decided against that moment of motherly leniency and weakness.

4 · Rabbit Feet

Deep down our mother was a romantic, no matter what bitterness she spouted in her later years. She was bitter because she was a romantic—there's no surer recipe for the former than having been the latter. She slept with POWs, with soldier boys coming back from overseas, with more soldier boys going off to Korea, and nurtured the hope, I think, that what had transformed these boys into soldiers—the uniform—would similarly transform her and her daughters. They would be accepted and liked and made to feel special. I have no idea how that was supposed to happen, and I don't think Francine knew, either, but at the time it was a common enough belief. Sleeping with a uniform was like rubbing a lucky rabbit's foot, finding a four-leaf clover, not changing your blouse after it's been touched by somebody famous, like Frank Sinatra or Nelson Eddy. It's just most women practiced that belief in moderation. Francine didn't.

And it must have rubbed off on us. For years Betty and I had rabbit's foot key-rings. Hers was dyed green. Mine was natural. You could feel the tiny bones through the fur, separate the hairs and see the toenails. To think that this had once been part of a living, breathing animal, its body quivering while it waited for the men with the jigsaw or hatchet to make it an amputee. I shuddered. I imagined they only took the feet of living rabbits, and each time they'd only take a single foot. I could see whole fields of animals hobbling about, each of them bandaged, waiting for the terror to strike them anew.

Feeling those hardened bones under my fingers! And yet I couldn't even think of giving it up. It was part of me. I was a part of it. I'd play with the beaded chain and finger the cap where it came down over the foot. And imagine it to be mine. Amputated but I'd keep it. The best part of me, no longer living but still alive. *The Revenge of the Killer Rabbit's Feet!* Coming soon to a theater near you!

I don't blame Francine for any of this. Francine was just doing what she believed. The beliefs might have been faulty—aren't they all?—but it's no crime believing them.

It carried further than that, though, her dreams for us, the superstitions she gave us. Betty was named for Bettys Grable and Boop, and I was named for Miss Hayworth, Orson Welles's wife, whom my mother believed was part Chippewa, like us, though why she would believe that, without even a whisper of evidence, I've no idea. When I was eight or nine I found that famous photograph of Rita Hayworth on her haunches in a slip in a *Best of LIFE* retrospective. I remember the dramatic cleavage of course, but I also remember her hands on her thighs, as though she were touching herself to make sure she was still there. And I remember her face best of all, the big eyes, the pouting lips. She wore a look of sultry indecision—should I be doing this or not? her face is saying, although it's already too late, she's already there, in a slip with black lace across her bodice, and that knowledge shows on her face as well. Francine told me I was named for her because I was going to be that beautiful, that desirable. I never believed it, but my mother insisted. I was going to look like that. And that's when my mother told me, "She's part Chippewa, you know." When I asked Francine what made her think Rita Hayworth was Chippewa she said all the dark-eyed, high-cheekboned actresses were. They were just keeping quiet about it.

"She's Italian," I told my mother years later when I'd looked it up. "Rita Cansino. AKA Margaret Carmen Cansino. She changed her name twice."

"Italians," my mother said. "They used to have this whole empire and now they're squashed into a silly little country that looks like a boot. They may as well be Indians." Then she tacked back to her old position. "She's Indian. That EYE-talian stuff is just a dodge. People hire EYE-talian actresses. They don't hire Indians except for when they want us falling off horses. You know why she married Prince Aly Khan?"

"Because he was fabulously wealthy?"

"Sure. But also because she was trying to get closer to her Indian blood. She couldn't say that, but that's what she was doing. She's Indian. She's not fooling anyone."

Betty and I would have needed a whole lot more than a rabbit's foot to get through Francine's beliefs intact. No wonder we IDed with the feet.

5 · The Decline and Fall of the Sabo Empire

Betty and I were of a piece. Named for movie actresses, the off-spring of impossible loves with empty uniforms, we were turned loose on the world armed with the idea that with our suspect beauty and luck, we could make it (meaning the world) suffer. At the very least it would suffer our beauty, and we would be prized for that alone.

Stupidly romantic like our mother, we didn't take long to tumble. Quickly married and divorced, Betty settled into a routine that was as frightening to me as it was plain. She worked on the labeling line at the Everfresh canning company when it was running, collected welfare from October to May when it wasn't, and had a baby every other year. Eight years later I followed suit. The same routine. Almost. I panicked when it came to the babies, though. I had my first, Garrett, at nineteen with—really without—a boy named Matthew Keillor. Then I got married to Kenny Newberry and had two more, though he was already leaving me while we were making number two. It would be pretty hard justifying that now, even to myself, so I won't try. Still, I was a faint copy of Betty. I had three; Betty had six. Two by her husband, four others by guys from the canning company and/or the toy factory, which in the '60s and '70s was turning out cribs and rockers, and those peg-and-hammer kits boys liked until Pong turned them all into couch potatoes. Betty's house was filled with this stuff. Like every guy who slept with her felt obligated to give her a baby rocker or a crib or a toy set of tools. Then came the fire. A space heater in the living room caught fire and it swept through the Airstream she was living in with Francine. Three of her babies died. The youngest, Celia, was nursing with Betty in the kitchen when it happened. They got out. So did Tina, the oldest, and Chip, the second oldest. They were rescued by neighbors—pulled through a window with the fire licking at their heels. They suffered a lot of smoke inhalation but came around in the hospital. The other three died inside the trailer. I didn't want to think of that, though. I didn't want to hear it or acknowledge anything about it. The fragility of life in general—don't tell me. Kenny and I were having our first then so I was weak and selfish, still holding out for the saving grace of romantic and married love.

It seemed so easy then, making babies. Kenny would come home from Nekoosa Paper in Neenah (two places with Indian names that didn't care much for Indians) and he'd love me right up, pregnant belly and all. He didn't seem to like me all that much afterwards, but I let him inside me just the same. After standing up so nicely to Matthew Keillor, who wanted me but not everything that came with me, I sort of crashed. I had a stupid and low period when any attention was attention enough. Kenny was infrequently nice and I accepted that. I was also exuberant with the newness of marriage, so much so that I was the willing self-sacrifice whenever he wanted to go out with the boys. Marriage, I think, addles you for a while. I was so full up with my own fecundity right then that I wanted to say to Betty, in my too-recently-married-to-be-anything-but-insensitive-and-foolish way, "Don't worry, Betty. We'll make more."

But right after the fire Betty went sort of crazy—wild in a self-destructive way—and I had a cesarean and Kenny was less interested in me stitched up than he was in me knocked up. I became wary again. Wary of Kenny, wary of more babies. Wary of all the men after and besides Kenny, who saw in me damaged but available goods. I said no to most everybody except Anderson Elliot, the town attorney. I met him while Betty was attempting to get a settlement out of the space heater company, and after he got divorced we started dating, off and on, which was fine with me. After having babies by Matthew Keillor and Kenny Newberry, I wanted to live inside my own mind, and not have these men taking up all the available room, making noise and constantly drawing attention to themselves, whining or crowing, it made no difference. Besides, the pickings were so slim among the available men. Better you infrequently make a series of one-night mistakes than try laboring over something that's not going to work anyway, simply because you're used to laboring and men are incapable of understanding you anyway.

No mistakes would be even better, but sometimes you do get lonesome for the company.

Betty had that lonesomeness in spades. She took all comers: Bob Notlinger, her shift supervisor at the canning company; tow motor drivers in the warehouse; some of the warehouse day labor—Byron Joe Gunther, Vernon Haight Jr., and others besides. Not what you'd call the town's finest. I'd see them sometimes at Poacher's Inn or Utke's, or at the time clock at the end of our shift. All of them sweaty, panting, resting their foreheads against their forearms, making those jokes that went two ways. It was like watching dogs scarfing down meat. When she was entertaining at her place it was like those boards you see in offices where you keep track of who's there and who isn't with color-coded magnets and tiny squares. During breaks they'd be by her machine, too, the cans whirling and clinking past until the labeling supervisor—Marcella Tschnauble, Ernie and Ellie's chubby daughter—sent them scurrying back to their own work areas.

I didn't hang out with that crowd. Right after work I'd leave. Go home to my kids. I was working 3–11 in the cook room at the canning company, and I got a job short-ordering lunches at Leeman's as well. Winters, when the canning company was closed, I worked at Jacks or Better as a set-up chef for the dinner rush. Francine moved in with me—I had a small bungalow by the golf course, the old caretaker's cottage for the cemetery—and she watched Garrett and Kenny Jr. for me while I was working. Betty would drop off Celia, Tina, and Chip and go off partying. I didn't have time for any of that foolishness. It wasn't any of my business, though, what Betty did with her time, as long as she came and got them sometime, preferably before Celia needed to be fed in the morning. When she didn't come to collect them, Francine would take them back to Betty's new used trailer that she got with the insurance money, and wait there. It was no great shakes as a trailer. It tilted to one side a little, like a boat in the trough of a swell, the result of resting it on cinder blocks on wet clay. It was as though Betty's life had tilted as a result of the fire, and Betty had found a home to match. A round object wouldn't stay still in that trailer. Everything traveled south, and Betty traveled with it.

Thank God for Francine. Francine had changed some. As a grandmother, she was willing to do for Betty's kids and my kids what she had been unwilling to do for us. Watch them, feed them, clean them. Late penance, a change of heart, I don't know. But I resented it a little. She was helping me so I could juggle two jobs, but she was also helping Betty juggle a couple more men. I told Francine, "Don't do that, you're only encouraging her," but Francine said, "She'll do it whether I'm there or not, so I might as well help out as not. Somebody has to be there for those kids." Francine took a long suck off a Marlboro. "I don't mind, Rita, really I don't."

I saw where Francine was coming from, but I just wanted to wash my hands of everything. I was too tired to keep up with my sister's doings. I didn't care what she did, as long as she didn't put me out doing it. A part of me did not want to feel sorry for Betty. I had acquired an essential meanness in regards to Betty, as though I could avoid what had befallen her if I kept my distance: misery loves company, so avoid the company of misery. I bet Job had a hard time finding people to hang out with, too. So I'd refuse sometimes to take Betty's kids. Like they would have been so hard, a burden. It's one of those things I live with now—that I thought I was doing the right thing about then—avoiding the near occasion of Betty as though she had cooties, as though whatever had touched her could rub off on you. Distance gives you safety. Something I didn't understand then, either: I was superstitious in the worst way. I was afraid her kids, having been disastered themselves, could infect my kids with their disaster. They were carriers. And certainly they knew something was up. All three of them, Celia especially, had that look of scared, preternatural alertness, like animals in the forest know something is amiss before they can even smell the smoke. I didn't want that rubbing off on my kids. As though I could have protected any of them from anything. As though Betty's kids wouldn't have turned out better had I helped more than I did.

That's what I told Matty Keillor—the town clerk and the mother of Matthew, the first boy I loved, the first boy who knocked me up—when I came into the town hall with Betty's three and my two to get a building permit. I was adding on to my bungalow. An extra room for sleeping—a bedroom behind the kitchen—and maybe a screened-in back porch if I could afford it. A behind for my bungalow, I told Matty. Some extra room for the kids—"I've got to put them somewhere," I said—and the screened-in porch so I could enjoy a smoke in the evening and pretend I was all by my lonesome, but still be close enough I could hear the kids if one commenced to wail. Matty offered that the one who needed looking out for was Betty "and her little one." She motioned to Celia, who was examining the stapler on Matty's desk. Tina and Chip just ambled around the room, flipping through record books, lifting pencils out of cups, and generally displaying their boredom. I was twenty-two at the time, and pregnant with what was to be my third and last. Betty was thirty-one. Who should be watching out for who? I wondered. "We could live with Francine," Tina said. "She likes us." Matty dandled Garrett on her knee and said she'd heard from some ladies on the labeling line—that would be Marcella Tschnauble and Lucille Marsdam, who were more Matty's age than mine—that Betty was falling down drunk on the job. She whispered this, as though Tina and Chip didn't know this about their mother. That she was plied with alcohol during her breaks until she couldn't hardly stand up straight, and then after work she was hanging around with the sanitation crew when they came on. "So?" I said, balancing Kenny Jr. on my hip. "She hangs out with everybody."

"You don't want her hanging out with those people. Franklin Spivey's harmless, but Vernon Haight, Byron Joe Gunther, Morton Brunner—they're bad news. Morton wouldn't be working there at all if his father-in-law Anselm weren't the managing director. And Byron is fired as often as he's hired, and the other two are just losers. You can imagine what kind of cleaning that plant gets at night with them in charge of it. That's $12.50 for the permit, Rita."

I wanted to say to her, "Hear from your son lately, the one who knocked me up?" but that would just be rubbing her face in it. What she said about Betty was meant to help, and I was just taking out on her what I felt Betty was taking out on me. I was going to lose Betty for good by the end of that summer, but the truth was I'd been losing her, and she'd been losing herself, ever since the fire. A sign of my age, and how selfish and stupid I was: she needed me and I wasn't there. I was hoofing it with Kenny, and didn't have time for her grief. I was having a gay old time being married, and didn't want anybody else's cloud to rain on my parade, such as it was; and Betty saw I wasn't trustworthy. I was just another somebody without time for her. I lost her as a sister right then, and I was so oblivious at the time that I didn't realize she wasn't ever going to forgive me. We had hardened ourselves to each other, tit for tat, and when it came time for Tina and Chip and Celia to live with me, they didn't want to. They came to live with me anyway, but not for so very long. Tina and Chip spent much of their time with Francine anyway, and with their great-aunt Ruth, who frequently came down from north of Green Bay on extended visits. Summers they spent with Ruth, and when Francine died they were seventeen and eighteen and wanted no part of me. I knew what that was like. Ruth said they could stay with her and so they went. Fine. I had my own problems.

I hadn't asked Matty about Matthew, how he was getting on. It would mean I still cared, for one thing, and for another, that I was not doing so hot in the loyalty department myself. I paid for my permit, gathered up the children, and took them over by Francine's. Most nights Francine would put them to bed, and I'd join Betty for an evening of working with and wading through the very perverts Matty said Betty should shy away from.

Not that you have much choice when the perverts come looking for you. You have to know what kind of place the canning company is, though, to know what kind of perversions are possible in it.

Let's say they're canning spinach. Big mounds of the stuff are heaped on the receiving docks. They are called docks but really they are just concrete aprons behind the plant, with grated sewage channels along the sides. Trucks come in, dump their loads, then elevators pile the piles till they're three stories tall. Rats and field mice scurry about in the slime of the crushed leaves. Snails, maggots, slugs, worms, you name it. Workers fork the leaves onto conveyors that whisk them into the washing/receiving room, where big aluminum tubs with serial paddlewheels tumble and turn everything. Thousands of gallons of water flush through those tubs, washing out the field grit, the slime, the worms, and snails. As mice or legless rabbits or broken frogs surface, the ladies running the washing line pick them out. Ditto for insects and smooshed animal parts on the sorting line, which is another webbed conveyor onto which the stuff is spit after going through the tubs. Dozens of plastic-gloved women, who pride themselves on spotting the tiniest gleam of bone, the bedraggled, sodden feather, the splintered webbed foot, pick through the shriveled and exhausted leaves.

Sometimes a whole snake is found. Sometimes just a section, washed clean of blood. Officially they're looking for unfit leaves, oatgrass, dandelions, mold, tiny stones. But when a lady hits the STOP button by her station, it's because she's found some animal parts and they're searching the line for the rest of it. Usually they do, and they punch the green START button, but sometimes it's half a mouse that's still missing, or the pieces of several mice chopped up in their nest, and they call the quality control guys who come in with bins, and they dump the whole line.

It's old ladies and women in their forties working the day shift. They're conscientious. Work like demons, picking, sorting, sorting, picking. They get along well with their supervisors. It's not only the company product they're protecting, it's the pride of their line. You expect them to ferret out a tiny snake scale clinging to a spinach leaf the same as you'd expect them to track down every bit of lint on a son's or daughter's sweater, or to pounce on three dog hairs trying to lie low together in a corner of the kitchen under a chair leg.

On the 3–11 shift, though, it's teenaged girls and single moms in their teens and twenties. People like me and Betty, only more so. The machinery's instructions are in English and Spanish—they take advantage of the migrants to keep everybody's wages low. The day women are used to this. They've been underpaid and under-appreciated all their lives. It's their pride they're working for, not anyone else's. They have husbands unionized in the paper mills even if they aren't, so being underpaid for cookie jar and Christmas Club money is what these women have come to expect. It doesn't change how they feel about the work—they've always hated it— nor does it change how they do it. They'd work hard regardless. It's what they do. But for the night-shift people, you pay an agricultural wage to factory people, and what you wind up with is a shitty factory. Half the time on the night shift the sorting belt is zipping by with parts of rabbit or snake out in plain sight, and the girl's got her ear turned into her boyfriend's nibbling teeth. Pieces of rat are scooting by and the boyfriend's reaching under her blouse to massage her boob with a grimy paw.

The boyfriends often are the Q.C. guys and the clean-up crew, so ostensibly they have a reason for being there. And every once in a while, after too much spot-checked product has rolled through, they'll shriek the whistle and stop everything. Everything gets dumped—what's on the line, what's in the canners, the cans already in the cookers—as much as they need to feel safe. Then they start everything up again, the machines and the boob-pinching both.

I wouldn't eat canned food if you paid me. Not unless I knew what shift it came through, which you can tell from the notches on the label. Still, I'd be wary. Plenty of workers, though, stop each week at the company store right after payroll and pick up damaged cans for cheap. It seems to me like they're buying back little pieces of themselves in #16 cans. Not something I'd want to admit doing.

Francine used to work part-time day-shift on that checking line. She had a metal stool she sat on as the stuff rolled by her. Betty and I worked second-shift in the cook room and in labeling, so Francine would always be home just in time to watch our kids before we went into work ourselves. It worked like that because of the time it took the product to roll through the lines. On breaks Francine would move her stool to an open doorway and sit with her legs crossed and her elbows crossed over her thighs. She'd smoke one cigarette after another and think of Betty. In her old age she had gotten sentimental about loss. By the time Francine was hooked up to the machines and they'd sucked away every penny of her pitiful life savings, Betty had been dead five years already. The burden of thinking about Betty, and of caring for Tina, Chip, and Celia, Francine passed on to me.

And I have never been good with burdens, my own or anyone else's.

6 · After the Fire

The fire—this is hard. You want to say nobody is at fault here. God's will. That something just happened and this is the something. Besides, guilt and responsibility aren't fashionable these days. You can talk it up all you want, but really, who's listening? The insurance claim, in fact, depends on there being nobody at fault except the manufacturer, and even then you can't go down the line and say to some schmo in a greasy apron and a paper hat, *There, you did it. It was you. You're at fault, you're responsible, fess up.*

You keep the personal out of this. That's what Anderson Elliott told me. "We're going to try to prove that the manufacturer of model A31—AGL147S manufactured a product that, by design, was unstable, liable to tip, thus resulting in the fire that swept through your sister's Airstream."

It would be so easy to believe that. The machinery is at fault, not the people. Some computer design program somewhere, locked inside some machine already, is the culprit. Nobody else need worry. The original computer punch cards from 1971 will be burned, and the machine itself will be unplugged, left out in the rain on a high, lonely hill. Lightning will strike it, its circuits will be fried, and eventually it will fall apart as surely, as irrevocably, as an abandoned farmhouse. Nobody else need be hurt. Oh, and here's a check for your pain and suffering. We're sorry. We're at the dawning of a new era and sometimes these machines don't know what they're doing. They need to be punished.

I could believe that if I didn't know Betty. I could believe that if I didn't know myself. I mean, I want to blame Matthew Keillor for a lot of things, I want to blame a lot of men for a lot of things, but it's not like anybody tied me down and made me, right? I mean, Matthew wasn't the first guy who got caught thinking with his penis. And it's not like I didn't know what I was doing, either. Even when I say I wasn't thinking, that doesn't mean I didn't *know*.

But getting knocked up is not the same thing as setting your house on fire, which is what Betty did. As with any story, there are at least two versions here. What Betty told Anderson Elliott happened, when she was trying to get a settlement, and what actually happened, which she never told anyone.

Anderson Elliott's office on Main Street is a neat little wood frame with an L-shaped porch. It used to be just his house, but now it's house and office both. When he and his wife separated, he closed down his office above the chiropractor's and had the house repainted robin's egg blue with white trim. Exorcizing his wife's demon, people said. She'd chosen the earlier colors, white with green trim. They were not yet divorced, and from time to time you'd see her car in the drive, which was two gravel ruts with a Mohawk of untrimmed grass between. The front entrance was at the back of the L. Betty and I stood on the porch, nervously smoking cigarettes. Betty liked to flick her butts, still lit, into the street or driveway or whatever looked handy. It was a dry day in August, blue and cloudless. Given what happened in June, I told her, maybe it wasn't such a bright idea, tossing her cigarette in the grass like that. Besides, I was trying to quit—I'd just had my second, Kenny Jr.—and the sight of her smoking while I was standing there with Kenny strapped to my chest made me want one.

Fuck off, Betty said, and flicked the next butt into the drive just as Anderson Elliott, dressed in a baggy white short-sleeve shirt and a black and red tie—this was a Saturday—opened his door and said come on in. He had a desk in the living room in front of the fireplace with a leather chair behind it and two wooden chairs facing it. Behind the chairs was a window that faced Main, and in front of the window a couch for waiting. Also a love seat off to one side. Anderson gestured to the chairs and took a seat behind the desk. "When it's cold I like to sit here and warm my fanny," Anderson said by way of explanation. Men without butts say that. They want to grant themselves a generosity of spirit they usually lack, and they think endowing themselves with a fictitious fanny will make them self-mocking and guy-next-doorish. Endearing. Not that it ever worked with me. I usually fell for some other equally stupid trick that I failed to see through. But that's another story.

From where I was sitting, on Betty's right, I could look down a short hallway to the dining room, with its book-lined china cabinets and a dining room table heaped with papers. Light poured in from windows I couldn't see and flooded that room. And behind that was the bright white and buttery yellow of a kitchen with white-painted cabinets above and below the sink, and a steel and enamel kitchen table with blue piping on the table's edge. It was all homey and quaint, like something you'd expect to see in a movie about the 1940s or '50s. June Cleaver or Donna Reed should be in that kitchen, mixing something in a Pyrex bowl, or talking with a neighbor on a Bakelite phone.

Anderson began by pushing an ashtray toward Betty and saying how sorry he was that we even needed to be meeting like this. He would have preferred, he said, happier circumstances. Then he leaned back in his chair, put his arms behind his head, and said, "Why don't you tell me what happened?" And as Betty told her story—it wasn't too much different from what she told the fire marshal—he kept nodding and tilting forward to jot something down on his legal pad. Every time he tilted back again and resumed listening, his chair creaked. Kenny Jr. would give a little start, and I'd coo into his tight little face to shush him. Eventually, as Betty was winding up, Anderson leaned forward and stayed hunched over his pad, writing and writing and nodding his head, like now he was taking dictation and wanted to get everything just right. I could see where he was going to bald. While his head was down I took the opportunity of opening my blouse and dropping my bra flap and getting Kenny Jr. hooked up. Only he didn't take it right away and he squawked that squawk that babies make when things don't go their way. Anderson looked up right then and got an eyeful of boob. A nursing breast is no great shakes as a sexual object, but it startled Anderson and when he went back to his legal pad I could tell he wasn't writing down anything important. Probably doodling a lazy "W" with nipples, the way teenage boys do in their notebooks to while away the fifty minutes of geometry or earth science. I could imagine the notation: "Rita Sabo's breasts: nice."

But when he finally spoke it was all business. "So what you're saying," he said, leaning back now with a cigarette of his own, "is you don't know how the fire got started, you were in the next room, but the space heater was filled and you think one of the children, or the dog, brushed past it, and in brushing past it, its design was such that it tipped easily, was even more tipsy when filled with fuel, and the jarring it received by child or animal caused it to fall and ignite the rug, which would not have happened had the heater been designed properly."

"That's right."

"And whoever jarred this space heater died in the fire."

"That's right."

"But you didn't see them knock it over."

Betty leaned forward with her legs crossed and knocked the ash off her cigarette. "That's right. But I think it was the dog."

"And the ages of the children who died . . ." Anderson was

consulting his notes now. " . . . Megan, ten, Morgan, eight, and Stanley, six."

I had been watching Betty as Anderson went through all this. But when he got to Stanley's name his voice quavered an instant and our eyes met. He did that eye dance around where Kenny Jr. was, then he looked at Betty as though to ascertain these facts in particular. And Betty, still with her arms and legs crossed, looked away, as though the edge of the carpet might contain something that required her full attention. But she nodded, and Anderson continued in a tone of utter calmness, "And there was a dog, a yellow Lab, Bunter Magee, who also died? Who you think caused the space heater to tip in the first place?"

"Right."

"Well, Mrs. Sabo—"

Betty leaned forward. She had a way of closing distance on a man that seemed both appealing and threatening. "No Mrs., Mr. Anderson Elliott. I dropped that when I got divorced. Remember, you handled it for me? I was a Hotchkiss when I was a Mrs. anyway. And you can call me Betty, if you still feel like it."

I could see understanding or something arc between them. As though there used to be a history and it was okay if they dropped all the bullshit and made use of that history once again. A part of me wondered right then if Stanley wasn't his kid, and whether he insisted the boy be called Stanley so the brothers were two halves of a joke. Morgan Stanley. Very clever. Very funny. I wanted to say it was even funnier in the cemetery, where you can see those names two in a row, but I bit my tongue.

He told Betty that he'd have to do some checking, but he thought she might have a case. He'd call her when he knew some more. Betty told him to call me, I was the one with a phone. "I see," said Anderson, as though he knew what kind of hardship she must be under. But she already had her new trailer, and the phone was the first thing she had installed. What it was, I knew, was that Betty wanted the wheels of justice to turn without her having to think about them. Keeping her informed was going to be up to me. I followed through on things and she didn't, and we both knew that.

When we came outside again there was an irregular circle in the grass from where her first cigarette butt had burned. It was the size of a quarter. "Your problem," Betty said to me as she lit another cigarette, "is you worry too much about consequences."

What really happened the night of the fire nobody will ever really know. But I do know what was likely, and it wasn't anything like what Betty told Anderson Elliott. I think that was the other reason Betty asked Anderson to stay in contact with me. She didn't want to go through all that again, especially as he and the insurance people started poking holes in her story. She could tell he didn't completely believe her when she told him what had happened that first time. He knew her. Knew when she was looking off to the side and twisting the ends of her long black hair into long sleek braids that she was probably lying. And it was only because he'd slept with her once upon a time that his mind was willing to offer her the "probably."

What followed, then, was a number of calls and visits between Anderson and myself. Betty couldn't have cared less after she stepped off his porch. If a check couldn't be cut immediately, she reasoned, why bother? But Anderson had the same idea I had. If any money could be gotten, maybe it could get squirreled away. Not for a rainy day, mind you—in Betty's life, when it rains, it pours, and Betty would just as soon stand out in the rain and get pneumonia as come inside—but for Tina and Chip and Celia. Eventually Betty would stop caring for them. And whether that happened by accident or design, we both knew it was surely going to happen. Celia especially would become too much for Betty and she'd be abandoned. Tina and Chip—you could see it in their eyes—had already figured this out by themselves. In fact, we had to pretend it hadn't happened already just so we had the feeling we were preparing for something yet to come, not scrambling after the past.

But it *had* already happened. Betty was falling off the cliff of herself, and most of the time when Anderson and I got together, the failings of Betty Sabo were our topic. I'd tell him what she was up to and he'd softly swear, "Jesus H. Christ. What in hell is she thinking?" It was like he was more disappointed in her than I was, and pissed that anybody could act that stupidly. Like self-destruction with her wasn't just an avocation, it was an art form, something the NEA might fund—Abandonments and Self-Abuse: A One-Woman Show.

Betty was rarely at home. She often dumped Celia with Francine or me—Tina and Chip were supposed to be watching her, but they took a page from their mother's book and frequently disappeared, not that you could blame them—and every time I told this to Anderson, how I'd ended up with Celia even after I told Betty she shouldn't dump her with me, he'd shake his head and say, "Sweet Jesus, sweet Jesus Christ."

After a while I realized I was making myself into the Virgin Mary for Anderson. And that I wanted to. Kenny always off with the boys, me with the house, the kids, my own and somebody else's, plus I had my jobs to juggle . . . I had suffered so, and here my sister was rutting like a whore on speed. And did he know Mary Magdalene in the early days, before she got all bashful and careful? And what did that make him, Joseph with a hard-on? It was funny. At first the comparison was unintentional, but then I played up to it. What I liked about Anderson—maybe Betty liked this about him, too—was that he'd always make a point of clearing his throat and looking away while I was nursing. I usually left Garrett and Celia with Francine when I came for these meetings, but Kenny Jr. was a clingy baby. I couldn't be out of a room five minutes without him noticing and wailing, so I took him everywhere. And when it was time to feed him, plop! Public Earth Mama. Usually I was discreet, but I took a guilty pleasure in embarrassing Anderson with my breasts. It wasn't like they were sexual things anymore anyway. How could they be, swollen and veiny like cantaloupes? But Anderson would look away whenever I rolled up my blouse or reached under my sweater, like I'd caught him peeking at a girlie calendar or that photo of Marilyn Monroe spread-eagled on the red velvet curtains or whatever it is she's posing on, her nipples pink and delicate. "Turn your head and cough," I'd sometimes say to him when he'd look away, and then he'd smile and murmur, "Hmm, yes," like that was exactly his level of embarrassment, but still, he wouldn't look back at me until I'd gotten everything arranged and Kenny was content.

His trying to be a gentleman strangely pleased me.

But that didn't stop him from offering his opinion of my sister. It was the same opinion I had, only it's different when it comes at you from outside your family. It made the lunches he was buying me go dry and tasteless. I'd drink water; it was the only thing that seemed worth swallowing. And after drinking a couple of glasses I felt both full and hollow.

So okay, I was attracted to him. To his harmlessness. But it felt weird. Like I was betraying Betty. Like I was seeing him for him, not for her. Like what was supposed to be business was somehow personal, even though we hadn't said anything about anything other than what Betty and the insurance company were up to. But I could feel it in our eyes, that sort of searching, feeling out, that comes right before connection. You know how it goes: *Are you thinking what I'm thinking? Are you feeling what I'm feeling? If I say what I'm feeling, will you tell me what you're thinking?* And like that.

Crazy.

We hadn't even done anything yet. And at the time I was still married to Kenny. And Anderson was still married, technically, to what's-her-face. His wife. I only met Marilyn a few times, but it was clear that as a couple they were not long for this world. You could see it in the set of her eyes—the longing for elsewhere, the disgust for whatever she was looking at. And whatever she was looking for, she was sure to be looking for it somewhere else. Augsbury for sure wasn't going to have it, didn't even know what it was. She was still living in the house, but they were separated. She was just using the house as a place to collect her mail. It was funny, but watching her breeze by sometimes, with her briefcase and overnighter and the utter disdain with which she regarded us—me with Kenny Jr. in my arms, his face nuzzled against me, Andy with this kindly, stupefied look on his face, as though he wanted to offer an embarrassed apology for his own weakness, his own neediness—it made me want to like him. I knew all about the harshness and dispatch with which he supposedly conducted the rest of his business, but here was something like vulnerability, and I filed that away for future reference. I do not as a rule like weakness in men (though all men are weak in one way or another; they just differ in how they compensate for it), but this was such a carefully contained weakness, and it had slipped out so accidentally—had I not been nursing, had I not been there concerning Betty's business, would it have revealed itself?—that I almost found it charming.

Our romance, if you want to call it that, moved forward awkwardly. There were calls and visits, usually monthly, on Friday afternoons or Saturday mornings. We would go over the most recent correspondence between Anderson and the insurance company, between Anderson and the space heater manufacturer, between Anderson and the Airstream makers, between Anderson and the county. Anderson was casting a rather wide net, and even if he wasn't hauling in anything, he felt obligated to keep me up-to-date. He'd filed suit, of course, but chances were that it would never come to trial. "Cases like these usually don't," he said, "unless the attorney is trying to make a name for himself, or the facts are solider than these." He held up Betty's statement. We both knew it was a crock of shit. Still, he would invite me over, "if I could spare a minute," and he'd go over the latest dispatches in

Betty's war against fate, waged in her absence. If it was Friday afternoon, Anderson might be having a beer, or if it was Saturday morning, tea. Either way, he would offer me some, and I'd lean over with Kenny Jr. still hanging onto my breast, and all the while we'd be making little eyes at each other, pretending like we weren't, and then we'd get down to business.

There was never very much to report, of course. Legal wheels turn slowly, and for people like Betty and me they barely turn at all. Anderson would tell me this, and I would nod seriously, like this was news, something I didn't already know.

We gave up the sham of meeting for Betty's sake when one day in March Anderson handed me my tea, then sat back with his cup on his lap. He indicated Kenny Jr. with a nod of his head. "How long is he going to keep on nursing?" he said. Just like that, flat out. Like this was a question of access—how long was somebody going to be at the bank window, making a withdrawal, or how long is somebody going to monopolize the phone when you want to use it. I had this sudden image of myself as a phone booth on some lonely road, lit up by a mercury lamp arching over it from a tar-slathered utility pole, and Kenny Jr. is inside, cooing into the receiver, and outside stands Anderson Elliott with his arms folded, his foot tapping, consulting his watch. We had been meeting for eight months. The fire had been nearly a year ago. I had been in his office maybe—what? a dozen times? Yet it touched me. The bald yearning in his voice, the impatient curiosity—it touched me. He was pussy-whipped even before he'd had a taste of the pussy.

Besides, I had a ready answer. "Not much longer," I said. "It's mostly comfort nursing. I'll be weaning this one soon enough. Kenny Sr. knocked me up again."

Anderson did a curious thing then. He went into the kitchen, rattled around in there, then stopped in the dining room/law library on his way back. A cupboard door opened and closed, and he returned with a bottle of scotch, a tray of ice, and two glasses. He made us drinks, nudged a glass over to me. He was still standing, his glass raised as though he were about to make a toast. He had gotten suddenly formal. "Your sister is an alcoholic, Miss Sabo." I didn't correct him, though at the time I was still Mrs. Rita Newberry. I didn't say anything about the other, either, because he was right about that. "Probably—in fact, in all likelihood—she knocked over that space heater herself. She is a careless person, your sister, I've seen her be careless. I don't doubt she was careless in keeping that heater filled, and when she got around to filling it, she probably spilled some on the carpet, or on the kitchen table. Probably didn't even notice. Probably she went back to nursing her own child—" here Anderson looked at some notations on his legal pad, taken, no doubt, the first time Betty and I went to speak with him "—Celia—buoyed by the warm glow of her own creation. A glow that was part alcohol and part heating oil. I put to you the possibility, Miss Sabo, that that fire was already on the carpet when she went into the kitchen to finish nursing the baby. And she was too lit to have noticed a goddamn thing." He took a big sip of his scotch. He was letting this sink in, pausing before continuing. I could see him addressing a jury this way, only without the scotch, and technically he was supposed to be arguing for Betty, not for the other side, but if he decided to switch sides—

For this next part he was looking out the window, casting little glances my way, gauging his speech's effectiveness. "Her kids were dying of smoke inhalation before she even noticed the fire. She didn't even think of getting out the ones who were sleeping until it was too late. She was plastered, wasn't she? You were there. After, I mean. Do you know where they found the dog, Miss Sabo? They found him with his teeth in the sleeve of Megan's nightdress. The goddamn dog knew more about saving those kids than she did."

Everything he was telling me was true. It squared with my own imaginings, with what I'd seen and what I believed. Still, for somebody else to be saying it—

"And nobody, Miss Sabo, is going to believe any different.

They'll take one look at your sister's statement, at her history, they'll get a few character witnesses up there—friends of hers, even—they'll get one look at the crowd she hangs out with, and then they'll look at her, and they're going to say, 'Self-inflicted. All this damage was self-inflicted.' But I'll tell you something. I'm going to pursue this, for a while anyway, on the off-chance that maybe some money can be squirreled away for the surviving children's education and welfare. Lord knows Betty won't be providing any, and though it's highly unlikely any insurance company is going to pay off on a claim like this, they might settle for something just so they won't have to drag it out. They can settle for a lot less than it might cost them to win this. That's what I'm going to be aiming for. I should have told you this earlier, but I wanted . . . I wanted . . . Hell, I don't know what I wanted." He put his scotch down. "Are you free for dinner Friday night?"

"I thought you were married."

"I am. So are you. Neither of us happily."

Kenny Jr., who was almost asleep, resumed suckling right then. His tugging pulled me back into myself, which is when I realized I'd been away. I'd been recreating the fire as he was speaking about it. The heat. The crazy orange light. The smoke. The screaming. Smoke gouging at your eyes so you couldn't see anything but the pain already inside them, a substitute maybe for the pain you felt elsewhere but couldn't acknowledge without going crazy. I had stood there on the edge of the shouting, holding Kenny Jr. in my arms as the firefighters and the ambulance people scrambled about. I looked at the other people for a minute, but all I saw was the fire reflected in their eyes and the grim wonder at this thing that was happening in front of them. Betty was alternately numb and wailing, and when she wailed you could smell the wave of booze on her breath. She could barely stand up. The baby was honking. She sounded like a goose—all that smoke. My own child was wide-eyed as the rest, amazed that things like this even existed, wanting to touch it, to see what it felt like. His fingers waved in the air, played patty-cake with the smoke. There was smoke mostly, then a leap of orange-tongued flames and a roar that sounded both near and distant. There wasn't the crackling you hear with barn fires. This was more like the mute cracking of enamel when a tea kettle is left on the stove and burns itself dry. The ruination is complete, the metal is blistered, beyond salvage, yet it lacks the drama of a big wood fire. An inferno in a beer can—what can you say? I didn't know what to feel. If there hadn't been children inside I'd have written this off as a joke on Betty. Ha-ha, Betty, your beer can got trashed. You turned it into a Polish cannon. That'll teach you. But it wasn't like that. There was the smoke and the dull roaring and the quiet intake of breath. Sparks went up into the bare branches of the trees. It was cold. The ground had partially thawed, then re-frozen. There'd been a fresh dusting of snow. Everything was black and white except for the dark slate of the smoke, and the smoky orange flames. You could see people's bootprints, the stiff little peaks where the mud had frozen in the boot's wake. The whole yard looked trampled. Then the children came out on stretchers, oxygen masks over their faces, firemen and ambulance people yell-ing things at each other, and then the children were whisked away, and Betty with them, stumbling with booze and disbelief. You wanted to believe right then that all the children were okay, that they were all going to live, yet knowing otherwise. I stood where I was, paralyzed with shock and fear and relief, relief that it had happened to her and not to me.

I had not gone to her. We had stood in separate places, and she had watched, with her youngest clinging to her, and I had watched with one child clinging to me, and me clutching the other, and we had not spoken. I think I knew that if I opened my mouth the first words out would have been recrimination, *How could you do this? How? How? Oh, Betty, Jesus, see what you've done, see? see?* and all my comfort would have been overridden with blame. So I held my tongue, and stood a little apart from her, and a little behind, and we watched the fire move across the ceiling of her trailer like a wave, like smelt during a run, only on the ceiling, and then the flames poured out the windows and weaved into the sky like an upside down waterfall.

Eventually I asked Kenny to take me home. Whatever comfort I could give could be given later. But I never got around to it. Instead of comfort in the days and weeks that followed, I gave advice. Betty was one person, I thought, who could use advice. Sure, she cried, and used my shoulder, and I patted her hair and said, There, there, and I'm sorry, I'm so sorry, but I was more interested in getting her to see Anderson Elliott than I was in her tears and her grief. I thought what she needed, and wanted, was a money poultice. I was wrong. It turned out she had no interest in the money, that what she really did need was exactly what I had withheld from her. What she had needed was what Anderson Elliott was offering me now.

"I'll have to think about it," I said.

Anderson turned his scotch glass on the table as though it were a screw. "I'll tell you something else. I used to think I was in love with your sister. I don't think that anymore."

"No? What do you think now?"

"I think I'm in love with you."

I gave out a short bark of laughter, then stopped. I knew what he wanted. I knew, too, that he was sincere in his belief. It was just that I no longer trusted sincerity. It wasn't enough for me. Nothing like that was ever going to be enough for me ever again.

I didn't do anything about his declaration for a long time. But I kept thinking about it. Which is what he wanted, I suppose. To plant the idea in my head and let it turn and turn in there, like a rock in a stream wearing away at a bigger rock over time. He was an attorney, after all. He could afford to be patient. I imagined all sorts of things. I've always had a good head for fantasy in the private part of my brain even while rejecting it in the part that reasons and makes sense of things. But in the private part of my brain it's all disarray and hedonism. Sex and love are two sides of the same coin. The one leads straight to the other, doesn't it? Sleep with somebody and then they love you. Or you hope they do, which is what you use to give yourself permission to sleep with them in the first place. If you like somebody, you are driven by a crazy logic. You read all sorts of things into minor moments—a hand brushing your forearm, a kiss on the nape of your neck, a squeeze of the hand—until you convince yourself it's love. Then to convince them you offer yourself up as a present. And *then* they're going to say they love you, out of gratitude? How could I believe this? I don't know. I can only say I did.

I have the ability, unique to myself I used to think, to believe what I want to believe, and to disbelieve it even while in the throes of belief. Now I know otherwise. Now I know most women have it, they just switch it off too often at the wrong times.

I set myself up, no question. Belief, disbelief, belief, disbelief, belief. Matthew Keillor, Kenny Newberry, Anderson Elliott—just variations in degree. And always, always, always, that thread of belief that loops its way through the tangle, that makes the tangle. *You don't love me. Yes, I do. No, you don't. Yes, I do. Well, okay then, if you really love me—*

But all that spring and summer I was good. The private part of my brain said, *Yes, yes, yes* while the conscious, reasonable part said, *Who are you kidding? Will you listen to yourself once? You're being ridiculous.*

And I was being ridiculous. I had three fantasies going simultaneously, juggled like oranges. The first: that Matthew Keillor, my first love, would come to his senses and love me. We didn't see each other anymore, but he hadn't left town yet, and in my Scarlett O'Hara fantasy he'd come to apologize and abase himself on my front stoop. I wouldn't take him in, but he'd break the door down. Breathing like an animal after a long chase, he'd plead his case with his tongue down my throat. I'd refuse him, but he'd take me in his arms, lift me up, and my murmurs of no, no, notwithstanding, that would be that. And, I reasoned, what happened after that would be of my choosing, not his. He'd have learned his lesson, ha-ha—he desired me more than I desired him—so I guess I came out on top in that deal, didn't I? Didn't I? The second fantasy was that Kenny would get his act together, turn over a new leaf, and save our marriage. I didn't spend much time thinking about that one. The third fantasy was that Anderson would divorce his wife and we'd rise in Augsbury society to something like First Couple. I'd volunteer at the library and Anderson—Anderson now, my dear, sweet Anderson—would become president of The Loyal Order of the Moose. Or maybe the Chamber of Commerce or the Rotaries—whatever would seal our cachet in amber. We'd turn his house into a happy home and Anderson would have his own office farther down Main Street, say in the abandoned community hall that someone was thinking of turning into a restaurant.

The funny thing is, the only one of these that I really couldn't see happening was Kenny coming around. That just didn't seem likely. It was no more far-fetched than the other two, maybe less so, but I didn't want to give it any credence. What did seem possible is what actually happened. In a moment of strength, I gave the boot to Kenny. And in a moment of weakness, I slept with both Anderson and Matthew.

Booting Kenny was the easiest. He had one foot out the door already anyway, and once Madeleine came and Betty was dead it seemed like he was embarrassed being related to me. He was gone almost that whole fall, drinking when he couldn't be out hunting. He was almost grateful when he came back one evening and I had the cardboard boxes and the shopping bags of his belongings heaped in the driveway, a mid-December rummage sale. The only thing he got mad about—enough to come to the door to give me grief—was that it was snowing and his tuner was getting wet. The wood veneer was spotting, and his eight-tracks were probably going to bind from the moisture. How could I treat his stuff so shabbily? he wanted to know. Didn't I know what that receiver cost him?

The rest of it was more complicated. Before Betty died the reasonable part of my brain didn't want to have anything to do with Anderson Elliott or with Matthew Keillor. But I kept nudging myself in both those directions anyway. I had always sent Matthew pictures of Garrett, usually one a month. (This even though we lived in the same town.) I did that now, too, only I was in the pictures as well. Francine took them. G. and me on the porch; G. and me in the garden; G. and me blowing bubbles, eating watermelon, swinging, going down slides, digging in the sand. Then I'd see Anderson and listen to him talk about Betty and pointedly not talk about his wife. He would ask me out, I'd say No thanks, I was married, and he'd say, But that doesn't mean you can't be happy. And I'd say, What makes you think I'm not happy? And he'd just look at me like, Who are you kidding? For short periods it was like he had direct access to the reasonable part of my brain. So I'd try a different tack. "What makes you think I'd be happy dating you?" And he'd say, "I don't know if you would be. I can't say for sure anybody'd be happy with anybody. But it beats being alone or miserable."

"Maybe," I'd say, like I was weighing the alternatives. "Maybe not."

That became a refrain for us: Maybe, maybe not. For some couples, the refrain goes, "I love you. I love you, too." For us it was, Maybe, maybe not. This is what we had instead of a romance. It was playful, like a romance, but it was performed at arm's length.

All that changed after Betty died. I didn't see Anderson for six weeks. Then it hit me. I didn't want to end up like Betty. I didn't want for things to just happen to me, for me to just wait like a cow on the tracks for the train to hit it. Francine had done that, and Betty had done that, and they'd both gone through their lives as though the word VICTIM had been stenciled on their foreheads. Like they were just waiting for the instrument of their demise to arrive. I wanted none of that. If my life was a train wreck waiting to happen I wanted to be at the controls. I wanted to see it coming. I wanted to have some say in how things collided.

I wanted to be the one in the train.

Anderson did not, as a rule, eat lunch out. Usually he had a sandwich at his desk, or heated up something in his kitchen if his wife wasn't around, but every once in a while he would stroll down the three blocks to Leeman's, where I worked the lunch shift—"Just stretching my legs," he'd say—and after a cup of coffee he'd pick up a menu and order more food than you'd think a skinny man could eat—a porterhouse with mashed potatoes and french fries, a chef's salad and green beans, coffee, milk, and pie with ice cream. He'd done this a couple of times since the funeral but I'd ignored him except to take his order. Then one day in late October I felt ready for him. The breakfast crowd was gone and the lunch people wouldn't be in for forty-five minutes yet. There were just a few farmers at the counter. Anderson sat in the booth nearest the restrooms. I poured him coffee and he looked up at me in that way of his that let me know that everything he'd said earlier still stood. I gave him credit for his patience.

"Tell me this," I said, taking two creamers from my apron and placing them on his saucer. "Did you sleep with my sister?"

He had his arms folded like he was protecting himself from a sudden blow to the chest.

"Yes."

"And Stanley—he was yours?"

He turned his face up slightly. He was contemplating his answer. His lower lip grabbed his upper and he sat there, turning the question or the answer around in his mind. Finally he said, "Yes, maybe. Yes." He seemed to be acknowledging this to himself for the first time.

"And Morgan?"

"Yes."

"And Celia?"

He played with his silverware. "I was mad at her. I never took the time to find out. If I was going to guess I'd say she was Morton Brunner's."

I went away and came back ten minutes later with a warm up. "And now you want to sleep with me," I said, as though I was asking for verification for some form I was filling out. I was feeling very lawyer-like, a minor functionary in the piddly-ass drama that was my life.

This time he didn't hesitate. "Yes," he said, and quickly added, "And you?"

Here it was, whatever it was going to be. I took out my order pad and wrote on it, then snapped the sheet off the pad and slapped it face down on the table. I was already walking away when he turned it over and read, "Maybe, maybe not." Then I'd drawn a line through that and written,

Yes, maybe.

Yes.

When the light by the bed was turned out you could feel the coolness of the air. October. Twelve hours had passed since I'd handed him my note at Leeman's. Eight weeks since Madeline was born and it was the first love-making since then as well. Since Madeline, I told myself.

Since when? Since Betty. Since I'd known Kenny and I weren't going to stay together. Since I'd stopped hoping—consciously— that Matthew Keillor was ever going to love me.

Anderson was asleep in my bed, his hands cupped over his privates as though even in sleep he was protecting himself. The baby cried. It must have been around midnight. I got up to nurse Madeline, and then Kenny Jr. started wailing, a sympathetic wail started by his sister, and when I went to his crib he patted my sore and enormous breast and said, Bite, Mama, bite. Mama, give bite. I found his pacifier and put him back to sleep. He needed to be

· 159 ·

changed and held and patted a little and I did that, too. He was jealous of Madeline, who so hungrily and happily latched onto me. No doubt in the scheme of things he felt I had betrayed him. Just as, I suppose, I had betrayed Garrett by having Kenny Jr. The whole world, I thought, was one betrayed relationship after another. I could feel the weight of them. Kenny—sure, I'd betrayed Kenny, but at this point that hardly seemed to matter. And Betty? Sure, I'd betrayed Betty, and Betty had betrayed me, and that almost seemed to come out even, only one of us was dead and it wasn't me. What was I doing with Anderson Elliott? I wondered. It seemed to me now as though she was throwing us together. Or maybe Anderson was working his way through the Sabo women as though he'd acquired a taste for us. That didn't seem likely. Still, there he was in my bed, sleeping the dead sleep of the happily fucked. He'd been so grateful. It being right after the baby, of course, I didn't feel anything. He just slipped around in me like a fish. What was I doing? Rewarding him for still being interested in me while I was knocked up with somebody else's baby? Just what was it we thought we were doing? I had a lot of questions like that. Like why was I sleeping with Anderson Elliott if it was Matthew Keillor I wanted? And why did I want Matt Keillor if all he wanted was to be away from me? And why, six months after sleeping with Anderson Elliott, did I sleep with Matthew anyway, and keep at it all that spring and summer when I knew these were the last acts of a desperate man? Did I really want to mess things up that badly with Anderson Elliot, even if he didn't know anything about it? Who was I betraying, anyway? And did it really matter if nobody came out of it cleanly?

Betrayal—yes, it matters. If it didn't, I wouldn't be messing around thinking about it so much. And it would be less of a problem if what I felt in my bones was the same as what I know in my head. Betty. Betty could use a word like betrayal. There is still so much I don't know, so much Rita Sabo, with good reason, has put off wanting to know.

7 · The Everfresh Canning Company

The Everfresh Canning Company does spinach, peas, beans, carrots, peas and carrots, peas and beans, carrots and corn, corn and peas, beans and carrots and corn and peas, and corn and corn and corn and corn and corn and corn and corn.

Corn is the worst. They start in July and they're still doing it in August and September, all hot months, and they take advantage of the agricultural exemption they get from the federal government to schedule their workers to sixty-, seventy-, eighty-hour weeks, and for the heaviest weeks they're not required to pay overtime till the clock hits fifty-four hours. The workers lose fourteen hours a week at time and a half, and the company thinks it's being generous, making it up to their workers, by selling them dents at a discount.

But the worst of it isn't something the company plans on. The worst of it is the heat. And the worst place for it is the cook room floor where Rita Sabo works second shift with Morton Brunner's wife Lilly and Bob Notlinger's wife Lila. All the machines give off their own heat—the hoppers, washers, blanchers, dicers, slicers, sterilizers—and all over the plant nailed to support beams are galvanized buckets of salt tabs, which people pop in their mouths like dinner mints, but the only place in the plant where they have to refill those buckets daily is in the cook room. The whole plant, with its yellow painted corrugated tin walls and corrugated tin ceiling, is a virtual oven, but you don't get really blast-furnace heat until you're on the cook-room floor.

Lilly and Lila and Rita. The two older women are aligned against the younger. Lilly Brunner has been working at the plant since before her husband Morton was hired, and Lila was hired right after hers. Lila is a spar woman with a dour, pinched face. It's as though she never eats from the salt bucket and she's dehydrating before your eyes. She should be over in labeling with that crowd, but they have too many fussy, beetling women over there as it is. It was easier adding on to the cook room, and Lilly is Lila's best friend, so even though they could get by with only two people on the cook room floor they have three. Lila, too frail to do Rita's job (she was too frail when it was Betty's job, too), is the record-keeper. She logs when the iron baskets of #8 or #16 or #32 cans go in the cooker, how many go in, how long they're in, what the pressure and temperature gauges read, and when they come out. Like Rita and Lilly, she wears a green plastic hard hat with a hair net, a badge number pinned to the hat band, a sleeveless blouse, leather boots, and jeans. The women elsewhere in the plant wear sneakers or Wellingtons, but here they wear work boots, same as the men.

Although Lila is responsible for the record-keeping, Lilly runs the floor. She's in charge of the hydraulic boom and the eye-hook that lifts the baskets of just-canned whatever into the giant cookers and lifts them out again. Then she transports them over to the cooling tank where Betty Sabo was found seventeen years ago, face down, her arms dangling loosely in surrender.

Rita Sabo ever since has been roaming the plant during her breaks. Everyone knows whose sister she is. She has been pointed out, the story told over and over. Since so many of the workers are migrants or college students, there for a summer or two and then gone, her roaming has taken on the status of legend. *There she goes, boy. You ever hear the story of Rita and Betty Sabo?* Like she's her sister's ghost seeking vengeance. Only it's not vengeance she's seeking. It's confirmation.

This is precisely why, in the first six or eight weeks following Betty's death Rita did not want to consider the circumstances of it. Why for weeks, months, years even, she kept putting it off. It wasn't only shock, disbelief, a certain unwillingness to know. It was that she already knew. She knew, once she started asking questions, that she'd become obsessed by it, which she has.

The fact is that for years Rita Sabo has pretty much known what happened. But the "pretty much" is what's driving her crazy. She's looking for corroboration, verification of her belief. It's doubtful that Rita would do anything with her certainty and proof if she latched onto it, but she wants to know, really know, how it happened. The most frustrating of desires, impossible to grant: to know in your brain what you suspect—no, believe—in your bones.

There is no ghost story here. Betty's ghost does not roam the factory floor, making machinery start and stop, causing lights to flicker, issuing disembodied moans from the vending machines in the break room, from stacked cases in the warehouse. But there is something haunting in the way her sister, Rita Sabo, floats over the factory floor. She appears, disappears. Saying nothing, changing nothing. Fixing everyone in the high beams of her accusatory gaze.

Though she never says so, Rita Sabo is looking for guilty faces. She's found plenty, she thinks, but her gaze has a hard time penetrating the opaqueness of her co-workers' faces. Really, who's going to own up to or rat on anybody having anything to do with a drunken, dead Indian? *What are you looking at?* the stonier faces say. *Let it lie,* the kindlier ones caution. *Just let it lie, girl. Nothing you find out is going to be worth the knowing.*

She had asked, long ago, for Anderson Elliott's help in ferreting out the truth, but what Anderson said was a variation on what all these faces say. Without evidence of a crime, there is no crime. Maybe it looks fishy, but that's not enough to go on. There are no witnesses, at least none willing to come forward, and the person who found the body says she was drunk. He says he left her to lock up the rest of the plant, and when he came back she was drowned. Anderson is not going to question the integrity of the principal officials—the coroner, the D.A., the chief of police—who agree with that statement and have labeled what happened an accident. He can't help, he says, what Rita feels. And what Rita Sabo feels is betrayal. She doesn't trust him; she suspects that even if he thought she is right he wouldn't pursue this. After all, he'd say, he has to live in this town. She also knows he is probably right.

So she does this still: roams the factory floor to where they're offloading peas or spinach, to the wash room floor where the ladies with their clear plastic gloves pick through the produce as it speeds by, picking out from the leaves of spinach or the cobs of corn the dandelion or milkweed or bits of snake and bird and mouse that come in with everything else from the harvesters. She goes to the hoppers, where things like peas are sorted by size, their shaking grates setting up a vibration you can feel in the soles of your feet, in your shins and thighs, in your ass, in your shoulders and ears. You can feel it buzzing in your brain. Then she goes to the people minding the gauges and watching for clogs at the blanchers, then to the canners, then past the cook room, which she knows intimately, then on to the labelers, which she also knows, having worked there, too, then to the boxers, and the warehouse, where men strung out on too much speed read sex novels while waiting for the next load, or ride forklifts and tow motors at breakneck speed, the wheels turned hard to the right so they keep doing the same tight circles, hungry as they are to be nowhere in particular, but desperate to get there fast.

She likes the blanching room best. Particularly when they're doing peas. When the sugar numbers are just right, Alma Beyes, who minds the gauges, will nod to Rita from behind her steamed glasses. The peas then are soft and sweet and slightly crunchy. Just blanched, their greenness slightly whitened, they pour hot down a chute into Rita's hands and she eats them like popcorn.

Then it's back to the cook room. Rita's worked there for going on twenty-two years, the last seventeen straight. Rita started off in labeling, and Betty had worked in the cook room, but during a pregnancy it looked like Betty would have to quit, and Rita had offered to switch jobs with her. In labeling you sat all day, fed stacks of labels into a machine, made sure the gluing machine that applied two thin beads of glue on the labels wasn't clogged, and watched thousands upon thousands of cans roll by. It was like watching cars on the highway, but only looking at their hubcaps. Then when Rita got pregnant again they switched back. And so it went, the two of them trading jobs depending on who was pregnant, or at least more pregnant. Rita inherited the job for good— asked for it back—after Madeleine was born. Lilly and Lila would just as soon she'd leave, but Rita refuses to give them the satisfaction of quitting. Besides, she rather likes being a reproach. The cook room has six cookers set like missile silos beneath the wooden floor, which is discolored black and gray from all the spilled water and steam. Only the rounded tops of the cookers hulk above ground level, and these tops are hinged and have an array of pressure and temperature gauges stuck on them like alien ears. Each spring the cookers are rustoleumed a bright silver, but they're a faded gray and leaking dry orange rivers down their sides by August. Above the floor, suspended from the ceiling beams, runs a track and a mass of cables for the hydraulic basket carrier, and at the far end of the room is the cooling tank, a huge trough two hundred feet long and four feet deep and maybe six feet wide. The corrugated tin and wood-frame walls of the cook room are tracked, too, so whole sections of the twelve-foot high walls can be rolled open in hot weather. In July and August it makes little difference, even after the sun goes down, but sometimes a cold front will roll through, or it'll be raining, and there'll be a forty- or fifty-degree difference from the blast-furnace heat when the cookers open to the edge of the outside air.

What makes the place ominous, though, is Lilly Brunner. Her husband Morton, who's pushing forty, still has within him the vague contours of the Hitler Youth poster boy that he had twenty years ago, when he first started messing with Betty Sabo. Lilly, though, who was always overweight, has become monstrous, obese to the point of having double chins for her double chins. Big rings of belly fat hang from her hips, held in, inner-tube style, by her jeans. She is a waddler, and her upper arms look like Rita's waist after a turkey dinner. Set in the wan, whiskery fat of her face are two coal-like eyes, small and hooded, and a tight little mouth that looks vaguely reptilian. Physically she would be a better match for Byron Joe Gunther, Augsbury's hulking layabout (though who plans these things?), and how she ended up with Morton is anybody's guess.

How Betty ended up with Morton is nobody's.

Fortunately for Rita, Lilly's hatred of her is confined to scowls and feigned indifference. It is too hot in there for real passion. Strong feelings, like anything else, dull quickly. They become sodden, limp. The work, too, beats it out of you. What happens on the cooking room floor is this: after the product—corn, say—has been cobbed and washed and pre-cooked and shot into the #16 cans and lidded, the cans are shunted onto a conveyor where a worker checks for dents and herds them with a sweep of her arm into a huge cast-iron basket. The basket is three-and-a-half feet in diameter, two-and-a-half feet deep, and weighs two hundred pounds. The cans are layered inside, each layer separated by a flat sheet-metal sieve with holes in it the size of quarters. A hydraulic foot-plate lowers each layer so another can go on top. When the basket is full, Lilly walks her hydraulic hook over, lowers it, then lifts the basket by its massive handle. The handle alone can crush your fingers if it drops onto the rim when your hands are there. Using a control panel that hangs from the ceiling on its own cable, Lilly walks the hanging basket along its track until it's positioned above the missile silo. Lila then writes down whatever numbers she needs to, and Lilly eases the basket down the shaft. She disengages the hook, it comes back up and she fetches the next. Once there are five baskets in the silo she closes the domed lid, turns the huge screws sealing it tight, Lila writes down some more numbers, and Lilly starts the boiler. Then she loads another boiler and another and another and another. Betty used to call it muzzle-loading the sperm.

There are three boilers on each side, arranged like a parentheses with a corridor down the middle. With all six boilers going at once, each throwing heat off through the floorboards and belching out great clouds of steam each time they're opened, it's like working in a sauna, only with constant pings and hammerings and buzzings and rattles and hums and clanks. There's no place you can be at peace except *inside* the noise. Three hours after your shift and your ears are still ringing.

Where Lilly's and Rita's work-lives intersect is when the mouths of the silos are thrown open and one by one Lilly sends the hook down the silo's throat. The baskets she hauls up she walks over to Rita, who is standing on a raised platform with an open diamond-weave floor and matching steps. Rita, wearing leather gloves, wheels a meat hook along the track above her head and fits it onto the basket handle. Then she removes the hydraulic hook and gives the thumbs-up to Lilly, who walks it back to fetch the next basket. Lilly's pushed-in grimace never changes. Then Rita leans way out over the steel-pipe railing and pushes the basket over the cooling trough's lip and into the water. There's a tremendous hiss when the basket splashes down and a cloud of steam rises into Rita's stretched out body. Rita has to shove the hook hard to get it to catch into the next track, which carries the baskets through the tank. It takes about twenty minutes for the hot baskets to reach the other end, by which time they're cool enough for the cans to be removed and sent through the labeler. Somebody at the other end—once upon a time it was Betty—sends the empty baskets back to Rita. The suspended track the baskets ride on through the trough is automated, but the track back to Rita isn't. So either the person at the far end walks them back to her or Rita goes to get them, pushing several in front of her like miniature railroad cars trailing hooks over her head, and dragging another behind her.

You develop a lot of upper body strength doing this. Rita can out arm wrestle a lot of men, though if she had to she doubts that she could out arm wrestle Morton Brunner, and he's the one person she'd like to take down. That, however, would require touching him, and she can't do that, either.

Somebody from lidding—Bobby Hussey usually—takes the empty baskets back to canning. There is a separate track for this final journey, and separate hooks. Rita wheels hers around a little switching yard of track suspended from the ceiling and keeps everything in order. Sometimes if there's a break between baskets Rita will get a drink of water from the big galvanized watercoolers—the kind you find on golf courses—and she'll chat with Bobby Hussey. She has to be careful, though. If she appears to be dawdling Lilly will try to clock her with a metal hook.

Sometimes Bobby Hussey grabs the baskets before Rita has a chance to wheel the hook back to her side-track. She has to retrieve them, threatening Bobby with bodily harm before he relents, grinning. He knows she could take him, and besides, he wears glasses that make him look bewildered and bug-eyed. She's not going to harm him. But if she's really upset, if the baskets are coming out of the cooker faster than she can get the empty baskets and hooks back, and Bobby Hussey is pulling these stunts, she'll say to Bobby that she won't be his friend anymore if he doesn't behave. Bobby is very quick to obey her then. Bobby Hussey is in love with her.

In addition to these baskets, Bobby's job is to keep the watercooler and the galvanized buckets of salt tabs in this area filled. It's a job he takes seriously. "Wan-na SAL tab, Ree-ta?" he asks. He has the slow-to-light eyes and unaligned, open mouth of the mentally impaired. "Wan-na WA-ter, Ree-ta? Wan-na WA-ter?"

At least Bobby Hussey has an excuse, Rita thinks. He was born that way. For the other men at the factory who are in lust with her—and they are in lust with anything with breasts—their grinning drool is an acquired stupidity. Dogs gone rabid with desire.

Something Rita Sabo has always wondered about: Why is it guys who wouldn't want you in their family want their family inside you? Rita was wondering that way back in high school. Betty shrugged it off. "Guys are like that," she said. "You either accommodate them or tell them to piss off. It's the same thing either way."

What Rita Sabo would like to do is tell everybody, each and every one of them, to piss off. Kindly take a hike. Take a long walk off a short pier. She has become Betty's surrogate on the factory floor. A daily ritual: guys stopping by with lewd suggestions and invitations. It's like these guys have never heard the word NO before. Or "Dry up and blow away." Or "Go fuck yourself." But then you said it, that word, the one they worship, and they forget, or are incapable of understanding, that what you requested is for them to be both the agent and the recipient, that you wanted no part of the proceedings. But they don't hear that. All they know, all they heard is you saying "fuck" like it was an invitation. They just don't get it. And it's not just her. Any woman in the factory under fifty is fair game. They don't get something else, either, and this is pretty fundamental: What Rita Sabo really wants, except for when she's roaming the factory floor like Betty's ghost trying to make people feel guilty, is to be left alone. Between baskets she sits on the scaffolding or dangles her feet over the concrete lip of the raised cook room floor. Her building is elevated to make space for the cook silos beneath the floor, so she has a place to sit and stare down the alleyway between the buildings. It's down this eight-foot-wide alleyway that the baskets are returned to her from labeling. Milkweed and nettles and dandelions grow up through cracks in the concrete and along the ends of the buildings where the footings have pulled away from the foundation. This is Rita Sabo's private space.

When the walls of the cook room are wheeled open the dying sun beats off the yellow tin of the building opposite. She will stare at the patterns of cracking paint, at the purple blossoms of the thistle, at the occasional dragonfly or cabbage butterfly that flutters through like a lost tourist. If she's tired of sitting, Rita will stand in the alley between baskets, her hair piled up beneath her helmet, her body sweated so clean she's shiny. (The only benefit of this job—her pores get steamed open daily.) She smokes cigarette after cigarette. Her favorite time is when it's raining. She stands outside and her body's steaming. Literally steaming. The water runs down her biceps and under her arms, cooling her off at least temporarily. She goes back to work with her sleeveless workshirt or her T-shirt plastered to her chest and in twenty minutes it's dry again unless she's popping salt tabs and drinking the water that Bobby Hussey is so earnestly pushing on her.

When Betty used to work here they'd sometimes take breaks together. Rita was already married to Kenny by then. She'd had the one baby with Matthew Keillor without marrying him and she wasn't in the mood for making any others unless she was married to the father. Betty was not quite so particular. She could get her coworkers to fetch her Orange Crushes, ice, cigarettes. It might as well have been panty hose and chocolate bars. They buzzed about her like bees around a honey pot. Rita and Betty would sit on the concrete stoop that faced the alley between buildings and drink their sodas in one gulp and guys would come by offering them more and making dirty comments. They even encouraged Bobby Hussey, then just a kid, to make suggestive comments he didn't understand. Betty seemed to drink it all in—"Talk dirty to me, sugar," Betty would say, "talk dirty to me"—but Rita, disgusted, would stare at the burning nettle that grew in the cracks between the alley and the tin wall of the next building over. When the nettle got shoulder high and the plant maintenance crews would come by with canisters of DDT on their backs and those directional sprayers with hoses that looked like skinny penises, Betty had to laugh and point that out. Then the guys—Morton Brunner, Franklin Spivey, Bob Notlinger, Byron Joe Gunther (between firings)—would hold the tubing as if it were and spray pesticide on each other, like whoever didn't die got the one flower smoking her cigarette in the doorway. Betty would laugh, would direct one man to spray another man's head. "That kills the lice," she'd say, and laugh, and then Morton or Notlinger would use the equipment to hose down the front of Franklin Spivey's jeans. "Fuckin' lice all over," Morton or Notlinger would say, and Franklin Spivey would jump back, "Fuckin' A—!" but not wanting to show in front of Betty and Rita how pissed off he was, or that he was scared of his pecker being sprayed. That was men for you, Rita Sabo thought—wielders of skinny penises, but so idiotically proud of the equipment, laboring beneath its burden, and everywhere spraying death.

Out loud she'd say, "It's about time for the nettles and milkweed to get sprayed again, ainna?" And they'd all know: she wanted them dead.

8 · A Prelude, Late July

The summer Betty drowned, Rita was pregnant with Madeline, her last. She doesn't remember a lot about that time. It was so hot that her head swam and swam. Crops died. When the rains finally came it was hail and what hadn't shriveled was shredded. Then came more heat. Rita could barely move. She was retaining so much water she felt bloated. Her legs ached and her eyes felt swelled shut. The canning plant was shut down. Peas ended early, carrots were wait-and-see, and corn wasn't ready to start. And if it did start it'd be three or four weeks behind schedule. Rita parked herself in front of a circular floor fan and let Kenny Jr., diaperless, pee on the carpet. He had a terrible diaper rash. The pustules were runny and he screeched plaintively every time she had to wipe him. Matthew Keillor was dropping hints again about making his way out east, fame and fortune, a life for himself, all that noise. Well, good riddance. She had an ace in the hole, didn't she? Anderson Elliott wanted her pregnant, and wasn't that something? Of course, there were no guarantees Anderson was ever going to marry her—hell, he was still married himself, for Christ's sake—but then she knew Matthew Keillor wasn't ever going to marry her, either. At one time he had said he was, but that turned out like most promises, broken. And besides, if Matthew hadn't broken things off like he had, before Garrett was born, she wouldn't have met—and married—Kenny. That was something, too, wasn't it? Not that Kenny was any prize, but then women who considered any man a prize were dim bulbs anyway. I mean, there was a certain necessity in their being around, but it wasn't like you could count on them for anything, could you? It just didn't work that way. Men were weak-willed, easily given to temptation. They did whatever they wanted, which she could sympathize with, even envy. What pissed her off was how they had it rigged so this was okay for men, and not okay for women, and how, once they'd done what they wanted, they couldn't just own up to it. Instead, they tried to lie their way out of it with mealy-mouthed oaths. Why do they feel the need to pull this crap? Obstinate denial, immediate forgiveness: what men started with on their part, what they'd settle for on yours. If women had the same kind of power men had, they'd do just what they wanted, no excuses. They wouldn't need to lie about what they did in weakness. That was the big difference between men and women, Rita thought. A man on top needs to pretend he isn't. A woman on top takes stock and says, Well, how did I get here? And then enjoys the ride.

Kenny was a broke-box operator at Nekoosa Paper. That meant that he carried a short curved paper knife like a miniature scimitar and policed the breaks in the paper as it came off the rollers. It was fast, hot, and messy work. He'd come home with bits of dried pulp spackling his clothes. He'd also come home way later than his shift ended, stinking of beer and watery paper and some other woman's perfume. And deny everything. Even the fact that he'd been drinking. Finally, when he told an approximation of the truth, it was like he was doing her this huge favor: "All right, already. Me and Al had a beer after work already. Satisfied? Jesus, woman, you're driving me crazy."

Catch them dead to rights and it's the same story, only they also work in indignant apologies: "Okay, okay, I'm sorry. Jesus, I love you already. What do you want me to do, bleed? I said I was sorry, babe. It'll never happen again, I promise. Forgive me?" And three nights later they sneak out again with childish relief and guilty glee.

She knew where Kenny was on his nights away. The same place Betty was. Traveling with the same pack. Byron Joe Gunther, Morton Brunner, Bob Notlinger, Franklin Spivey, Vernon Haight Jr. All those men Matty Keillor had warned her about. Or rather, four men and a boy. Vernon was just a teenager then, a hanger on. A Bobby Hussey with enough brains to get himself into real trouble. The same was true of Franklin Spivey, only Franklin was old enough to know better. His weakness: going moony over Betty in public. Like she really was a raven-haired Betty Grable. Poster girl for a new generation. Morton had beaten him up a couple of times already for giving Betty the eye. Franklin was a slow learner. Sometimes he'd ask Rita what he could do to get her sister's attention. "Don't worry," Rita told him. "Once you get it she'll strap herself on you like a utility belt." "But how do I get it? How do I get her to pay attention to me?" And Rita told him, "Stop being so needy. Start acting like you're bad news. Start acting like you don't give a fuck. Then maybe she'll get curious." "Curious, right," Franklin said. "Curious." Then he toddled off with this gleam in his eye like he was contemplating how to put some new plan into action.

Betty never told Rita what Kenny was actually up to those nights out, though, or who he was up to it with. Live and let live, that was Betty's policy. What people do on their own time is their own business. She would let Rita know where he was, however, taking pleasure in reporting the location of his doings if not the doings themselves. "Kenny was out at Poachers' this evening." Or, "I saw Kenny at Utke's." That was all she would say. Rita knew enough not to push. Betty was not above sleeping with somebody's husband, her sister's included. The fire had been a year ago and she had run through so many men since then that the shorter list would have been who in town—besides Bobby Hussey and Franklin Spivey, evidently—*hadn't* she slept with? Her steady partner for knocking boots, though, was Morton Brunner. Morton Brunner had married Lilly right out of high school—the rumor was she'd turned out *not* to be pregnant, she'd just packed it on senior year— and it had all been downhill since then, only he was too weaselly to leave her. He depended on her too much. Her old man ran the show at Everfresh, and he knew if he wanted to keep his job he'd better stay married to the old man's daughter. So instead he became king of the "I'm sorry, I couldn't help myself, can you ever forgive me?" apology theatrics. Him and Kenny. Probably out comparing notes about their fat wives the way men do when they get together. The baby rolled its weight around inside her, shifting from one side of her belly to the other and Rita thought, At least I have a reason for being fat. That was how Rita thought she could distinguish herself from Lilly Brunner: will versus weakness.

One night late in July, Betty told Rita that she wanted to make it up to her (make it up to me for what? Rita wondered) by giving her some relief from the heat. "It's not right you should be here sweltering by yourself all the time. Come on. We'll get Francine to babysit, and Morton'll let us into the plant. We can go skinny dipping in the cooling tank."

"We can do that at the quarry."

"Oh, but everyone'll be there. All those kids with their pert little fannies, I can't stand it. This will be so much more . . . private." Betty rolled her eyes suggestively. They made the arrangements and Franklin Spivey met them at that weed-choked alleyway where the cement footings were chest high. He hauled Betty into the doorway of the cook room and the two of them pulled up Rita. Franklin continued to hold Betty's hand until Betty noticed his thumb was caressing the back of her fingers and she shook him off. Franklin was in a pair of cutoff jeans and he was skinny as a twelve-year-old chowing down twenty-four hundred calories a day. You could see everything—ribs, scapula, the bone in his sternum. He had scraggles of orange hair up his belly and curling around each nipple. He tried throwing back his orange-speckled shoulders but that only accentuated how skinny he was. "Glad to see you could make it, Betty. Rita," and it was when he came to the full stop at the end of Betty's name that Rita knew he was in love with her. The poor boy, Betty would eat him alive. That is, if she ever noticed he was alive. Franklin backed off, ducking his head like a menial servant as he went, and rejoined the others at the far end of the cooling tank.

"Look there," Betty said, pointing out Morton Brunner. "There's my honey."

Rita had to admit it. Morton Brunner had a body that could have won the war for Germany. Sleek and hairless and well-thighed and tightly-buttocked, his pectorals perfect half-moons and his stomach a washboard, Morton Brunner was a sight to behold coming or going. Rita's first look at Morton naked was from the rear. He was hoisting himself out of the cooling tank down by the labeling machines and the cheeks on his bottom were as sculpted as the cheeks on his face. He was twenty-three—nearly a decade younger than Betty. All the men hanging out with Betty were younger than she was. Betty said she would know she was losing it when she couldn't entice the young ones any longer and had to settle for the pussy-whipped, big-gutted forty-year-olds.

The factory lights were on down at that end and the half-light in between emphasized the perfect V of Morton's torso from his shoulders to his waist. As full up with Madeline as she was, it took Rita's breath away.

He must have rubbed himself against the tank's lip getting out. As he approached her she could see a big stripe of orange rust down his belly that disappeared behind his penis as it rose in greeting.

"How nice to SEE you, REE-ta." In mid-sentence he'd changed his voice to ape Bobby Hussey's. "Can I offer you some wah-wah-WAH-ta?" Rita settled her eyes dismissively on his cock, hoping that would make it shrink but the attention didn't faze him. He went down on one knee and put his forehead to the back of Betty's hand. "Oh, my lady," he said, mock knight-errant, "please join us in the healing waters." He was holding two beer bottles in his hands and offered one to Betty.

Betty peeled off her T-shirt and flipped it onto her shoulder. She had a blue bikini-top on underneath.

"Oh, come on, Betty, it's hot. Show us some tit."

"Animal," Betty said, but she undid the clasp holding the cups together and shrugged off the top of her suit. Then she flipped that onto her shoulder, too, like it was a pelt, and strutted to where the others were waiting. They hooted and hollered but made space for her, as though Betty deserved her own distance.

"Much better," Morton said. Then to Rita, "Care to join us?"

"I'd prefer it up here," Rita said, indicating this end of the tank.

"Lonely at this end," Morton said, "but suit yourself."

Pregnant as she was, Rita needed help getting into the tank. She couldn't climb over the tank's lip nor over the railing of her platform. What Morton finally did was have her grab hold of the eye hook on the hydraulic and he raised her up that way. It was awful. The cables only went to the end of the trough, and Morton had raised her up too high, so suspended in air, Rita had to feel with her feet for the tank's lip and beg, literally beg, Morton to lower her again so she could find a foothold. "Morton," Betty called from the other end of the tank. "She's pregnant." "Oh, all right," Morton said, hitting the DOWN button. Then Rita fell forward and belly flopped into the tank. Morton roared.

"Catch you later, REE-ta. Holler if you want company. I'll be sure to hear you if I ain't doin' submarine races with your sister."

Morton Brunner and his perfect body padded off to where Betty was hand-paddling about on an orange and green air mattress. It was not quite dusk yet and the tin and wood-frame corridor sheltering the cooling tank was much lower than the cook room or the labeling room. It was a shed, really, low and dark and tunnel-like. Morton had turned on some of the ceiling lights and as he returned to Betty he moved from a bar of light to a bar of shadow, a bar of light, a bar of shadow till it almost seemed he was strobing in the darkness. Between the ends of the cooling tank hung three or four baskets of well-cooled peas. Must have been an off-brand for them to have been left there. Whenever the peas got too high in sugar content or too low, or when their diameters didn't fall within certain specifications, or they failed the hardness test, Everfresh subcontracted and canned for the off-brand label. Rita could check— those labels would still be in the machines—but why bother? Right now she was concentrating on becoming indistinguishable from the water in the tank. The water inside her belly and the water outside it. It was the same thing, really. Why did it seem so odd to be in this container?

She tilted her head to see the top of her belly. To escape the heat she peeled down to her underwear and a T-shirt. She felt her tummy. A too-hard pea. Pea? Right, if peas were the size of watermelons. She touched with her fingers the dark seam running from belly button to pubic wedge. The *linea negra,* they'd called it when she had Garrett and Kenny Jr. She remembered all those words. Rectus muscles—those were the muscles in her belly that were separating, the thickened seam where they would cut if they needed to for a C-section. Perineum—that was another good word. It sounded like something they'd have at a college in which the students would study stars or flowers. "Today at the perineum . . ." Kenny called it her "taint." Taint? She was afraid to ask. She was showing him where to massage her when she hurt. The books said your partner should help you with these things. "Taint your clit and taint your ass," Kenny said. "But all the same I'd like to lick it." He laughed so hard getting that out he snorted Pepsi out his nose.

Kenny in the late stages of a pregnancy was a real prize.

Rita reached with both hands behind her head and found the water tank's welded rim. Elbows flanking her ears, she did a slow bicycle kick. It felt good to be moving with so little resistance. Her bottom floated slowly toward the surface. She sucked in some of the lukewarm water and spit it out. It tasted of rust. If we were out west, she thought, this might be a watering trough for some huge spread of cattle. It would have to be mossy, though. All watering troughs out west are made of wood and are mossy. It goes with the general coolness of the atmosphere once the sun goes down each evening. All that heat just escaping right into the sky, right into space.

She closed her eyes and tried imagining the heat from her belly escaping into space. From the trough's far end she could hear her sister say, "Morton!" but it was punctuated with a giggle. Great, Rita thought. I'm trying to take a nap in a cooling tank for cows and my sister's fucking in the same canal.

Maybe she did fall asleep. She had water up to her temples and her eyes were closed. She was still bicycling very slowly. At one point she felt herself being watched. Who would watch a pregnant woman floating in her underwear? Bobby Hussey, she thought, or Franklin Spivey, and her eyes cut over to where there were baskets still suspended in the water—that's where somebody who wanted to look would hide—but there was nobody there, and the feeling went away after a while, though not completely.

She heard other people arrive, heard muffled laughter and screeches, but didn't lift her head from the water. Really, she didn't want to know what was happening. Whenever there was a noise at the far end it came to her in long, separate waves. Bong, bongg, boonnnggg, like sonar. Was this how dolphins did it? She tried to imagine herself a porpoise or a dolphin, but it was too great a stretch. They were sleek and purposeful. A whale, she thought. Maybe a great blue whale. Certainly nothing graceful.

She hears a louder screech and something like the syllables of her husband's name, but that seems unlikely. It is coming from so far away, too. Besides, why think of Kenny when she's enjoying herself? Her legs move lazily and the throb of thickened blood vessels in her breasts and vagina is dampered, quieted. She feels wonderfully less swollen, less sticky. Then she hears it again.

"Kenny! Kenny, stop that!" It is her sister's screech, and this time there's no giggling.

Rita swings her feet down till they touch the trough's scaly bottom. Her head comes out of the water, her hair streams down her back. At the tank's far end, past the hanging steel baskets in various stages of submersion, she can see Morton and Vernon Haight Jr. and Franklin Spivey and Byron Joe Gunther, all half-submerged themselves, all splashing water like this is the kiddie pool. Only they're also swilling beer. And there's Kenny. Kenny reaching out to tweak Betty's teats. Teats—yes. That's the way she thinks of Betty now. They're cattle down there, come to graze on whatever's available. In a second if Betty lets them they'll lugubriously mount her, lumbering and lowing with pleasure. She's reclining still on the air mattress and is being spun in a series of lazy half arcs. Whoever is closest touches her in some way—they grab a thigh, pinch a hip or fold of belly, try to kiss her ear. Their tongues hang out and Betty is giggling, having a gay old time. She anoints each guy with a shake of her beer bottle like she's the Archbishop and they are her faithful.

Then Kenny pours his beer on the triangle of hair between her legs and yelling out, "Muff dive!" goes for her crotch. The air mattress shoots up out of the water and they are on her. There is a lot of splashing and yelling and at one point Byron Joe Gunther has hold of Kenny by the top of his head and Morton is pummeling his belly. Morton has done this before, outside Utke's, and another time at the Tiny Tap when he thought Franklin Spivey was getting too chummy with her. Now Betty is standing in the trough's corner with her hands up by her mouth, her forearms covering her. Franklin Spivey is standing next to her, his hands on her shoulders. He looks like he is almost in ecstasy. Betty doesn't even notice him. She's saying, "Stop it, guys! Just stop it! Quit it, will you? Kenny! Morton! Stop it! Jesus, Byron Joe, let him go!"

Eventually Byron Joe did so. He threw the exhausted Kenny into the water face first, shook him like a dog, then tossed him out of the trough. It wasn't until Kenny's body sailed over the side that Rita could see he was wearing jeans. They all were, except for Morton and Betty. Small comfort, Rita thought. He'd kept his pants on.

"Okay, party's over," Morton said. "Everybody out of the pool. Newberry's gone over the edge and ruined it for everybody."

"It's always somebody," Vernon Haight Jr. said.

"Like you wouldn't have," Kenny said. He was hunched over and trying to breathe.

"Not without being invited to, asshole."

"There's your problem," Kenny grunted. "Lack of initiative."

"This will be on your permanent record," Bob Notlinger said. "It will reflect on your merit review."

"Walk carefully, everybody. There's a lot of broken glass down here."

Rita absently scratched herself, then realized she was vulnerable. She shrank back into the water. Nobody had seen her yet, and nobody would have if Betty hadn't yelled, "Hey, where's my sister? I nearly forgot. Hey, Rita! Hey, el blimpo! You need a ride?"

"Rita's here?" Kenny asked. He squinted, trying to see all the way down the cooling tank. "Jesus, Rita?" He touched his stomach gingerly, as though just now remembering the pummeling he'd taken on Betty's account.

"Yes, Rita, you oaf." Franklin Spivey handed Betty a towel and she held this to her chest. Then she took a bouncing step to launch herself over the tank's edge but collapsed back into the water before she got there. "Oh, shit, I stepped on some glass. Oh, shit, oh Jesus," and they had a fresh crisis to worry about. Betty lifted her bleeding foot high out of the water and Franklin bounded out of the tank and produced his T-shirt to use as a bandage.

"I'll get some tape," Vernon Haight Jr. said and ran off to get some.

"Some bandaids is what we need," Morton called out after him. "Some bandaids, you fucking idiot!"

"Oh, criminy, do you think it needs stitches?" Betty had gotten herself up on the tank's rim and was balancing herself there with her foot straight out in front of her. Franklin Spivey was propping her up from behind so she wouldn't keel over to one side or the other. "Please, somebody kiss it and make it feel better," Betty said. She was moaning and wince-giggling all at the same time. She leaned way forward holding onto her big toe while Morton wiped at her foot with Franklin's T-shirt. Finally he gave up getting it to stop bleeding and just pressed the T-shirt hard against her instep. By this time it was a very bloody shirt.

"Decent slice, man," Byron Joe Gunther said. "I couldn't have done any better with my knife."

Rita took opportunity of the distraction to get away. She had to grab hold of the lower pipe-railing on her platform and pull herself out of the water, then roll over the trough's edge on her belly, sliming her belly orange and scraping herself something horrible, but she made it. Everything stuck to her and she felt heavy, wet and squishy, like that whale she'd thought about, trying to move about on an empty beach. But nobody was paying her any attention now and she walked away from them, into the darkness of the cook room and around the corner into the washing room. Everything was stopped dead where it was. The stainless steel tubs and aluminum sorting tables with their green-stained white conveyor belts that not even bleach could get clean gleamed a dull watery red under the glow of the safety lights. Rita walked around all the equipment and to the far door marked EXIT. She set off an alarm getting out.

The police—if you could call Clayton Jones the police—arrived just as she was pulling out. Whether Clayton noticed she was barely dressed and soaking wet she didn't care. She leaned across the passenger seat and shouted out, "Quick! Somebody's breaking into the factory and they've hurt themselves!" Then she drove off. Jones drew his gun and went to investigate.

The evening's upshot was that everyone except Rita got arrested, and those who worked for Everfresh got fired. Since the plant was on downtime anyway, it hardly mattered. It simply meant that when things started up again in late August they all had to beg for their jobs back and they lost their seniority and were back closer to what was considered starting wage. The only people it adversely affected were Bob Notlinger and Morton Brunner, who as foremen got paid whether the plant was operating or not. Their wives, Lila and Lilly, were furious.

After everybody posted bail they drove Betty, who'd wormed her way back into her hip huggers and somebody else's T-shirt, to the emergency room. They took thirty-eight stitches in her foot. "A doozy," the intern doing the stitching said. He had hair as long as Rita's and a full beard. "Good clean glass cut, though. Put a fresh dressing on that every couple of days and stay off your feet."

Betty said she'd have no problems with that. "I like staying off my feet," she said. "It gives my ass something to do besides look pretty."

"Amen to that," Morton Brunner said.

Thirty-three days later she was dead.

9 · What Happened to Betty

Some things you cannot know even when you think you have a right to know them. You think you have the power of prescience, the ability to stare down the future and win, but then I always believed I was going to win the lottery, too.

I didn't see any of it coming. And what I did see coming I was wrong about. Betty was the same way, though with her it's hard to say. After the space heater fire I don't think she much cared what happened to her. If fate were a freight train barreling down on her, and Betty was enjoying a beer in a chaise longue spread across the track, I doubt she'd do much to get out of the way. How else could you explain her almost complete indifference to four or five men spinning her about on an air mattress, each of them plucking at her nipples as though they were trying to get the pin feathers off a chicken?

Or this, in early August, ten days after she'd cut her foot: she comes home one evening and says to me, while rummaging in the back of my fridge for a beer, "Morton Brunner says he wants to leave Lilly and take up with me."

"What'd you say?" Francine and I have been babysitting Garrett, Kenny Jr., Tina, Chip, and Celia. Madeline is still two weeks away and it's not like I feel like going anywhere. Even Anderson isn't bothering me right now.

"First you have to know how he asked me." She pops the beer and slumps on my couch. Her back's almost on the seat cushion and she hitches her legs up till they're resting on her chest. I'm looking at where the seams on her jeans meet. "He was licking me here," Betty says.

"And what did you say?"

She laughed. "I blew farts in his face."

So perhaps it should come as no surprise when the last week of August, three days after I gave birth to Madeline, Betty was found drowned in the cooling tank. An accident—that's what they called it. An accident. There was a large contusion on the side of her head, and smaller ones on her shoulders, but these contusions, the coroner said, were consistent with the victim hitting her head on a blunt, flat object, most likely the top rail of the cooling tank. Nasty looking but not fatal. Not nearly enough to kill her. She drowned, the coroner told the *Press Star* and the *Post Crescent,* plain and simple. Breathed in not air but water. Easy enough to do—her blood alcohol was high enough to qualify her for orbit. She could easily have gulped gallons of water like it was air and never known the difference. So pronounced Melvin Jenks, the coroner, a portly man given to pursed lips and cornpone pronouncements. That was Anderson's assessment, and he should know. Anderson could tell me all sorts of things, things that never reached the paper. For example, that the coroner's report noted that her vagina was full of semen, and that there were abrasions on her shoulders. Or what Morton Brunner told Jenks and Clayton Jones (for the police report) that never reached the paper, or that the paper chose to omit, this being a time of more delicate tastes. We had just gotten out of Vietnam and people had had their fill for a while of horrors being splashed across the front of their newspaper. People were breathing a collective sigh of relief and closing their eyes. Things like that happened in other places, far away, where the names had too many vowels or too many consonants or they came in strange combinations and were in general too hard to pronounce. The Fox River Valley was not exactly a hotbed for homicide then, and the occasional farmer suicide or spouse beating were scandals that people didn't really want to know about, not in the detail they would be reported on later, when the frequency made the details more important just so you could keep track of which horror you were talking about: the one where the body parts were found in the black plastic leaf bags alongside the road, or the one where the woman was impaled on a meat hook. Anyway, Morton's official statement, or testimony, or whatever you want to call it—it never ran in the paper, at any rate—was, "We were pretty drunk. I left her sitting up against the tank, sort of woozy, and I told her I was going to get us some sodas, close up shop, and then I was going to take her home. I was gone, what, twenty minutes, half an hour? Christ, next thing I know she's in the water, drowned." Both the *Press Star* and the *Post Crescent* left out the part about their being drunk, and Morton's invoking the Savior's name in vain. They already had Melvin Jenks's statement about her blood alcohol level, and his line about the victim's being qualified for orbit seemed to put the right spin on things.

Something else the papers left out, or maybe they were never told, was what Morton had said about the semen and the bruises. "Betty," Morton told Jones and Jenks, all confidential, "liked it woolly, if you know what I mean. I mean, a lot of that—them contusions and things—could have been from her rubbing her back on the tank while we were locked up like that. But then we got out of the tank, I swear. I left her propped up against the tank. Christ, I'd asked her to move in with me. I was gonna get a divorce. Then she hit her head. I don't know any more. I called you, I told you all this once already. What more do you want?"

"So when are they going to bring charges?" I asked. I was in bed with Anderson. We had to be up soon and he had gotten the paper off my porch and brought it in to me along with a cup of coffee. It was one of the few nights he slept over. Usually he liked to walk back home at two or three in the morning.

"They aren't," he told me.

"But what you just said—"

"Jenks has already ruled it was an accident. Jones has no say in this, and he'd defer to Jenks anyway. So would Milt Stevens, our D.A. He's already announced there won't be an inquest; he's satisfied with Jenks's autopsy report."

"But you just said—"

"That I know more than was in the paper. Chalk that up to my knowing Jenks and Stevens. Over lunch they'll give me more information than they'll give to some reporter. But that's all it is—more information. It doesn't change the conclusion."

"But I've been hearing stories—"

"Stories? You mean hearsay? So and so said so and so said such and such to so and so? I know somebody who heard it from her second cousin whose sister's girlfriend was the sister of the girl? That's how we get the stories of the hook and the hanging, you know. You know those stories? The couple who drives off to a lover's lane, but they feel all nervous, there being a psycho out in the woods who has a hook for a hand, and after a little while they get really nervous, and they start hearing noises, and the girl says, Take me home, and they drive off, and feel all better, and then they tell themselves they were silly for being so scared until they get home and the boy goes around to the girl's side of the car—this still being an age of chivalry in dating—and there's a hook hanging from the door handle? Or how about the couple parking—you know this one?" He was having a good time with this. I could see how he would be in court, belittling somebody's take on things, honing in on their insecurities about their own stories, the holes in their testimony. Something they'd say would be the bait he'd use to make them say something else—something that wasn't quite right—and that's what he'd hook them with, the misstatement, and then they'd flop around like a fish on the stringer, and anything they said earlier, even if that part had been right, would now be in doubt. It was amazing to me, really, how few cases he took to court. Maybe he had a reputation and didn't need to. Not that it mattered. I was trying to make him stop and he wasn't listening. He had a sip of his coffee. He was going to see his pretty examples through to the end.

"You've heard this one," he said. "I'm sure you have. It's another couple parking—you ever notice it's always a couple parking? That way we get the two great American obsessions, sex and violence, into the story, plus we satisfy our puritanical cravings at the same time. Amazing." He had a sip of orange juice. "Anyway, this couple is parking and they hear this noise and the boy says, I'm going to check this out. He's being big and brave because he's thinking it's his buddies come to bother them, but he's scared, too, so as a precaution he says, Don't open this door for anything, I'll go see. And then he steps out into the darkness and he disappears. He's gone, completely. And he doesn't come back and he doesn't come back and after a while this girl hears a noise on the roof of the car. All night long she hears this noise, thick-thick, thick-thick across the roof of the car. And the boyfriend doesn't come back and he doesn't come back, and she's thinking this is one of his elaborate pranks, he's got some long branch he's making this sound with, only Christ if this is a prank it's going on way too long, and she's going to kill him if he's been out boozing with his buddies in the woods, playing tricks on her, only deep in her heart she also knows it's not that, no, it's not that at all. So she stays there all night, scared out of her mind, wild with fright, listening over and over to that sound, thick-thick, thick-thick, it's like water dripping on her brain, it's driving her crazy. So finally it's morning. The darkness turns gray and finally it's light. Birds are making their noises. And although that other noise is still going she can breathe easy. It's over. She's going to find her boyfriend and really give him a piece of her mind, scaring the bejesus out of her like that. And she opens the door finally and in the bright sunlight she sees her boyfriend swinging from a tree directly over the car, his arms loose at his sides, this hideous look in his eyes, and his shoes are slowly swaying over the top of the car going thick-thick, thick-thick." Elliott smiles, letting this register with me. He sips his o.j., then he says, "Or how about—"

"Stop it. Will you just stop it?"

He grins, pleased to be making his point. School's in session and I hate him for it. "None of those stories were ever in the paper, were they?" he says. "How could they be? They're just stories. They made the rounds for a while. Stories do that. Lots of stories make the rounds. And the details change from one telling to the next, don't they? You know that as well as I do. Christ, not one of these stories can even give you an exact count of who all was there, can they? That's because none of the people telling these stories *know*. They don't *know* anything. They speculate and then they make up a story that fits their speculations."

"But won't there be an inquest or a grand jury or something to find that out? And then a trial?"

"You watch too much TV. A trial only happens if an inquest jury—six citizens—decides something's worth having a trial for. And an inquest only happens if the D.A., after considering the evidence provided by the police and the autopsy report, calls for one."

"So what's the problem?"

"Don't you get it? There isn't going to be an inquest because Jenks has already said it was accidental. And Stevens concurs. Besides you, who's going to quibble with that?"

"I thought you were."

"Me? What for? Why? Jenks is the coroner, Stevens is the D.A. If they say it was an accident, it was an accident. Case closed. Think about it, Rita. I mean really *think* about it. You know Betty. And you know that if she took it into her head to walk that tank rim there were any number of things for her to have hit her head against.

Those pots half-submerged in the cooling tank, the tank rim itself. She could have clocked herself a doozy and never known what hit her."

I thought about that. He was being reasonable now rather than a know-it-all and that made it harder to hate him. I thought about how during slow times at the plant Betty liked to show off, use the rim as a balance beam and walk on down to where I was sitting feeding labels into the machine. Or, if she was feeding labels, she'd come over to where I was launching steaming baskets of just cooked cans into the trough. Everybody knew this. She even did it when she was pregnant, or drunk. She'd fallen in more than once. Lost her footing, yelped, gotten soaked. Morton might come by, see her in the tank, and if Lilly wasn't watching, give her a dunking as she tried to climb out. I nodded slowly to Anderson, the same way I later nodded to Kenny when he told me he wasn't there. I didn't believe him, I didn't believe either of them. I said I did, but only because I thought I had to. I was still woozy from the delivery, couldn't even hold the baby hardly. I felt addled, slow. So for a while there I concentrated on what I wanted to believe, rather than on what I knew to be true.

And it wasn't like I could concentrate anyway. Anderson kept me apprised of things, but really, all that investigatory stuff—Jones, Stevens, Jenks—happened without me knowing it was going on. Then poof! Jenks's announcement was made public and it was business as usual. Another drunk Indian doing herself damage. What is it with those people anyway? You'd think they'd learn.

That was when I asked Kenny, straight out, if he was there that night. I was thinking about how I should have seen it coming. Kenny said no, he'd only been there the one time with her and them, but he couldn't look me in the eye saying it. I think what happened to Betty scared him. It scared me, too, but I didn't kick him out right away. Though I didn't want to have anything to do with him, he was at least around some, and for right then I needed that.

So whether I believed Kenny or not, for a long time I put all my doubts about what happened out of my head. Or at least tried to. I had another talk with Anderson and he convinced me there wasn't any point in pursuing things, at least not unless I had more to go on than I did, which I didn't. I could suspect all I wanted, and yes, those guys were scum, but then she was hanging out with them, and even scum have accidents. Jenks's report was pretty thorough. Was I going to argue with the elected coroner for Outagamie County? On what grounds? That I had a hunch? The two papers would love that. *Sister of deceased claims foul play—'I have a hunch,' sister says.* "Look, I agree with you," Anderson told me. "You've got emotional logic on your side. But that isn't enough. It's not a substitute for knowing the facts. Even I can't squeeze blood out of a turnip. I did all I could with the space heater fire, and we both know she lied about that. I'm sorry."

"You could talk to Jenks."

"And tell him what? Melvin, I think your medical opinion sucks. You're a nice guy and all, but you screwed up royally. Nope, no can do. His explanations brook no disagreements, and even if he might be wrong—which I'm willing to grant you; he's no M.E., he's just some well-liked elected flunky who does this on the side—what he says is at least as plausible as anything you'd care to insinuate."

So the bottom line was that Anderson wasn't going to help me. Not anymore, not in this. He was being nice to me in all sorts of other ways, though, so I had to juggle my feelings: not trusting him in this one thing, sort of depending on him in others. If we've stayed off-and-on since we first started being on, you could probably trace it to this. In a backhanded sort of way he helped me. He reconfirmed for me my wariness, my sense of doubt, without which you tend to be taken advantage of.

Anyway, in other ways he took my mind off things, and I needed that. In December I threw Kenny out, and in the spring Matthew Keillor showed up at my door again, and though that wasn't going anywhere, for a while at least it went where it used to go; and amidst all that I just didn't want to think any more about Betty. I wanted to blame her, too. I did want to believe the official story. There had been a party, it got out of hand, she'd drunk too much— she frequently did—she banged her head a good one in a drunken stupor while doing her patently stupid cooling tank rim-walk, and then she slipped quietly into unconsciousness, into the water, and there wasn't anybody around to save her. I wanted to accept that at face value. It wasn't true, but for me, for a while, it was the right story, the story I wanted to hear. The story everyone already believed anyway. And I already had these other things happening to me: Kenny, Anderson, Matthew. If I filled my head up with guys and with the subsequent trials and tribulations, then it wasn't filled up with Betty. I didn't see this at the time, but I was doing exactly what Betty had done after the fire: I was stocking up on men.

The story that winter was that Kenny left me. I had the house, I kicked him out, but because he was inside it and then he wasn't I guess that gives people the right to say he left me. The funny thing is I could almost believe it. Why not? The way I was acting, had he tried coming back anytime soon after I'd booted him, I'd have proved myself three times an idiot and taken him back.

Something inside me had broken down. Of the two of us, Betty and me, I was supposed to be the strong one. School, work, kids, drinking, men: I was the strong one. I could swear off anything faster than she could, apply myself, discipline myself, limit myself, push myself—anything and everything—better than she could. *Need to shoot an arrow hard and straight? Here, let me lop off this breast first. There, that's better.* The only thing in which she could exceed me was extremity. And yet I had broken down not once but twice. With Anderson in the fall—I felt nothing but it felt good— and again six months later with Matthew, which felt both so wrong and so right that I let that continue until he left me. I wanted him so bad, even though I knew it was going to turn out badly, that I was willing—I wanted—to look the other way for as long as it lasted. As though I could get what I wanted if I just played dumb enough. My one moment of resiliency was tossing Kenny out, but if he'd balked we'd have been right back to square one.

So maybe it wasn't so strange that with Betty I was willing to believe anything. That she and Morton had been alone, just the two of them. That they'd fucked and that she'd been very drunk, and when he left her she'd climbed up for a cooling tank balance beam walk and after that there'd been an accident. She'd fallen. Clunk, ka-lunk. Splash, splash, she took a bath.

It became known to everyone as "the night Betty drowned in the cooling tank." Eventually people started telling it like she'd been there all by herself, like this was something she'd engineered all by her lonesome. A drunk woman rim-walking, swaying and swaying, then falling like a sack of potatoes, like a felled tree, like a bag of cement. Then they tried to put more distance between themselves and the event. "What happened to Betty," they said—not as a question, but as a statement of belief in an ordered universe. I started saying it, too. What happened to Betty. What happened to Betty. As though there was no preventing it. It had been written in stone, irrevocable even before it happened, and yes, like all victims, she was partly/mostly to blame for being there in the first place.

What happened to Betty, what happened to Betty. No one supposedly knew anything. Yet they seemed to understand everything. What did they understand? I wanted to go up to people's faces and scream in them, WHAT DO YOU UNDERSTAND?

And then it hit me. Everyone was in agreement here. It was already settled. Probably had it settled even before Melvin Jenks started looking her over. However it happened, everyone agreed: Betty had it coming.

I began having visions. The one of Betty in the cooling tank was the worst. Seventeen years later and I still have it. I'm up on the scaffolding, easing a pot filled with steaming #8 cans over the cooling tank's lip and I see her. It's not the way they found her, but it is the way I see her. She's on the tank's bottom, spread-eagled, her hands slightly raised and held forward, floating. She looks like she might be ready to conduct a symphony. Or do jumping jacks. In the rippling of the water her hands sway ever so slightly. Only the look on her face is horrible, horrible, as if she'd seen something right at the end there and it registered with her for all eternity. Her feet are raised, too, and there's a crease in her belly from where she seems to have been folded. In the rust-colored water her skin seems more sallow than usual. And then something else hits me. She's not conducting anything. She's frozen in the last position of emotion she had, which was, is, a piercing cry for help.

Her eyes are open, which means we've failed her.

When I see her like this I have to step away for a moment. I need to catch my breath. Then Lilly, who has the next pot ready to go, is yelling over the whistling and thrum of the machinery, "C'mon, idiot, let's go." And when I look in the tank again Betty's not there. I see a faint orange outline in the rust maybe, a ghost's ghost. I let the basket splash on top of her. Its weight carries it forward. The next pot quickly follows.

10 · Possibilities

It was only with hindsight that I started reconstructing other possibilities. What happened to Betty: any number of things. That's the
problem. Maybe Morton really did want to marry her. That could
be both true and false—he's told other women he was going to leave
Lilly for them when all he really wanted was to get into their pants.
But maybe this time he was serious. Who knows? And did Lilly
find out? I mean before the story became public knowledge. Had
she heard the rumor about Morton and Betty running off together?
(Running off—what a laugh! They'd probably get as far as Green
Bay and check into the Hiawatha Motel for a weekend of hot sex on
a vibrating bed or on an orange carpet with headboard-size paintings of ships in stormy seas over their heads.) Or had she heard
about Morton's and Betty's dalliance in the cooling tank? From that
she'd know all she would need to. She could have followed Morton
and Betty to the cooling tank. Waited for Morton to leave for those
sodas. Or maybe she did it with him. Betty was stealing her husband, Betty was blowing farts into her husband's face, then brag-
ging about it. She was humiliating them both. I bring Lilly into it,
too, because the drowning happened right beneath my station.
Lilly's home turf, not Betty's. Betty liked the cooler dark of the

labeling room. Sure, she filled in for me because I was pregnant, but she hated it up at this end. "Too much like work," she always told me. "It's not worth the extra thirty-seven cents an hour." So I always wondered why Betty drowned just beneath my scaffolding. It wasn't like she had far to travel, but still, she always preferred labeling as the place to party.

I can see it, though, however she ended up there. Betty turning this way and that in Morton's grip, him shrieking at her, "Bitch!" as Lilly comes running up with the steel hook that she bashes into the back of Betty's head. Or Morton going for those sodas in the break room and coming back he runs into Lilly, who's looking down in the water at what she's done. "If you know what's good for you," she'd say, "you'll say nothing except that it happened accidentally." And since to Morton everything does happen accidentally, he would have no trouble believing this and saying in all sincerity that it was so.

Or Morton did it himself, believing, as too many men do, that killing is akin to possession.

The coroner's report? We went round and round on this. Anderson got a copy for me from Melvin Jenks. It had a lot of medical gibberish on it, probably plain enough if you spoke that language, but I didn't, and Anderson, in translating it, seemed to take Jenks's word on everything. "But what did he find when he checked Betty's head for damage?" I asked Anderson, and he told me the results were inconclusive. The contusions were consistent with her striking her head, and given the patient's history, a sublateral hematoma caused by her head's striking the cooling tank's rim was most likely, and any other conjectures would just fuel needless speculation.

"Is that him saying or you saying?"

"It's me saying what his report's saying," Anderson said, holding it up like he was going to start singing from it.

"But it could have been a blow *to* her head rather than her hitting something."

"Sure, it could have been. It could have been anything. Her brains could have been plenty scrambled without much showing except for a blue-purplish bruise, and she did suffer a concussion, but there were plenty of things about for her to have hit her head against, and that cooling tank rim is Exhibit A. Melvin Jenks says the drowning was accidental, the drinking and the head blow contributory, the abrading of her shoulders incidental. Nobody's going to question that account, Rita. Nobody. Except you."

"And Clayton Jones is only too eager to put it down as an accidental drowning, right?"

"It's the commonest form of misadventure in Augsbury, Rita. Drunk and drowned. Guys in snowmobiles on spring ice, people in cars any time, even folks at the quarry. Clayton and Milt both know that. They've hauled their share of kids out of the river, out of the lake. I mean really, Rita, what did you expect?"

A good question. What did I expect. Even without Anderson telling me what was plausible, I knew what was likely. Lilly Brunner was Anselm Hacker's daughter. Anselm Hacker was the managing director at Everfresh Canning. He owned shares. He wanted to buy it outright from the parent company. I knew that. Everybody knew that. And even if she married badly, it wouldn't do anybody any good for a CEO's daughter and son-in-law to get charged with accidental homicide when it would be extremely hard to prove anyway. Negligence, sure, but whose? Drunken Indians were always falling sideways and hurting themselves. Why, there was a story once of this old Indian getting so drunk he slept through the removal of his leg, which his nephews had chained-sawed off as a prank. That story got revived once Betty drowned. And Betty Sabo came from the same stock. Remember that guy who wound up with the knife in his eye for knocking up her mother? Real no-accounts, those people. Besides, Betty slept with too many people. Everybody knew she had it coming. Farting in a man's face, Jeez Louise. How many people had she told that story to? And how many had repeated it?

Other possibilities I toyed with: another of those all-hands-on-deck, all-hands-on-Betty drinking extravaganzas that turned first into a fiasco, then into a tragedy. Each of them taking turns dunking her until they noticed she'd stopped breathing. Only that requires too many people who were in on it to keep quiet. Maybe if it had ended in rape and not in murder they could have more completely closed ranks: "It's a guy thing, you wouldn't understand." But they didn't close ranks. And once it had been ruled accidental, a drowning, not a homicide, they could all breathe a sigh of relief. Even if they were implicated, it was in a tragedy, not a felony.

Eventually stories did leak out. Each story a slight variation of the one previous. There had been other people there that night, but earlier. Betty was still very much alive, still giggling hysterically when they took off. "Bye, Betty. See you tomorrow, girl."

I worked with these guys. I asked them. I waited for people to get drunk and in the right mood to speculate, and even then what I got were answers that somehow sounded pat, maybe even rehearsed. Like they either really believed what they were saying or they were really good at lying.

"We was just horsin' around," Bob Notlinger said. "Like the time before, remember that, Rita? You were there. There was horseplay, but nuthin' like this. I don't see how that could have happened except it was by accident."

"She was pretty plastered," Vernon Haight Jr. said. Just eighteen, he was the youngest out there. "She coulda drowned and not even known it. I believe that, yes, ma'am, I do."

Byron Joe Gunther folded his arms and simply grunted. "She was a crazy woman," he allowed. "Stupid things just came to her natural."

It was like each of them was giving personal testimony. Like after they'd spoken with Jones and Jenks they knew just how to answer somebody who was nosing around, asking questions. Play dumb, be forgetful, remember it's an Indian they're asking about. Nobody's curiosity is going to last long or get them very far.

Franklin Spivey and Kenny Newberry chose not to say anything at all. "I wasn't there," Kenny told me. "Whatever happened, happened without me being there."

"Everything happens without your being there, Kenny." I think it was right then I decided I was going to jettison him. Fair enough. He'd already jettisoned me.

And Franklin? Franklin just kept his head down and tried to let everything slip over his head. He'd been in love with Betty. Everybody knew that. The pain on his face was obvious. He was like a man in mourning, sack cloth and ashes. He hid away in his trailer and took up with raising animals. Something safe. Something that you could love and appreciate and it would love and appreciate you right back. Something that if it took up and died on you, well, you expected that. You could always get another animal.

So that was how it was. They were all gone, they said, before Betty drowned. They had left her all by her lonesome. Even Morton Brunner. Morton Brunner gave his statement, as did the others, first to Jones, then to Milt Stevens, and after that Melvin Jenks gave his report to Stevens, the D.A., who declined to press charges seeing as how there were no charges to press. I was furious. Wasn't Milt Stevens a friend of Elliott's? How could they do me this way? How could they do Betty's memory this way? "Why can't there be a grand jury or an inquest, Elliott?" I had taken to calling him Elliott. "At least give me that."

"I told you already, Rita. It's not going to happen. How am I supposed to convince Milt an inquest would be worth his while when his own coroner says it isn't?"

"You could at least try."

"Okay, fine. Let's suppose for a minute that I could. I can circumvent all the procedures already in place and I get you your goddamn grand jury or your inquest or whatever the hell it is you want. So what do you have now? I'll tell you what you get. You get Morton up there in a suit and a tie, you get Melvin's report that signs off on an accidental misadventure—"

"Oh, I like that. 'Accidental misadventure.' What, she was climbing Everest and she fell?"

"Some Everests are smaller than others, Rita. For Betty, anything four-and-a-half feet off the ground is too damn high. But I digress. You've got your inquiry, just like you want, and you get Morton up there all dolled up, and an inconclusive coroner's report—but *he's* calling it an accident—and a reluctant D.A., and to top it all off you've got some defense attorney who can call any number of witnesses, including you, the deceased's sister, who can testify that Betty was a drunken sot *given* to misadventure in the first place, and add to that six of Morton's peers who are supposed to be sifting that evidence, and what do *you* think is going to be the result? Huh? What do you think?"

"At least let me try!"

"Let *you* try. I like that. You try. Since when did you become a trial attorney? Since when did you get elected D.A.?" Like many of our discussions, Elliott and I were having this one in bed. We were at his house. He got up and left the room, and when he came back it was with a bottle of scotch and two glasses. "Look, Rita, I talked around and around on this with Milt Stevens. He thinks it's a waste of time and money going after a guy when you're never, ever going to get past reasonable doubt. You can't. It's impossible. Jenks wouldn't even grant you reasonable doubt as to whether it was an accident or not. He's already said it was." He offered me a glass, then got back into bed and laid down with his glass on his belly. "You need to just give this a rest."

"So what do you think happened to her, Elliott?" His last name sounded more like a first name than his first name did. I liked that. It gave me distance from him, which I needed.

Elliott looked at his fingers, which were laced over the hillock of his belly. The tips of his fingers kept his glass in place. The glass rose and fell with his breathing. When he looked at me his eyes were hard and glistening. "What I think doesn't matter." And then he went back to looking at his glass' rise and fall, and I knew. He had decided to cut his losses.

"What you can't explain you don't. What you can explain nobody listens to or believes in anyway." Betty told me that when I asked her once just what in the hell did she think she was doing. She was so calm when she uttered this, as though she'd discovered a principle around which she could organize her life. Which is funny given that Betty was a willy-nilly person. And I don't think she'd care if I knew or could explain what happened to her or not. But I wanted to anyway. If not for her, then for me.

Here is the start of what I think happened, though you could never prove it. And maybe I only want to think this is how it happened because emotionally it fits: Betty is holding court at the tank's far end with the regular yahoos, the—what did they call them in *Casablanca*?—the usual suspects. God knows what they do to her or she does to them or they do to each other but eventually most of them leave. No doubt that cooling tank was a private Playboy Club and Betty their personal bunny. Betty had a high tolerance for outrageous behavior and a willingness in most things to go too far. Blowing four or five guys under water, or getting them close and then shutting them off just before they came might fall into that category. So would laughing at the size of their endowments once they got their pants off. That she might be at the mercy of these guys wouldn't even occur to her. "Hey," she'd say. "They're my friends. What's a little comedy between friends?"

Their thinking exactly as they form a loose semi-circle around her. Morton Brunner, Bob Notlinger, Franklin Spivey, Vernon Haight Jr., Byron Joe Gunther. Morton and Bob are both respected men in the community now, their wild days behind them, forgotten, forgiven. Seventeen years ago, though: they were kids then, twenty, twenty-one, twenty-two, twenty-seven. "Sowing their wild oats," people would say. Everybody does some of that.

As to their raping and drowning her: no, I don't believe that, or at least not the drowning. And you wouldn't have gotten a rape charge to stick under those circumstances anyway. (Given Betty's reputation, not under any circumstances.) Not that they weren't capable of it. Five drunk men are capable of just about anything, especially if one of them is Byron Joe Gunther, who's capable of anything while stone cold sober. But I do think of them as accomplices for having been there and scrupulously avoiding finding out what happened after they left. They can tell themselves they have clean consciences, but that is a state of mind anybody can acquire with the right amount of beer in them. Or maintain through repeated denial. Ask Matthew Keillor. Ask Kenny Newberry. Ask anybody with dirty hands if their consciences aren't clean. See what they say, and how easy they say it.

11 · The Stars at Night

It would have been two or three A.M. when it happened. Corn, though it's up and running again, is only running one shift. The sanitation crew is done early, say ten-thirty the latest. Morton makes sure all the employees have punched out, then he makes some phone calls. He props the door to the labeling room open. Everybody steals down the alleyway between the cook room and the washing room. There are no weeds now. A slow time at the canning plant means the grounds have been policed. Things have even been repainted, the machinery regreased.

It's something like the one month anniversary of Betty slicing her foot open. Not all the guys have been rehired yet. Everybody's pumped. Add to that the illicit thrill of being in the factory again after it's closed. They're pissing on the equipment and breaking bottles on the loading dock.

They party for three or four hours doing God knows what. Mostly it's drinking and horseplay. They have underwater contests, most of them sordid. Men can't get together without making a competition out of something, even sex. They make sure Morton's gotten all the glass out of the tank, though, and they're wearing sneakers. They wade around in the tank like the colonizers of another planet. Finally, exhausted and dead drunk and shriveled up from being in the water so long, everybody gets out and gets their clothes on. They shout goodbyes to each other, say they'll see each other the next day, maybe find one of those high school beer parties and crash that. It's a Thursday, the next night should be a good one. They can run up to Pappy's Rock and pick on some long hairs with that stink weed they're all so high on smoking. "High is right," Franklin Spivey says. "High is right, high on life." He laughs, holds his head between his fingers. That's all he can stand to have touching him—the very tips of his fingers. "High, all right," he repeats. "Jesus Christ Almighty." He repeats this several times before throwing up in the parking lot. "Cheer up," Bob Notlinger says. "It's not like it's the end of the world. Come on, I'll drive you home." But Franklin shakes him off. He's going to be okay, he says. Driving clears out his head. Just give him a minute. Just give him a goddamn minute! "Okay, okay, easy, easy up there," Vernon Haight Jr. says. Byron Joe just laughs. "If the little shit can't handle his beer he shouldn't be drinking it," he says. "Next time we bring a jug of kiddie cocktails for the little weenie."

"Look at Betty Sabo, will you," Bob Notlinger says. "She's done as much as you and she ain't coughing grits. You could learn a lot from Betty Sabo, Franklin."

"Amen to that," Vernon says. "Where is she, anyway? Maybe she can teach *me* somethin'. Class is in session and she can make me clap her erasers any time."

Morton comes out of the plant and says Betty is staying behind to help him tidy up.

"But she came with us," Franklin Spivey says, meaning himself and Vernon Haight Jr. He's still half in love with her. Everybody is but Franklin wears it on his face. The alcohol has pasted his need to his face where everybody can see it. He wants Betty and he knows he will never have her. High on life, he thinks. What a stupid thought. He'd rather be high on Betty. He'd say that, but Morton would beat the shit out of him. Instead he repeats himself. "She came with us, Morton."

"And she's going home with me. After she helps me tidy up. Anybody got a problem with that?"

Nobody has a problem with that but Franklin. Betty's a woman, and good with a broom, and hey, she is Morton's main squeeze if you don't count Lilly. She's just playing with the rest of them. Even Franklin Spivey, stupefied, with ropes of saliva hanging from his lips, knows that. It's a game, really, how far she's willing to go with them and how far they're willing to push it before Morton says, "Okay, that's enough." Considering all that goes on, Morton's pretty possessive. Unless they're really drunk, they know when to lay off. The couple of times Franklin and Kenny each went too far Morton beat the crap out of them.

The wild card in all this, of course, is Betty. She can say, Take a hike, Morton, and hoist herself onto Franklin's astonished hips and ply his mouth with her tongue if she feels like it. She'll jump off him three seconds later, laughing, but by that time Morton's livid. She's been doing stuff like that a lot lately. It pisses him off. He's trying to feel free of Lilly and all Betty's doing is reminding him of how chained he is, how fucking tied down he feels.

"Don't sweat it, sweety," Betty says, toweling her hair as they walk out to Morton's pickup. The others have gone, their cars all parked on side streets are gunning to life, roaring off. Betty feels the night air hot in her hair and on her body. She's wearing her shorts, that's all. It was nicer in the cooling tank. Morton's dressed but he's carrying the rest of her clothes in a bundle which he sets on the open tailgate. "Ain't nobody really free," Betty says. "Or else everybody is."

"What the hell is that supposed to mean?" Morton asks. Betty selects her bra from the pile of clothes and bends over to put it on. Straightening up, she shrugs. "It means we do what we like, babe, and let the chips fall where they may."

"That's easy for you to say," Morton says and Betty laughs and says, "Yes, ain't it now?" She's sitting on the pickup's tailgate and getting her arms through the armholes of her T-shirt. "My kids are a weight, for example, but they don't weigh on me half as heavy as Lilly must weigh on you. 'Course, nothing on this planet must weigh as heavily on you as Lilly. You always do missionary with you on top, right? Or have you found yourself a way of breathing out your ass?"

She says this to be funny but Morton tackles her backwards into the pickup. She skids into the toolbox, which tips over. Its contents scatter behind her head. Part of her back rubs over a coil of rope. "Ow, that hurt, you bastard."

"Weight?" Morton says. "I'll show you weight."

"Ow!" Betty says loudly, but she's still laughing. Morton isn't until her shorts are shucked off and he's astride her. Morton, the Hitler Youth, has a cruel, self-assured smile that lasts for fifteen seconds. It melts once he's inside her. He becomes pure need and his smile turns into a grimace. He thrashes and kicks things. The clankings and clunks of things thrown aside in his urgency echo in the warm night air off the railroad cars sitting on the embankment than runs past the parking lot and behind the factory. His need has become a violence.

"Jesus," Betty breathes, "slow down why don't you and let somebody else enjoy it."

But Morton Brunner can't. It's anguish he feels, anguish and then brief happiness and then more anguish. The woman beneath him will never truly be his. He knows he shares this feeling with Franklin Spivey but it seems more awful to Morton because he knows Franklin's never had her, and if you have something but you know it's temporary, know it will never really be yours it's terrible, terrible, almost like a madness. She will always be smiling at him, amused, maybe even laughing, and worst of all, she's right. He will never escape Lilly's weight, not ever. She will always be astride him; he will always be suffocating beneath the voluminous rolls and folds and mounds of his wife's flesh. And he can't do a damn thing about it.

And then, from beneath him, a gurgling of laughter. He's had his

eyes closed all this while, his ears stopped up with pain and ecstasy. He's not seen what Betty, lying in the pickup's bed, giggling
and staring up at the stars, waiting for Morton to finish, has been
able to hear: the crunch of a car approaching over gravel with its
lights off.

Betty says, "Looks like we're about to be arrested again, hon."

Only it's not Clayton Jones or even his deputy, Bud Willers,
come to arrest them. It's Lilly Brunner, who's already called or
personally checked out all the places her husband usually hides.
She has checked out every stray road she and Morton used to park
along when they were still in high school, every farmer's field that
has a turnaround in it, every cemetery lane that's not watched by
the police, every bar he likes to think he's got a friend in. She has
been driving for three hours straight and the coils of her neck sit
heavily on her collar and where flesh meets flesh she's sweating
profusely. Her dough-like skin gleams dully. It's not until she's
driving down River Road by the fishing shanties that it occurs to
her—the bastard hasn't left the canning factory yet. He's such a
creature of habit he didn't even think that eventually she'd look
there too.

Betty says, "Better get off me, hon. Otherwise it'll look un-
seemly." She has her hands on the truck's gunwales, composing
her Hi, hello, how are you? for Officer Clayton Jones of the Augsbury Police when Morton lurches past her, knocking her flat. He's
got hold of her wrist and he's pulling her down and with his arm
across her belly he's trying to keep her from getting back up. As
though hiding were going to do any good. "What," Betty hisses, "if
you keep your eyes closed they aren't going to see you? That only
works for little kids whose parents are playing along. C'mon, Morton, up and at 'em. Time to face the music." She's pulling back,
trying to get Morton to sit up. Her right eye is half-blinded by the
high beams that have just come on from Lilly's Chevy. "Come on,
Morton, quit it. The jig is up. Hiding's not going to do any good."
But Morton's not hiding. He sees who it is behind the steering

wheel and panicking, he reaches past Betty, seizes a wrench, and clocks her on the side of her skull.

He's still trying to get his pants up as Lilly disengages herself from her seat and approaches him, the same slurred sound of gravel crunching under her feet as when she drove up.

"She made me," Morton Brunner whines. "She made me get on top of her. She said she was telling on me if I didn't."

"Shut up," Lilly says. "And zip yourself." She looks away, at the Main Office across the street from the parking lot and at the place where the railroad makes a bend to run behind the factory toward the warehouse. The two empty cattle cars there have their doors open like mouths. "You make me ill," Lilly says. "You disgust me."

"Yeah?" Morton says, and his voice is almost a screech. "Yeah? Well, you make me sick, too."

"Shut up," Lilly repeats, "and I'm not going to say that again." She looks into the truck-bed as though she might be checking on how well a batch of cans might be doing in the cooker. Betty's eyes are closed, her head facing the direction Lilly's car came from. It's almost as though she were dreaming of its arrival. Drool has pooled in the corner of her mouth and is starting to spill over, a thin rope of saliva onto her shoulder. There's an ugly knot on the side of her face where her hair comes down by her ear. The skin's not broken and the hair is covering it, but it looks nasty just the same. "How hard did you hit her?"

"Hard enough!" Morton Brunner cries. His girlfriend unconscious, maybe dead, in the truck-bed beside him, his wife seemingly calm as she sizes up the situation with her beefy forearms crossed, Morton Brunner is beside himself. Nearly out of his mind, he starts crying. He will do anything, anything, that will release him from this agony. But what to do, what to do? He sees no way out.

Lilly jerks him out of the truck-bed and to his feet. The back of her hand slaps into his belly. "Pick up her feet."

"What?"

"I said, pick up her feet. And stop sniveling."

Morton is slow to respond but he does it. They spin her around and Morton watches Betty's bouncing chin as they carry her, Lilly leading, back inside the plant. Lilly's backpedalling, looking over her shoulder for the doorways and turns. Morton's eyes drop from Betty's head to her chest, her breasts flaccid now beneath her T-shirt, her belly, soft, her panties, caught partway down, partway up, her thighs. His head will no longer nestle there, not between her thighs nor where her thighs meet. He feels a maddening sense of longing and loss. By the time they get to the cook room he's sobbing again.

They carry her across the floor. Morton thinks of the hideless carcasses of deer he's carried this way just before they toss them on the newspaper-covered kitchen table for butchering.

"Take off her panties."

Morton is sobbing as he does this. They crush like a flower in his fingers. Lilly snatches them away. She's wadding them up with the T-shirt she's already stripped from her body. They've got her back against the tank, her feet straight out in front of her as though she were all tuckered out from volleyball and she was resting in the gymnasium. "Shit," Lilly says, as she struggles with the bra's snaps. She tilts the body forward till it folds on itself, undoes the hooks behind, reaches around in front and peels it free. "Fancy," she says, examining the bra. "Okay, get her up."

The last Morton sees of Betty Sabo is Betty's head, tilted to one side so he can see the knot just below her temple, then her breasts, splayed to either side, then her sagging belly with its marbling of stretch marks, and finally her feet. He watches her chest heave once as they balance her on the tank's lip and then he sees the long purple scar that runs like a river up her foot from heel to instep. The other foot has a big toe with a bunion on it. He has kissed that foot, his lips have brushed those toes. Lilly gives a push to Betty's torso and Morton helps by lifting the heels. The heels go over the side with a splash and both Morton and Lilly take an involuntary step back.

Lilly wipes her brow with the mass of fabric she holds in her hand. Her hairline grows very close to her eyebrows. She asks, "Where are the rest of her clothes?"

"By my truck, I think."

"Bring them here."

They leave everything bunched in little piles as though it had all been discarded in haste.

"Nobody's going to believe she got into this building by herself, so here's your story, Morton—" and Morton listens as Lilly proceeds to tell him what to say. "Where are those beer bottles you cleaned up? Get them." They arrange these so they look natural, and plenty enough to indicate the drinking had been extensive. "Don't forget to buy a soda, too, and drink all of it before you call the police."

"Where will you be?"

"Home, of course, waiting for a phone call from my darling to tell me where in the fuck he is when he belongs with me, only it'll probably be from the police, telling me where the fuck my darling husband really is."

She goes out to the pickup then and sits on the tailgate, which drops an inch or two beneath her weight. She has always been a heavy girl, and marriage has just seemed to bring out this natural tendency in her. Morton has always said he liked her weight. "There is more of you to love," he's told her on numerous occasions. But she's also heard him call her a fat sow when he thought she wasn't listening. It grieves her terribly, that he would turn his affections away from her like that. She can't understand how for some people it can be that simple. It can't be that simple. You're big, you weigh too much, he doesn't like you. Why should that suddenly be an impediment?

She thinks he's looking for impediments. He always has. She could feel it in the way he lay on top of her the first time they made love. She was offering herself up to him completely and he was holding something back. She could feel it. And the more she opened herself up for his love the more he resisted her. She had to let him think she was pregnant before she could get him to marry her. It has always been like that. His resisting her, resisting the enveloping arms of his own wife. She has tried to make allowances. She knows he's weak. She knows, for example, that it's going to take a while for Morton to gather himself enough so he can call Clayton. She can just see him in there, pacing back and forth, going over his lines, nervously sipping his soda and steeling himself to make the call. He'll be fine once he's crazy mad enough at her and at himself to toe the line, to make the call. She knows he knows it needs to be done.

There are still some beers left in the cooler on the floor of the cab. She pops one and sits on the tailgate again. It occurs to her that she could sit right here till Clayton comes and tell him everything. She could get all hyper and short with her breathing and cry a little and say he made her help him get rid of the body. Who would believe Morton over her? And then she'd be rid of them both, Morton and Betty both. He's cheated on her for the last time. He's done unspeakable things to their love for the last time.

It would serve him right, she thinks. Serve him damn right. And that woman! She's glad Morton clocked her. She didn't think he had it in him. But then clocking a defenseless woman is pure cowardice, and Morton has that in abundance. He has all kinds of weakness in abundance.

But as Lilly Brunner sits there heavily, sipping a beer, the heat oppressive, bearing down on her, with only the lightest of breezes to bring relief, something gives way inside her. She takes in a great suck of air and with a great groan starts sobbing. She's losing or has lost Morton, maybe for good, he'll never love her now, not any-more, not with this between them. But why, why can't it bring them more closely together, why can't it be that way, why? Why? And she has no idea—no, that's not true, she knows it's not true, she saw the chest heave—if the body she tossed into the cooling tank was living or dead.

For the longest time this evening her anger has sustained her, has kept her going, has seen her through to what needs to be done, and she did it, but it's ebbing away now, all that anger, ebbing away, and what's to replace it?

Jesus, God, but she loves Morton! How could he do this to her? How? How could he? How could he do this to her love? She loves him! Doesn't he know, doesn't he understand what that means? Doesn't he understand what she's just done for him? Doesn't he understand that she'd die without him?

She's shaking. She couldn't move right now if she wanted to.

And what has she done? My God, what has she done? She's shaking and her feet feel very cold. She feels very cold, all over. She's seething perspiration and yet she's shivering. When did the night turn so cool? Where did that breeze come from? Why are the trees alive with whispering? Why do the stars cry out with grief? They are pinpricks of grief a long ways away, shining in a sea of velvet. How can this be? How could these things have happened? Morton, oh Morton, why don't you believe me when I say I love you? Why isn't loving me enough for you? Why is it you always want more, and why is it you don't want it from me?

Still grieving, for the girl, for herself, for the love she bears her husband, a love that won't ever, she can't ever wash clean of shame, Lilly Brunner stares at the night sky, and her wet eyes look with longing on stars whose patterns she cannot name.